TYE WATKINS

IN

DRUMS ALONG THE BORDER

BOOK FIVE OF THE TYE WATKINS SERIES

By

Gary McMillan

COVER CONCEPTS AND DESIGN BY MICHAEL MCMILLAN

Authors' Discovery Cooperation, Inc.

165 Cherry Lane

Robert Lee, Texas 76945

325-453-4595

ldudney@nwol.net

This book is a work of fiction. People, places, events and situations are the product of the author's imagination. Any resemblance to actual persons, living or dead, or historical events, is purely coincidental.

Copyright March 2009 Gary McMillan

No part of this book may be reproduced, stored in a retrieval system, or transmitted by any means without the written permission of the author.

Published by: Authors' Discovery Cooperation, Inc. March 2009

ISBN Number 978-0-9800854-7-1

Printed in the United States of America

Dedication

I would like to dedicate this book to the memory of my mother-in-law, Carolyn Emerson, who was my number one fan and whom I dearly loved.

April 3, 1915-November 22, 2008

I would like to thank Terry Retherford of Odessa and Charles Fields of Del Rio for their critiquing of this book and a big thank you to Dane Jones of Odessa for the help he gave me.

Acknowledgements: The Lonely Sentinel: Fort Clark
By Caleb Pirtle & Michael F. Cusack
Apaches, A History and Culture Portrait
By James L. Haley

Other Books in the Tye Watkins Series

Border Trouble

The Crossing

Yancey

The Desperate Trail

Preface

This is the fifth book of the Tye Watkins Series. In all of them I have tried to portray just how dangerous it was for our forefathers who had the courage to settle along the Texas/Mexico Border in the years after the Civil War. These men and women knew the perils that awaited them around every bend in the trail and over every hill but they still came. They slept at night with a loaded pistol and rifle beside their Bible.

The books are fiction but the places described in the book are real. There is no question that the Army and the homesteaders had many conflicts with the Indians and the bandits that roamed the land along the Border. According to records, Fort Clark had more engagements with the Apache than any other fort on the Border. Every once in a while a patrol may have had as many as three skirmishes a day but most of the time they chased the Apache who were like ghost that were rarely seen and left few tracks. Sometimes the army was the hunter and sometimes they were the prey.

Fort Clark can still be visited and is the home of about 2,000 residents. A large number of the buildings built in the 1860-1880's are still there. Many now are homes and the enlisted men's barracks is now the fort's motel. The fort is located on Highway 90 thirty miles east of present day Del Rio, Texas.

On the following pages you will follow Tye Watkins, who is Chief of Scouts at Clark, as he tries to put an end to an unusually large band of Apaches. Tye will learn that the Apache leader is Ke-ah who Tye, as a young boy living on the Border had befriended. He had found the young Ke-ah who had been seriously injured from a fall from his pony. The two became best friends and spent many nights camping out together. Ke-ah learned English from Tye and Tye learned Apache from Ke-ah.

The friendship lasted until Ke-ah became of age to become an Apache warrior. By that time the relationship between the Apache and the whites that were settling the area had ended and the trouble began. They have not seen each other since that time.

Now, years later Tye would be forced to try and track down Ke-ah and his warriors and hoped that it did not come down to a face to face confrontation with his old friend.

Chapter One

The light rain did not help the disposition of the soldiers standing beside their mounts, each one cursing this young Lieutenant under their breath as if it was his fault that it was raining. The subject of their disgust was Second Lieutenant James Braddock who also stood beside his mount with his rain slicker on, anxiously waiting for his scout to return from the canyon that opened before them. Being the first day of April, the morning air was still a little on the nippy side and the darkening skies promised even heavier rain later in the morning.

The cold drops of rain, that found their way down the soldier's collars, caused shivers to run up and down their spines. They hunched their shoulders and pulled their slickers tighter around their collars. Pulling their hats low on their heads they stared straight ahead saying nothing, but wishing like hell they were somewhere else.

There had been no reported Apache trouble for three or four months and the men were not happy about standing around getting soaked, especially since they were only three or four hours from Fort Clark. They had been on patrol for four days and each yearned for a drink at Jim's Saloon in Bracket and not standing in the damn rain freezing his butt. They were veterans of a number of patrols and most had encounters with Apaches and understood about being careful but with no reported trouble, this seemed stupid and a miserable waste of time.

It was not only the weather that made them irritable but also the problem of being on a patrol with a green lieutenant leading his first one. There was not a single one of them that had not lost a friend because of mistakes made by these know-it-all stinking lieutenants fresh out here from back east. These young officers were smart, knew all about making the right maneuvers and right decisions as far as army policy and procedures but they didn't know squat about fighting the Apache. Only a very few of them would listen to the veterans' and scouts' advice or suggestions. The only way to do things was by the 'book', or so they thought. The only problem, they would eventually learn, if they lived long enough, was that the Apache hadn't read the book on techniques and strategies of war. The Apache made their own rules, fought their way, and were damn good at it.

The Apache had been fighting for a hundred years or more against other Indian tribes that greatly outnumbered them. They had become the best guerilla fighters in the world, feared by the other tribes as well as the Mexicans, and the whites who settled on what they considered their land… Apache land.

The Apache, because of small numbers, depended on surprise as their best ally. Their war plan was to hit fast, do as much damage as possible, and quickly disappear with as little damage to themselves as possible. Always being a little short on numbers, survival was the important thing to them. They could not afford the big losses they would incur in a direct, all out assault on a troop of bluecoats who usually had them bested in firepower. On most patrols, the troops never even saw them but when they did, it was hell on earth for a few minutes and then they were gone. A veteran trooper would tell you, "You only see an Apache when he wants you to see him".

The army had learned the Apache warrior was the most adept of all the Indian Tribes at ambushing their enemy. They could blend in with the terrain and their ability to go for hours without moving was well documented and every soldier knew it. The canyon ahead would be a perfect place for an ambush…if there were any Apaches around. To the man, the troops didn't believe there were.

The Fort Clark Post Commander, Major Thurston, knew these veteran men would be upset about a young inexperienced lieutenant leading them. With no reports of any hostile Apaches since back in the fall, he wasn't worried about the young lieutenant's lack of experience. The fact of no reported trouble didn't squelch the men's anxiety about Braddock. They knew that sooner or later all officers had to make their virgin trip; they just didn't like the fact they had been chosen to be part of this officer's first experience.

This was to be a routine patrol where Thurston figured the youngster could become familiar with the area and meet some of the families settling along the Border. Also, by placing him with the veterans, he would find out if he had the mettle to make it out here. Not all soldiers were the dependable, order obeying, yes-sir, no-sir, type that one would expect. You had malcontents, alcoholics, criminals, and sometimes men just trying to escape their past. Thirteen dollars a month sounded pretty good and then throw in free lodging and meals, it sounded great. Fortunately, there were more good soldiers than bad and the misfits were generally held in check. He knew that some of the malcontents would test Braddock. He had sent Jason Miles, an experienced scout, along with the veteran Sergeant Baker to 'baby sit' him and keep him out of trouble.

James Braddock was not a green lieutenant just out of the Point like the men figured. He had served two boring years on a post in Virginia. He wanted action and made it known he wanted to be assigned to a frontier post. He had finally gotten his wish by being assigned to Fort Clark. Having come from the lush green hills and mountains of Virginia, he was shocked at first by the harsh, barren country surrounding the fort. All he could see was cactus, sage, small trees called mesquite, sand, and rocks. It was a land that looked like it could not grow even a single blade of good green grass. He would learn it was a harsh and unfriendly land. It was an unforgiving land that could kill you as quick as an Apache could. The land was vast with seemingly no end and if one was not careful it could swallow a man up and he would never be heard of again.

After a couple of patrols to the south of Clark with an experienced officer, he found that everything out here can scratch, bite, or stick you. That had been back in January, but now he had become accustomed to the country and actually saw a certain attractiveness in it. He could see how some of the men who had been here for awhile liked to talk of staying after their stint with the army and try to make a home out here.

Speaking of making a home out here in this land, he was shocked at how many families were making a go of it and seemingly more coming every day. The terrain was generally flat around Clark; with low mountains to the north and Mexico only thirty miles to the west. To the east, toward Fort Inge, you had gently rolling hills as well as to the south. Despite the land, he had been amazed at the wildlife that a man could find; deer, coyotes, rabbits, turkey, panthers, snakes, and an occasional bear and buffalo. There were countless other varmints including some of the two legged type.

Today was the first day of spring 1869 and it marked a big day in his life. He was on the frontier and leading a patrol of twelve good men. It felt great! He was proud and content.

He came from a family that had always stepped forward when their country needed them. His grandfather and his grandfather's brother, as young men, fought the British during the Revolutionary War. They both survived the bloody conflict and moved near New Orleans when the war was over. Once again, in 1812, they fought beside Andy Jackson at the battle of New Orleans even though his grandfather was sixty and his brother was fifty-eight years old.

James's father, before moving his family to Virginia, had been with General Sam Houston when they defeated Santa Anna after the fall of the Alamo in 1836. Shortly thereafter, he left Texas for Virginia, met the lady he would spend the rest of his life with and settled down to raise a family.

His mother and father settled on a small piece of land and the future Lieutenant James Braddock was born in 1847. He had two older brothers and a younger sister. His oldest brother, Billy, still lived on the farm and took care of his mother. His dad had died two years ago and his last words to James were how proud he was of him becoming an officer. His sister was married to a good man who owned a general store and his other brother was a law officer. They all had families and seemed content with their lives when he last spoke with them before he left. He had received one letter from his sister since arriving at Clark, telling him his mother was well and they all missed him. After receiving the letter he had sat down and wrote a letter tha…Shots! Coming from inside the canyon, brought him from thoughts of the past back to reality.

He turned to Sergeant Baker who was beside him.

"Wha…what do you make of it, Sergeant?" He asked, trying to keep his voice from betraying his anxiety.

"Not sure Lieutenant but it ain't good. We had better mount up." Baker replied.

"Give the order, Sergeant," Braddock said as he mounted his horse.

"PREPARE TO MOUNT," Baker hollered at the men. The men placed their left boot in the stirrup and their left hand on the pommel of their saddle, their right hand holding the reins. When the order "MOUNT" came, each man swung his right leg over the back of his horse and settled his butt in the cursed McClellan saddle. The soldiers and officers out here felt like a demented group of men back east designed the saddle and they sure as hell never had to sit their butts in it for any length of time. The soldiers, to a man, wished for a good western saddle like they had before joining the army.

There had been no more shots fired and the only sound now was the occasional snort or whinny of one of the horses and the restless stomping of their hooves. The rain was forgotten now as the men stared at the opening of the canyon, anxiously looking for their scout. Sergeant Baker moved his mount up beside Braddock's horse.

"I think we're in trouble, Lieutenant. Up there," Baker said nodding to the rim of the canyon on the left. Looking up, Braddock saw, for the first time in his life, an Apache warrior...about twenty of them. "Over there," Baker said pointing to the other side of the canyon. Braddock turned his head right and saw a large number were there also, sitting on their horses...watching. The soldier's mounts, possibly sensing trouble, were more restless, snorting and stomping their hooves, forcing the soldiers to exert some effort to control them.

"GOD HELP US," one of the soldiers hollered from the back of the patrol. "THEY ARE BEHIND US TOO," he cried. Each man turned to look and saw forty or so Apaches sitting on their ponies, watching them.

"What are they waiting for?" An anxious Braddock asked Baker.

"They have us trapped and they know it," he answered. "They will attack when they are ready to." He then added, "We're in for it, Lieutenant." At that time, their scout, sitting on his horse, came walking out of the canyon. He was sitting straight as a pole in his saddle. The men could not believe it...then they all saw at once. His face was a bloody mess under his hat that was pulled down low over his eyes or where his eyes used to be. Two empty, bloody sockets could be seen where his eyes had been. He was riddled with bullet holes and he had at least half dozen arrows in his back.

"Get him down," Braddock ordered. The scout was tied to a wooden cross to hold him upright in the saddle. Two troopers got him off his horse and laid him gently on the ground. The men turned away from the sickening sight. Braddock was thinking what could be done to get out of this situation. He looked at Baker and the expression on his face told him that the sergeant thought it was hopeless.

Braddock studied the surrounding terrain looking for a defensive position. Forty yards to his left was a pile of large boulders. He pointed toward them and shouted to the sergeant. "Over there. Get the men and horses behind those boulders."

"FOLLOW ME," Baker screamed at the top of his lungs. He kicked his mount in the flanks and the excited horse bounded toward the boulders, almost unseating the sergeant. The men followed Baker's mount's heels and when they were behind the rocks, they leaped from their mounts and scrambled for the cover. Two men were dispatched to take the horses farther back into the recesses of the huge boulders to keep them out of the line of fire.

Braddock stood behind a large boulder beside Baker. He looked at the Apaches who had been behind them. They had not moved. He looked at the canyon rims where the Apaches had been looking down at them; they were gone. "When will they attack, Sergeant?"

"They ain't in no hurry. They'll be coming soon enough." As he spoke the Apaches that had been on top of the canyons joined the others. There were now over eighty warriors and a man could tell they were preparing to charge because of all the yells, shaking of rifles and bows, and the strutting of their horses. Even a greenhorn like Braddock knew they were fixing to come.

The Apaches charged and the pounding hooves echoed off the canyon walls and shook the ground. Above the pounding of the hooves, the men could hear the cries of the Apache. Braddock looked at his men and could see fear in their faces, even though he knew they had seen this before. Braddock stood up, his torso above the rocks and exposing himself to enemy fire. "HOLD YOUR FIRE TILL I GIVE THE ORDER," he shouted over the noise of pounding hooves and Apache screams. Bullets were splattering the rocks around him and an arrow took his hat off but he stood steadfast.

"Sir," Baker screamed to be heard over the deafening noise of the charge. "GET DOWN, SIR…GET DOWN."

The men didn't know if the man was an idiot or the bravest man they had ever seen. Whatever the case, they took courage from this young lieutenant and lay their Sharps across the rocks and aimed at the charging horde.

At forty yards, Braddock screamed, "FIRE." Twelve guns roared as one and six Apaches cart wheeled off the back of their mounts and two slumped over their pony's necks. The charge turned and went to the left of the trapped troopers. As they passed, several troopers fired their revolvers and two more fell off their mounts. A shout went up from the troops as the charge broke. Baker pulled the lieutenant down behind the rocks. "That was a fool thing to do, Sir."

"The men needed encouragement, Sergeant Baker. I figured if they saw the officer in charge unafraid, it would rub off on them." He looked at the dead Apaches on the ground and then at his men who had not suffered a single man lost, not even a wound. "Looks like it worked." He sat down behind the boulder and started to open his canteen but his hand was shaking so badly he put it back down. 'Baker was right, that was a damn fool stunt,' he thought to himself.

Braddock looked at Baker. "I heard the Apaches would not attack the army like that. They would rather ambush the soldiers and suffer as few casualties as possible."

"Normally that's right except when they feel they have an advantage like just now." Baker replied.

"Advantage…what advantage are you talking about?"

"Twelve of us and almost a hundred of them; that's a fair advantage I'd say."

Braddock understood and looked back at the Apaches.

They sat on their ponies just out of effective range of the Sharps. They were obviously arguing about the next step in ridding their land of these bluecoats. Braddock figured the odds were about seven or eight to one.

"We can't stay here long, Sir." Baker mumbled.

"Why not?" Braddock asked. "We have good position and some water. Besides, when we don't return to the fort, a relief patrol will be sent out."

"The patrol won't be sent out until day after tomorrow, Sir…maybe even the next day. It's not unusual for a patrol to be late coming back. With limited water, we will be buzzard bait by that time. Besides, it ain't going to take the Apache long to get some men up there," he added pointing to a cliff that towered above them. "They can take their time up there and pick us off."

Braddock thought on this new development. He knew he should have thought of that and now instead of being a hero and leading his men to safety he had led them into a trap. He glanced to where the horses were and then back up the cliff. He didn't think the Apache could hit them from up there. That was one problem that he could put out of his mind, he knew the Indians knew a cavalryman on foot was easy prey out here plus they would want the horses to ride…and eat. He thought they had some time before they received fire from the rim and when or if they did, the men could scramble to where the horses were.

"Do you have any ideas, Sergeant? You've fought them before." Baker looked at the canyon before them, the tops of the canyon walls, and all the surrounding terrain. He figured the canyon was a blind one with one way in and no way out, or, the Apache had plenty of men inside to prevent the soldiers from getting through. He spit a wad of tobacco juice from his ever present chew in his mouth.

"I think our only chance is to charge them. I don't think they will expect that and maybe some of us will make it through and get to the fort to tell Thurston." Braddock looked at Baker like he was out of his mind. "Charge them? You are suggesting we charge from eighty to a hundred Apaches with twelve men and actually think we might get through."

"No, Sir. I think some, even if its just one of us might make it through to the fort. Thurston has to know about this. We can stay here and fight till hell freezes over but in the end, we're all dead and no one knows about them," he said nodding toward the gathering Apaches.

James thought on this for a moment before speaking to the men.

"GET YOUR MOUNTS AND FORM A SKIRMISH LINE ON ME," he shouted. "USE YOUR PISTOLS AND DON'T STOP UNTILL YOU GET TO FORT CLARK."

The men scrambled for their mounts. Baker let out a tremendous yell and the patrol charged the surprised Apaches. It only took a couple of seconds for the warriors to react. They cut loose with their terrible screams and charged the patrol. At twenty yards, the troopers cut loose with their pistols. Firing from a running horse and scared to death did not help their accuracy. Four Apache were knocked over their ponies' rears and two horses went down. Before the soldiers could fire again, the two charging groups were together. With horses rearing, men hollering, and the wounded screaming in pain, it was a sight seen only in a soldier's nightmare. No soldier, with any sense, wanted a hand-to-hand fight with an Apache but this was what it had come to, man to man, knives, tomahawks, and pistols. The twelve soldiers were firing their pistols at point blank range. Braddock was swinging his saber savagely and with deadly affect with his right hand and held a smoking Navy Colt in the other. It was all close in fighting now and with the dust it was hard to tell friend from foe.

Despite fighting valiantly, the troopers were overwhelmed by sheer numbers. The soldiers were being knocked off their mounts and hitting the ground hard by the warriors who were flinging themselves from their ponies like battering rams. Once on the ground, with three or more Apache on each of them, it was over quickly with a knife in the chest or a war club busting their skulls.

Braddock, Baker and a Private Sayles were the only ones to make it through the charging warriors. Braddock was hanging on desperately to his horse's mane and the pommel of his saddle. He was only half conscious because a club had hit him a glancing blow on the side of the head. Baker had taken an arrow high in the back.

of his right shoulder. Sayles had an arrow in his left thigh and his horse had one in his right shoulder. At a quarter mile from the battle scene, his horse stumbled and went down. "DON'T LEAVE ME... OH GOD, DON'T LEAVE ME," Sayles screamed.

Braddock and Baker reined their mounts around. Braddock, having regained his senses, hollered to Baker, "Get to the fort and tell Thurston what has happened." Before Baker could say anything, the lieutenant slapped Baker's horse on the flanks with his saber and the horse almost jumped out from under its rider. Baker held on lying low over the saddle as he galloped away, the feathered shaft flopping back and forth. Braddock reined his mount to the man who was on the ground behind his horse. Braddock jumped from the saddle and lay down beside Sayles.

Braddock yelled so Sayles could hear him over the charging Apaches. "We have to slow them down and give Baker a chance to get to the fort." That being said, both men fired their Sharps with each knocking an Apache off his pony. Throwing the Sharps aside, they fired their pistols with deadly accuracy and broke the charge. The Indians retreated to regroup. Braddock turned to Sayles to tell him to reload his pistol and was startled to see an arrow imbedded in the private's forehead. His lifeless eyes stared straight ahead and his mouth was open as if he had been trying to say something. The lieutenant glanced over his shoulder and could not see Baker. 'Good for him,' he thought.

In the seconds he had to live, he thought of his decision to come out here so far away from his family. He could have stayed back east but he wanted to see action. 'Well,' he thought, 'I'm seeing action.' He smiled, despite knowing he was about to be dead. "I won't be taken alive and I won't go down easy," he said out loud as the large war party charged. He was mesmerized for a couple of seconds as he watched. Everything he had heard about the Apache was true. They were absolutely fearless. He was sure the charges he had seen so far, and the one he was now watching come his way, was going to be his last. It was a sight that would make a man's blood run cold as ice, but it was still a fascinating sight.

He knocked two off their mounts before they were on him. He stood up and was beginning to swing his saber when a lance struck him in the chest and protruded two feet out his back, the bloody point dripping with blood and gore. He dropped his saber and grasped the shaft in his chest with both hands attempting to pull it out. He raised his eyes only to glimpse a war club that bashed him in the forehead, knocking him backwards. The point of the lance stuck into the ground when he fell. His body, suspended off the ground by the spear that had impaled him, twitched once and then was still.

It was all over. Braddock, his scout, and eleven troopers were gone as was twelve or fourteen Apache and several more wounded. The warriors began their butchering but when one of the braves grabbed Braddock's hair to scalp him, a sharp command from Asay, their leader, stopped him. He told the brave to leave the officer alone. Not butchering an enemy was the sign of respect by the Apache for a fighting man. Asay had seen this man was a warrior.

Asay looked in the direction the soldier had gone. He knew they would never catch him with the lead he had. The soldiers' grain fed horses were better conditioned for long runs than the grass fed Apache mounts. He signaled his braves to come to him. When they were all around him, he ordered them to bury their dead brothers by covering them with rocks to keep the coyotes away. This was a common practice with the dead if they were a war party and not going back to their camp anytime soon. Otherwise, they would take then to camp and given a proper burial with a great ceremony fitting an Apache warrior. After taking care of the dead and tending the wounded, they rode off into the hills, yelling and waving the bloody scalps of the soldiers. They had plenty of bullets, rifles, pistols, and sabers which made excellent points for spears.

Camped along the banks of the Rio Pecos later that evening, Asay reflected on today's events. He also thought of the past, and the future. He was a man of over thirty winters and known for his ferocity in battle and cunningness when it came to planning strategy. The Apache bands sometimes had no formal chiefs as other tribes but had leaders who led them by their skills in war and vast experience.

Asay was a Chiricahua Apache, considered the best fighters of all the Apache tribes. He, as all the Apaches, was tired of the white man pushing them off their lands. Five moons ago, warriors from all the Apaches tribes had met along the Rio Grande River to decide what their future would be. Would they submit to the white man or would they fight for their land…their way of life? Representatives from the White Mountain Apache, Northern and Southern Tonto bands, Cibecue, Chiricahua, Membreno, Mescaleros, and Jicarilla tribes from Arizona and New Mexico were there. From Texas and northern Mexico, the Lipan and the Kiowa Apache were also present at the council. A well known and respected Lipan medicine man, Juh-nah, presided over the council. This was the first time almost all of the tribes had come together for council. After Juh-hah and several other well known and respected warriors had spoken, the overwhelming choice was to eliminate this danger to their homelands and the Apache way of life. They would fight until the wave of whites was gone or there was no more Apache blood left to spill.

The Apache hated to fight during the winter so the council decided they would all attack in each one's homeland when the warm winds begin to blow. The time had come, and Asay and his band had ventured south to find homesteaders and soldiers to kill. He had almost eighty warriors with him; all of one mind…'kill' the white man.

This council had been witnessed by Tye Watkins. He and Dan, one of his scouts, were on a cliff across the river from the camp. They could not hear what was being said but over two hundred warriors from several different tribes meeting in one place was highly unusual. The two white men knew that whatever the reason, it was not good for the army and the settlers along the Border.

CHAPTER TWO

Tye and Shakespeare had just finished eating a fine supper that Rebecca had cooked and sat on the porch drinking coffee and watching the rain. It had been raining all day.

"Yu kno whut tha say abut rain on tha ferst day uf spring?" Buff asked.

Tye figured another one of the old sayings from the days Shakespeare was trapping beaver in the Rockies was coming. Since Shakespeare, or Buff as he liked to be called, had come to live with him and Rebecca he had heard many old truisms and Indian folklore stories. Surprisingly, many of the things had actually come true. He leaned back in the chair and took another sip of coffee before answering. "What does it mean, Buff?"

"Rain on tha ferst day uf spring means thangs or going downhill."

Tye laughed. "What do you mean by things going downhill?"

"Meens tha bad thangs or going ta be comin…real bad thangs." Rebecca came through the door at that time. "What bad things coming are you two talking about?"

"Buff said rain on the first day of spring means things are only going to get worse," Tye said smiling and winked at Rebecca.

"Why do you say that, Buff?" She asked.

"Seed it my own self too manee times not ta beleeve it. Old Bridger his own self tol me tha way bac in '24 or so. Seed it ta be tru mor times than not."

"Someone is coming, Tye," Rebecca said. Tye turned and looked. He was surprised to see Captain McClellan coming. He immediately looked at Buff because it was a little late for visitors so it caused him to wonder what was wrong.

He stood up as McClellan arrived and shook the captain's hand. "Good to see you up and around, Captain," Tye said. On the last patrol, when Tye had brought in the outlaw Yancey Cates, McClellan had been shot in the right shoulder. He had almost died before he got back to Fort Clark to receive medical attention.

McClellan swung his right arm in a circular motion, grimaced some, and then smiled; "Almost good as new." He looked at Rebecca and then Buff. "Good to see the three of you also. You're as pretty as always, Rebecca."

Rebecca smiled, remembering when the captain could not stand Tye, but that was before the patrol he was leading got into an ambush because of his stupidity. Tye had pulled him and his men from the ambush and saved not only his life but possibly his career.

"Thank you, Captain," Rebecca answered.

Tye asked. "What brings you over at this time of day and in this weather?"

"Bad news, Tye." He sat down on the porch. Tye and Rebecca looked at each other and then at Buff.

Buff looked up and said. "I knowed it…I just knowed it." He shook his head and stood up.

"Knew what?" McClellan asked.

"Never mind," Tye said. "What's this bad news?"

"You know Sergeant Baker?"

"Sure, I know him. Good man." Tye answered. "He's on patrol with the new lieutenant."

"He was on patrol with Lieutenant Braddock when they were jumped by close to a hundred Apaches."

"A hundred?" Tye repeated. "Was he sure of that?"

"That's what he said. They were waiting outside of a canyon while your scout, Jason Miles, scouted out the canyon. They heard shots and then the scout came out of the canyon tied to a cross to hold him upright in the saddle. He had been butchered something terrible. There were Indians in the canyon, twenty or more on both sides and maybe forty or so behind them. Braddock did the only thing he could do. He led his men into some rocks that offered some cover. They beat off one charge but he knew they could not last where they were with limited food and water. He got the men mounted and in a skirmish line, charged the Indians. Baker said that the men were told not to stop and if they got through, to head to the fort and warn Thurston. Braddock, Baker, and a private made it through the Apaches but the private's horse went down. Baker and Braddock reined in to help him but the Apaches were gathering to charge. Braddock told Baker to get to the fort and before the sergeant could argue about it, the lieutenant spanked Baker's horses across the rump with his saber. The lieutenant dismounted and stayed with the private to slow the warriors some. Baker had taken an arrow in his shoulder and was in bad shape by the time he got here."

He stood up. "The major would like to see you and Buff right away."

Tye turned to Rebecca. "Honey, would you get Buff and me our slickers?" He looked at Buff thinking what he had said not ten minutes ago and shook his head. He decided he was going to start believing everything this old mountain man said. They put on their slickers and with McClellan, headed to see Thurston.

Arriving at Thurston's office, everyone took a seat, waiting for Thurston to speak.

"Gentlemen, we have a problem. Maybe the biggest one since the fort was regarrisoned." He walked to the wall map and pointed at

Fort Duncan, about fifty miles south of Clark and right on the Border.

"I had a courier from Duncan ride in about an hour ago. A patrol from Duncan was hit hard by a large number of Lipan Apaches two days ago. Only thing that saved them from a massacre was the quick action of their scout. The scout ended up being killed along with nine troopers. As you know, we had some terrible news ourselves. Young Lieutenant Braddock was killed along with all his men except Sergeant Baker who was seriously wounded." He picked an arrow off his desk and handed it to Tye "Is this a Lipan arrow?"

Tye took the arrow and studied it. "No, Sir. It's Apache alright but I don't recognize the markings. If you asked me to take a guess, I would say it was Mescalero or Chiricahua."

"Your scout, Dan August, happen to be here when Baker rode in. He looked at the arrow and said the same thing." He looked at Buff. "Buff, several months ago you said something about the Indians getting their business lined up to make a push." With a sigh, he sat down and continued. "I think you may be right." He leaned back in his chair and looked straight at Buff. "Buff, just what caused you to think this? I mean," he paused for a couple of seconds, "You said you've seen it before."

"Yes, Sir, I have…twice. Tha last time wus in '67 when I wus scouting out uf Bents Fort. Tha Cheyenne all over Kolorado started raiding in all parts uf tha kountry. Forts kud not send help ta uther forts because uf tha mess all over tha they wus causing." Buff stood up and walked over to the map on the opposite wall from the one on the wall behind Thurston's desk. This map showed all the forts along the Border plus other forts farther in from the Rio Grande. The map behind Thurston's desk was an enlarged version of just the area around Clark for fifty or so miles.

"Yu take this here Fort Davis and Fort Stockton," he said placing his finger on each. "If tha Injuns hit within forty or so miles all around each fort, Davis can't send troops to help Stockton. Same thang tha uther way, Stockton can't help Davis."

"I would bet Buff's idea is right," Tye said. "Why else would all those warriors from the different tribes and from as far away as Arizona get together last fall. There had to be a reason and I'll wager that's what it was. Dan and me were at that camp in late fall when they held council. All of you know the Apache don't cater to winter fighting. It's spring now and we're getting reports from all over of trouble."

"Wal, if I'm rite abut it, yu can bet tha are prepared with plenty of guns, ammunition and food stored all over tha kountry. Tha have had a few months ta prepare. Injuns I dealt with my whole life never did nuthing tha wusn't planned and I bet these heer Apaches are no different. As yu kno, most of tha Injun leaders are smarter than a lot of high ranking army officers…present company excluded," he chuckled, looking at Thurston.

"Thanks for the vote of confidence, Buff," Thurston said smiling, then added. "I didn't know you were scouting for Fort Collins and Bents Fort before you came here. Were you at Collins when the flood occurred?"

"Yes, Sir, I wus thar; I wus skouting fer tha 11th Ohio Cavalry. It wus a day tha I wud never ferget. It wus June 9th, 1864 when a twenty foot wall uf water kame out of tha canyon whar tha camp wus on tha banks uf tha Poudre River. Two kumpanies of men, all thar horses, and mules' wus swept away. Tha onliest reason I'm heer is becauz I wuz on patrol. We never found all tha men to bury them."

"I heard about it a few months after the fact," Thurston replied. "It was a sad day for all…a total waste of men and animals." He leaned back in his chair and puffed on his ever present cigar; "Back to the problem at hand." He looked at McClellan. "Have you recovered from your wound sufficiently to lead a patrol?"

"Yes, Sir, I'm fit for duty sir and anxious to go."

"Good." Thurston said leaning forward and putting his hands on the desk. "Tye, I want you to lead McClellan and a company of men and find the place where Braddock and his men fell. I will send enough men and extra horses so you can afford to spare some to bring the bodies back here to the fort. I then want you to find these savages and bring hellfire and damnation on them. I will have the supplies and an ambulance with a medical team ready by daylight. You will leave then." He looked at the men. "Any questions?" No one said anything. "Then, if there are no questions, you will excuse me because I have a lot of paperwork to do to get things together. Captain McClellan, please get Senior Master Sergeant O'Malley to pick the men and get them ready to leave at first light."

"Will do, Sir." The men filed out of Thurston's office with McClellan heading for the O'Malley's and Tye and Buff toward their house, leaving the major to get things rolling. Tye was thinking about Rebecca and how she would react to his leaving. They had gotten used to being together a lot lately because of the lack of trouble. He knew she would not be happy about it but then, she knows that is what he is paid for.

CHAPTER THREE

Twenty-two miles northwest of Clark, Jarrod Cavender and his wife of twenty years, Laverne, made camp with their two teenage sons, Jerry and Mason. Jerry was thirteen and Mason was almost eighteen years old. The family had left Georgia two months ago. The draw of free land in Texas was just too much temptation for a man who had worked for another all his life. Jarrod longed to have his own place; a place to raise his family and most of all, something to leave his children when he was gone.

They had made camp early tonight because it was Laverne's thirty-nineth birthday. A deer had been shot earlier by Mason and the aroma of fresh meat roasting over the fire had each of their mouths watering in anticipation. The last few days, their meals had been mostly beans and biscuits so the prospect of beans and fresh meat sounded like a feast. Jarrod studied the area around the camp while the meal was being prepared. A row of oak trees or maybe pecan or both indicated a creek about a quarter mile to the north of where they were camped. High cliffs beyond the trees would protect the home from bitter north winds in the winter. The land was fairly flat and appeared to have good topsoil which was unusual for this area. He walked to the wagon and picked up a shovel. Digging holds in different spots he found the top soil was about eight to ten inches deep before one hit the rocks. Barely deep enough to raise crops but it was as good as he had seen in the last hundred miles. He replaced the shovel and looked at his wife busy fixing the meal.

Jerry had walked to where Jarrod had seen the trees. He came back and said there was a small stream, maybe fifteen foot wide and two to three foot deep. When he said he could see some fish swimming in it, Jarrod was sure this was the place. Fish meant the stream had water the year around which would be important out here.

Laverne had been hesitant to leave the cozy, safe home they had in Georgia even though it was not theirs. Jarrod had worked the fields for the Jefferson family almost his whole life. He wanted to be his own man, make his own decisions, and be able to pick up a handful of dirt, smell it, and know he could call it his own. He had great respect for the Jefferson family, and his family had wanted for nothing…but something was missing. It just took the allure of free land that made him realize what it was.

Both Mason and Jerry had heard the two discussing leaving. They had never argued about it, just each giving their opinions. Pa had finally won out and Laverne had reluctantly agreed to leave their home. The Jefferson's understood Jarrod's dream and had been generous to the family when they left. They had given Jarrod an extra sturdy wagon and a pair of oxen to pull it along with a bonus of three hundred dollars for his years of service.

They had loaded what furniture and tools they felt were necessary in the wagon given them, which allowed more space in the other wagon for food, water barrels, and even some privacy for Laverne. They had four horses broke for the harness and three for riding. A bull, seven cows, a rooster and chickens along with several goats made up the rest of the little caravan. Jarrod had used some of the money to purchase ammunition and food staples such as sugar, flour, beans, bacon, and of course coffee…lots of coffee. Jarrod figured they could find deer or antelope to keep them in meat, and he had been right until the last few days.

It was almost dark when the meat was roasted. After a great meal and lots of birthday wishes, they settled in for the night as darkness engulfed the camp. Even though they had not seen another living soul, they were still watchful and Jarrod and the boys took turns on watch through the night.

Jarrod took the first watch this night. As he sat there in the darkness listening to the animals munch on the grass he looked up at the sky. There was no moon and no clouds, nothing to hinder the brilliance of a million stars. He was shocked at just how big the sky seemed and he knew there had to be a God to create such beauty. He was memorized by the beauty and the serenity of this land. As he stared at the sky he realized this was it…this was where he and his family would stop and spend the rest of their lives. For the first time in as long as he could remember, he felt relaxed. He would break the good news in the morning after searching the area to see if any other homesteads were located nearby and had possibly homesteaded the land.

~~~

Four Apaches from Asay's party were on a hunting trip when they came across the deep wagon tracks that belonged to the Cavender's. They knew the tracks were made several hours earlier. There was some discussion as to whether to continue their hunt or report back to Asay. They deducted the wagon was moving at a slow pace and would not travel more than a few miles before stopping. They could catch up quickly so they decided to continue their hunt. They would kill the white invaders tomorrow or the next day.

Back at the Apache camp, Asay sat away from the rest of his men. He wanted to not be disturbed while praying to Ussen, his One-God, the Creator and Life Giver. Asay prayed for wisdom and strength to lead his people to victory over the white-eyes and once
~~~

again be free to roam the land as his father and his father's father had done. He had eaten nothing this day and would fast until Ussen spoke to him or gave him a sign as to what he should do. He had his magical hoop with four eagle feathers equally spaced around the hoop, which the Apache believed, gave the hoop magical powers. The hoop itself represented the cycle of life from birth to death. The circle is an important symbol to the Apache and other tribes. Their wickiup's were circular, religious ceremonies were performed in circular structures, and dances were performed in a circle. They believed birth, life, and death of all humans and animals revolved in a circle. Asay believed that Ussen would listen to him calling up to Him for the strength and wisdom to lead his people and would answer him or give him a sign. He would wait.

~~~

At Fort Clark, Tye, Rebecca, and Buff sat on the porch, discussing the situation with the Apaches. The rain had stopped and the air was cool, clean, and fresh smelling. The clouds had moved on and as always, after a rain in this country, the ever present dust in the air was gone and the stars were exceptionally bright. It was a absolutely beautiful early Spring night. However, the situation prevented the three of them from enjoying it as they could have.

Rebecca was sitting on the top step of the wooden porch with Tye, her head on his shoulder. "What time do you leave in the morning?"
~~~

"I'll go to the stables about an hour before first light. Thurston wants us headed out by daylight."

"Whut uther scouts ar going with yu?" Buff asked

"Only need one more besides you."

Buff looked at Tye through the dim light that filtered through the open door from the lamp on the table inside the house. "Yu meen yu want me ta go?" he said.

"This could be bad Buff. I need the best scouts I can get. I figure you and Dan August will be enough. I just figured you wanted to go.

"Shor as God made little green apples," Buff said, the excitement showing in his voice. "Wuldn't won't ta be in tha way tho."

"I need the best, Buff. From what I have seen and heard from some of the men you were on the last patrol with, you are the best. You sure as hell won't be in the way. I figure with Dan's and my experience with Apaches and your experience with all the other tribes you have encountered, there won't be any situation come up that we can't figure out and correct." Tye stood up and placed his hand on Buff's shoulder. "Yeah, I want you to go."

Buff, excited as a school kid, stood up quickly. "Guess I'd better git my thangs tagether." Tye laughed and Rebecca forced a smile at the old mountain man. When Buff went inside she turned to Tye.

"Do you think he is ready to go physically?" she asked thinking of the knife wound a couple months earlier Buff had gotten from an Apache.

"That old man is the toughest sonofa..." he stopped in mid sentence and then corrected himself. "I mean he is the toughest man I have ever known. You saw how he acted. Men like him can never sit for long."

"Men like you?" She said laughing. Then added a serious note; "Tye, you will be careful won't you? Stay safe and come back to me."

Tye kissed her hard on the mouth, holding her tight. "You know what I have said before, nothing or no one could ever keep me from coming back to you." He picked her up and carried her into their house and into the bedroom.

Predawn found Tye, Buff, and Tye's best scout, Dan August at the stables with fifty men and officers along with a supply wagon, medical ambulance, and a surgeon ready to move out. Six men and two other wagons were there to tag along and bring the dead soldiers of Braddock's patrol back to the fort. The only sound that broke the early morning silence was the snorting of a few of the horses and an occasional cough from one of the men. Just as the eastern sky was turning gray with the coming sun, the men crossed the bridge over Los Moras Creek and turned west on the Old Mail Road. Each man knew what they would find at the scene of the massacre and the knowledge of that made each one of them determined to bring these red devils to justice. Most of the troopers had seen what had been left of their friends before this and were convinced, the only good Apache was a dead one. This was not Tye's opinion and it galled him most men thought that way.

Tye, Buff, and Dan led the soldiers down the old mail road. They would follow it for about fifteen miles then turn north. Tye understand the feelings of the soldiers. The men killed were their friends and comrades, but Tye also had strong feeling for the dead men even though he was not on friendly terms with each of them. He would lay down his life if need be to save each of them and the men knowing this, loved him. They respected the job he did knowing how dangerous it was. Each trooper knew that the Apache wanted to kill the scouts first and especially Tye. They considered him a great warrior and it would make any Apache who killed him 'big medicine' to his people.

Captain McClellan and Lieutenant Garrison headed up the patrol which was made up of veterans only. Sergeants Christian, Arnold, Phipps, and Absher were riding behind them to make sure their every order was carried out. Absher was the grandson of Stumpy Absher, one of Buff's friends when he was trapping beaver with Tye's father and the famous Jim Bridger forty years earlier. Christian, Phipps, and Arnold had been on several patrols with Tye and had proven themselves many times to be capable of handling any situation. McClellan felt good about the men and felt proud as he looked back at the blue clad soldiers riding two abreast with the Flag of the United States flapping in the early morning breeze above them along with the smaller company guidon. He also knew, as did the men, that some of them would not be sitting upright in the saddle when the patrol returned.

Chapter Four

When the troop turned north off the Old Mail Road, Tye, Buff, and Dan moved out in front about a quarter mile. McClellan put riders out on each side a hundred yards or so out from the column. These out riders would warn the troop of any hostiles and they could give the column a few extra seconds warning they would ordinarily not have. Within an hour, the terrain changed from fairly flat to broken hills and arroyos. Cedar and cactus covered the rocky ground. From a quarter mile away, the scouts could hear the horses and wagons of the column.

"Sorta noisy ain't they," Buff said, more of a fact than a question.

"Exactly why the army can never surprise the Indians," Dan said smiling as he looked over his shoulder at the approaching column.

"How much futher ta whare tha men wure kilt?" Buff asked, nudging his horse with his moccasins to keep up with Tye and Dan's horses that had gotten a couple steps on him. At the crest of a hill, they stopped. Tye nudged Sandy a couple steps closer to the rim of the canyon. Stretched out before him was a huge valley that's floor was covered in sage, cedar, cactus, and huge boulders that apparently had been spewed from the bowels of the earth thousands of years ago. Tye had been here many times and he knew the area well. He had found many bones from huge animals that appeared to be very old, maybe thousands of years. They were from no animal he had ever seen. He had learned this small valley was a sacred place to the Apache so they would not enter it. The Apache felt like the spirits of the ancients still lived here and they would be asking for more trouble by entering it. He turned Sandy to the left and started moving west, around the rim. They could continue north after a small detour around the valley.

Dan, knowing of the valley, spoke. "It is good to bypass this place. If Apache eyes were watching, there would be bloodshed for our violating it by entering into it."

"This heer sum special place fur them?" Buff asked.

"They believe the spirits of their forefathers still live here along with the great beast the bones belonged to. They will not enter it and will kill those that do when they leave," Tye stated.

Buff nodded. "Seed that befor bac in tha montons with tha Blackfut. Tha can git pretty damn touchee on sum thangs like that." He looked down the slope at the column following then on the flat land below them. “Thos thar wagons gonna be able ta sta with us, Tye?”

“For a few miles; if the site of the fight is where I think it is, they can go that far but not much further from there. There’s some high ground near there. I think we could leave the wagons, supplies and the medical team there with a few soldiers for protection.”

“We are already outnumbered, Tye. Reducing our numbers more…is that smart?” Dan queried.

“We’ll be stopping for a break here in an hour or so,” Tye said. “We’ll discuss the situation with Captain McClellan and go with what he feels best.” Nothing else was said and the three men continued along the rim. As far as Buff was concerned this was the ‘purtiest’ country he had seen since he left Colorado. The canyon was deep and wide and one could tell that it was a place that had been uninhabited for a long time. This fact made it even more intriguing to an old mountain man like Buff. It was not covered in towering pines or the beautiful aspens but rather, it was a desolate beauty. The floor of the canyon was fairly flat but a man on a horse would have trouble navigating through it because of the boulders, some of which was larger than a house. The canyon walls were what caught most of Buff’s attention. They appeared to be free of dirt and were almost pure white in most places. The walls were almost vertical from the rim for about a hundred feet and then a steep slope for another two hundred to the canyon floor. There was almost no brush to be seen anywhere except for some cactus that drew his attention and wonderment. They appeared to grow straight out of the rocks.

They traveled for several minutes before they came to the end of the canyon and turned north. They were traveling slowly so the wagons could keep up.

"Ya'll go down the slope and wait for McClellan. I'm going up there," Tye said, pointing to the high rim that was probably a half mile off, "to see if I can spot anything from there." Both men nodded and turned their mounts down the slope. Buff turned in the saddle and hollered.

"Yu best be karful, Tye. Yu heer me?" Tye waved his acknowledgement and kicked Sandy into a fast trot. A few minutes later reaching the summit, he reined up, dismounted and loosened the girth on the saddle to let Sandy blow some. Several minutes crept by as he sat on his heels, studying the terrain below him. He could see maybe a mile toward the west and east but only half that distance ahead to the north. He saw nothing but more sage and cactus…at first. A wisp of what appeared to be smoke could be faintly seen to the northwest, maybe three quarters of a mile off. He could tell there was a creek there by the number of trees that snaked along the canyon floor following the banks of the creek. The smoke came from an area on the far side of the trees. It wasn't a campfire, there was too much smoke. It wasn't a grass fire because there wasn't enough smoke. If it was a burned out homestead, it was probably set on fire late yesterday and had just about burned itself out. He figured that's what it was. "Damn," Tye swore. "Damn." He re-tightened the girth and mounted Sandy. He turned him back the way he had come and headed for the column.

~~~

Jarrod Cavender studied the burned out homestead from behind some trees along the creek. He had set out this morning to see if any homesteads were near the spot he had chosen to make his home. He could see nothing moving, only the barely visible remaining flames from the caved in roof of the home. He sat there several minutes, wanting to go but afraid if he did what he would find. He sat there five more minutes before standing up and walking toward what remained of the home. His horse followed with Jarrod holding the reins loosely in his left hand, his pistol in his right.

Entering the yard, he stopped abruptly. His gut turned over and he thought he was going to vomit. Before him, lying in the yard was a woman, or what he thought was a woman. She was mutilated beyond belief. Beyond her was what he figured was her husband. He had his hands tied behind his back and a rope around his neck and wrapped around one of the post that supported the porch. He was in a sitting position, legs stretched out in front of him on the ground. Jarrod swiveled his head to look where the man's wife lay and cursed. The heathens had probably raped his wife repeatedly
~~~

and made him watch before killing him. "Damn them to hell," he uttered when he walked to the corral. A boy, maybe ten or twelve was tied to the railing around the coral. 'They must have used him for target practice,' he thought. At least twenty arrows were in the boy from head to foot. All had been scalped.

Recovering from the shock, he jumped on his horse to head back to where his family was. He rode a hundred yards before stopping. He couldn't leave these people for the buzzards and coyotes. Cursing, he reined his mount around.

Tye had reported the smoke and they were a quarter of a mile from the homestead when they saw the house, or what was left of it. They also saw a man riding a horse toward the house. Surprised anyone was still alive; Tye, Buff, and Dan kicked their mounts into a gallop and closed on the home. Jarrod saw them but it was too late to run. He grabbed his rifle and swung it toward the men. Tye, seeing this, reined in quickly, raised his hands and shouted. "WE ARE SCOUTS FOR THE ARMY. WE MEAN NO HARM."

The man hesitated and then lowered his rifle. The men rode toward each other, and Jarrod was watching the men closely, ready to simply raise the barrel and fire if need be. The men stopped twenty yards away. The big man on the oversized sorrel moved his mount a step out from the rest.

"Tye Watkins the name. I'm Chief of Scouts at Fort Clark. These men here are my scouts, Buff and Dan." Both men nodded. "Who are you?" Tye asked.

"Name's Jarrod Cavender; we just came into this country yesterday. There's a valley over the hill yonder," he said pointing with the rifle, "and I want to homestead it. I rode out this morning to see if there were any neighbors that might have homesteaded it already. I found this," he said sweeping his arm toward the home.

"Anyone left alive?" Tye asked already knowing the answer.

"None," the man said shaking his head. "None."

"McClellan's coming," Dan said. Jarrod turned his head and saw the large column of soldiers and wagons.

"From Clark?"

"Yes," Tye answered. "We had a patrol wiped out yesterday morning. We are going to retrieve the bodies and see if we can find the hostiles." Jarrod nodded. Tye continued. "I think you had better get back to your family Mr. Cavender. We'll take care of this," he said nodding toward the homestead. Jarrod turned his horse to leave. "You be careful and take care of your family." Tye said. "We'll be by before dark and probably camp close to your camp." Cavender didn't answer. He was hurrying to get back to his family.

The bodies were retrieved, wrapped in blankets and buried. Every man had figured out the man had had to watch his wife being used by the Apache. The married ones understood what it must have done to him more so than the single men but all were highly upset. "We catch them red-bastards, there won't be any prisoners," was uttered by more than one trooper.

Buff overheard some of the talk and when he, Tye, and McClellan were alone, he mentioned it. Tye pushed the front of his hat up with his finger. "They are upset about their friends being killed and this only added to the anger. We'll probably see more of this before it's over," he said pointing toward the graves. "These Apaches are mad, Captain. Apaches will scalp their victims and maybe torture them to find out how tough the prisoner is but mutilation like this comes from pure anger and hate."

"I've often wondered why they torture their prisoners so much," McClellan said, more of a question than anything else. Dan walked up at that time.

"Apaches feel they get power from an enemy they kill. The longer it takes the more power they get. They will kill a prisoner immediately if he is weak. They feel there is no power to be gained from killing a coward."

"I may be a coward then if I'm caught," McClellan said smiling, bringing a laugh from the scouts.

"Yu jus mite be smarter than I figgered," Buff said laughing. They mounted their horses. McClellan spoke to Lieutenant Garrison who was standing by his mount a few feet away. "Get the men mounted, Lieutenant," he ordered.

"Yes, Sir." He turned to Sergeants Phipps and Arnold and repeated the order. The troops were moving out a minute later trying to keep the scouts in sight.

Chapter Five

Tye saw the two wagons and the people moving about them long before they spotted him. The scouts waited for McClellan and the men to arrive, and then headed toward the wagon. He saw the man named Jarrod coming to meet them with an attractive lady by his side. Tye, Buff, and Dan dismounted and shook the man's hand. The man was genuinely glad to see them and introduced his wife.

"Honey, these are the men I told you about. This big feller here is Tye, and that's Buff and Dan. This lady here is my wife, Laverne."

The men tipped their hats and as one said, "Pleased to meet you maam."

The two boys came up and the introductions were made. The younger boy shook Tye's hand.

"We spoke with some homesteaders a couple days ago and they spoke of a man that was a scout from Clark. The scout was named Watkins. You him?"

"My name is Watkins and I scout out of Clark. I hope what you heard wasn't bad," Tye said smiling.

"No, Sir. They said you were the best and if we were ever in trouble to look you up." Jarrod snapped his fingers. "Tye Watkins. Sure they spoke of you. When you introduced yourself I thought that name was familiar."

McClellan walked up at that time and shook Jarrod's hand and tipped his hat to Laverne. "I'm afraid you come into this country at a bad time Mr. Cavender. We believe the Apaches are making their big push to rid this country of the homesteaders, towns, and soldiers. It would be very dangerous for you to stay right now." "We sold everything we owned to come out here, Captain. There is no place for us to go back to."

"I'm sure that is true, but I must insist yo…"

McClellan was interrupted by Tye.

"The captain is right, Mr. Cavender. It is very dangerous right now. You saw that with your own eyes earlier today. I know you want this land," he said sweeping his arm above his head in a circle, "and I can't blame you. It's a good place to build a home. But I think it would be smart if you waited till this Apache problem is solved."

"I understand, but what are we to do?" Cavender said, shrugging his shoulders, desperation showing in his voice.

"I think I have an answer," Tye replied. He turned to McClellan. "Sir, where we are heading it begins to get rough country pretty quick. The wagons cannot go more than a mile or so farther. This would be a good place to set up base camp." He pointed to a sheer cliff with large oaks around the base. "There's a good spot and the Cavender's can stay also."

"There's a spring there too," Cavender said, glad his problem might be solved. McClellan, never one to make a quick decision, pondered the situation for a moment. He valued Tye's opinions and quickly decided that would be what they would do.

He turned to Lieutenant Garrison.

"Lieutenant, get the wagon and ambulance over to the base of that cliff." He pointed in the direction he was talking about. "Have the medical staff set up a field hospital and then pick ten men to stay here to protect them. Also, the Cavender family will be camped with them for protection."

"Yes, Sir." He turned and shouted for Sergeant Christian to come to him. While the wagons were being moved to the cliff and camp was being set up, Tye was learning more about the Cavenders. The family was like all the other families out here, hardy, brave, and having a strong will to make a home regardless of the dangers. He made it a point to meet and visit all of them he could on his travels through the countryside.

It always amazed Captain McClellan when he pointed to an area on the map and Tye could name the families living there. He realized quickly the scout had an uncanny knack for remembering names. The captain knew Tye had strong feelings for them that stemmed from his own family's experience as homesteaders many years ago. He had felt Tye's misery every time one of the families was killed. He knew this quality Tye had endeared him to all the homesteaders but it didn't stop with the many families settling in the area. The soldiers knew Tye would do anything, including endangering his own life, to protect them.

Garrison reported about thirty minutes later that the camp was set and the men selected to stay behind as guards. Sergeant Christian would be in charge.

"Good." McClellan said. "Have Christian keep a man up there," he added, pointing to the rim. "They should be able to spot any trouble coming." Garrison nodded and walked to where Christian and the men staying behind were.

The men gathered around Garrison. "This is not a holiday for you men getting to stay here instead of on the patrol. There is close to a hundred angry Apaches roaming the area. You had better stay alert and be prepared to defend yourselves at any moment. Sergeant Christian will be in charge. You will follow his orders without question. IS THAT UNDERSTOOD?" he asked raising his voice to put emphasis on that point. Every man nodded his understanding. Garrison turned to Christian. "Use our wagons and the Cavenders for protection. Have the men pile up rocks for protection and dig in for a possible attack. There will be plenty of supplies for you." He shook Christian's hand and walked away.

"You heard the lieutenant. Let's get the wagons moved to form a barrier and start pushing some dirt and rocks for protection. Private James, you find a way up that cliff and take the first watch. Take a canteen of water with you. I will set the sentry duty roster in a few minutes." He told each man to make sure he had a full canteen of water when he started his watch. "Now," he added. "Lets get started making this place a fort."

The column had moved out, heading north. They were making much better time without the wagons and Tye figured they could get within five or six miles from the site of the massacre by dark and then locate it early in the morning. He was surprised that with the number of Indians supposedly in the area that they had seen no signs of them.

~~~~

Asay was a fierce and crafty warrior. His scouts had reported the wagons that the Cavenders were traveling in and also he knew where the bluecoats were. Very few things transpired in Apache land that the locals did not know about. Sometime, the army,
~~~~

including Tye, thought the birds such as the hawks and brown eagles spoke with the Apache.

Asay squinted toward the setting sun from atop the hill he was on. He had been up here for over 24 hours with nothing to eat or drink. He was waiting for Ussen, the Creator and Life Giver, to speak to him, or give him a sign to tell him what he should do. He prayed for strength and wisdom to lead his people

Just before sunset a brown eagle circled high over his head. Watching, he noticed the great bird getting lower and lower with each circle until finally, just at dark the eagle was almost a arms' length above his head, and suddenly, letting out a great cry, flew west…toward where the bluecoats had camped on the creek.

Standing up, Asay raised his arms wide to the heavens. Ussen had given him a sign. He let out a great war cry that caused every head of his warriors below him to look up to the rim where their leader was. They knew what had happened and the brave with the drum began a fast rhythmic beat…BOOM, boom, boom, boom, BOOM, boom, boom. The warriors began chanting and dancing, shaking their bows and rifles above their heads as they circled the fire. Asay made his way down the hill, knowing what he was going to do at first light.

~~~~

Tye had found a good place to camp just before dark. There was no water but they had plenty with the packhorse carrying two
~~~~

barrels. The camp was against a cliff and a deep arroyo ran along one side making it impossible for an attack to come from that direction. If they were attacked, with only two directions to defend, they could hold off any Indian attack. Forty or so rifles could create a deadly fire when the enemy had to cross open ground.

There was no coffee as it was to be a cold camp much to the agitation of the troops. A hot meal and coffee was always looked forward to after a long day in the saddle. Disappointed as they were, they were veterans of many a patrol and they understood why there would be no fires.

McClellan walked over to where his scouts were sitting and sat down on his heels. "Do you know how much farther it is to where the fight took place," he asked Tye.

"If it's where I deducted from Baker's description of the area, I'd say we are less than five miles away. We should be there by an hour or so after daylight."

"Good," McClellan said, and stood up to leave.

"Best have the sentries warned they had better be alert, Captain," Dan said. "Remind them there's a hell of a lot of Apaches around."

"I thought they don't fight at night."

Buff laughed. "Thar's manee a dead soldjur that tho't tha same thang, kaptain. Most Injuns don't because tha beleeve if'n tha git themselves kilt at nite, tha will wonder aimlessly fer ever in darkness. Don't thank fer a minute tho they won't try and sneek up and kill an enemee if they feel safe in doing so."

"I'll tell Lieutenant Garrison to speak to the men who have sentry duty tonight."

Tye smiled. That old mountain man had a way with words. He stood up and walked to the edge of camp. He looked up at the sky in wonderment at how big it was like he had done a thousand times before on a thousand other nights camped under the stars. He stood perfectly still letting his ears become attuned to the normal night sounds of this land. He listened to the night breeze for any sounds. He knew there was a difference in the sound of a leaf being rustled by the wind and a man brushing against it. These old hills are always changing with rocks falling or dirt shifting but being dislodged by a man's foot is a different sound. Small animals move with a rustling sound and if a snapping of a stick is heard, it would be a much larger animal moving in the darkness… probably the two-legged type. He stood there a few more minutes listening but the only sound was a sentry's footsteps. He walked back to his bedroll and lay down. He was asleep almost immediately.

Chapter Six

The night passed quietly and an hour after first light of the new day found the scouts looking on a sight that Tye had hoped to never see again. Twice in the last year he had found soldiers that were like these. The bodies were ripped apart by buzzards and coyotes, and lay scattered on the ground. The birds rose into the air and circled over head waiting for these intruders to leave. Tye sat on Sandy and girded himself for what he was fixing to see up close. They dismounted and tied their horses to some cedar.

"If we let them get a whiff of the smell they would be hard as hell to control so let's leave them here." Approaching on foot they found Lieutenant Braddock and the private first. Braddock's body was still suspended above the ground on the spear with only the backs of his legs and his dangling arms touching the dirt.

"Tha didn't butcher him, Tye." Buff stated. "I don't kno abut these heer Apaches, but in the mountains tha was a sign of respect for a fighting man."

"Same here Buff. Things looks exactly like what Baker said happened. The three of them got through and the private's horse went down. Braddock stayed to stall the Apache long enough for Baker to get away."

"Man had a lot of guts, I'll say that for him," Dan added. Buff and Tye nodded just as McClellan and the column rode up.

"My God," McClellan said. "Is that Lieutenant Braddock?"

"Yes Sir," Tye answered. "Looks like things went down just like Baker said. The rest of the men are about three hundred yards down there where all the buzzards are. It appears Braddock made a choice to try and buy time for Baker to get away."

"You mean he stayed knowing what the end result was going to be?"

"That's exactly the way the signs point, Sir. He knew he was a dead man but he also knew it was his responsibility to let Thurston know about the Apaches and someone had to live to tell the story. Baker was that man."

"Remarkable," McClellan mumbled. "Remarkable." He dismounted and turned to Garrison. "Get a couple of men and get Mr. Braddock's body off that damn spear and wrap him in a blanket…and do it carefully and respectfully."

Tye smiled. McClellan had come a long way from the arrogant, self centered bitter man he was a year ago. He was hated by the men and had no respect from the other officers. That feeling all changed when his arrogance got himself and his men in an ambush. They survived only because Tye got them out. Tye had a long talk with McClellan telling him that something good had come out of the mess and that he wasn't the only officer that had committed the mistake he had made. The good was that the men had never seen McClellan in a battle situation and he handled himself well in this one. They would respect him for that, and if he would listen to the men who had been out here and quit doing everything 'by the book', he would be okay. He changed and had proven himself to be an excellent officer and Thurston's go to man in a time of crisis.

Braddock and the private's body had been wrapped in a blanket and the men made their way to the others, shooing the buzzards away. Very few got through the next hour with their breakfast still in their belly. Body parts, blood and the terrible stench of death that one never forgets hung heavy in the early morning air. While the men wrapped the remains of their friends in blankets, the scouts circled the area, searching for the direction the Apaches had traveled. It was not hard to find the tracks…seventy or so horses left a trail even an Apache could not hide.

~~~
~~~

Asay lay on his belly, studying the lay of the land, but more important, studying the bluecoats. He lay hidden, behind some sage on the crest of a hill about three hundred yards from where the soldiers were. The soldiers being there had been a surprise. Asay and his men had been following the tracks of the white man and his family. Now, they would kill all of them and pick up much needed guns and bullets.

Asay lay with his lifelong friend, Naiche. "This will be a good day, my friend," he whispered to Asay. "We will kill all the white eyes…and if we fail, it will be a good day to die." Asay turned his head and looked into his friends eyes and smiled. The two of them had spent many nights under the stars; they both had killed many enemies; and they had taken sisters for their wives six winters ago. During those nights they had spent together they had many talks of the old ways, of their fathers and grandfathers. They talked of the battles they had fought together against the Comanche, Mexicans, and the white eyes.

Theirs had been a good life, an Apache's life. They each had one child and were content to hunt, occasionally go raiding, and most important, taking care of their families. This seemed a long time ago. Their world crashed around them when the bluecoats had raided their camp while they were away hunting and slaughtered the old men, women and children that were left unprotected in the camp. Both men had lost everything, parents, wives, and tragically, their children. The day they buried their families, they took an oath to kill the white man wherever they found them…kill them without mercy… men, women, and children.

That had been the start of the killing. Their bravery and daring had not gone unnoticed by their fellow warriors. The younger warriors had been drawn to them like a magnet. After many battles, Asay had emerged as the leader of this elite fighting group. They had killed over thirty whites and until yesterday, had not lost a single man. This was due to Asay's cunning in planning battle strategy plus the fact they were all excellent guerilla fighters. As the two studied the camp below them, Asay's thoughts drifted back to the previous night. Around the campfire Asay had spoken of why they were here. He spoke of their dead friends and families killed by the white eyes and spoke of the Apache way of life and how the white man was intent on changing it.

They were insisting the Apache disregard Ussen as their creator and worship their God. Finally, he had picked up a handful of dirt and let it slowly sift from his hand to be blown away with the night breeze. He told them this is our land and like the wind is blowing this sand away, the white man is taking it away from us. This cannot happen…we will stop them or die like an Apache should…killing his enemies. He would not die from old age taking hand outs from the white man. His short speech had been followed by much shouting and celebrating from his fellow warriors.

That was last night and now; his men were waiting to see what plan he had to kill these white intruders. As he studied the lay of the land and where the soldiers had camped, he became slightly impressed with whoever had chosen this spot for a camp. They had a high cliff behind them that had a slight overhang which would prevent his warriors from shooting straight down on their backs. A sudden flash of light caught his attention on the rim of the cliff. 'So, the white soldiers had a man up there to give warning.' He brought his attention back to the camp. He knew from seeing the trees that there was probably water by the base of the cliff. He figured the wagons had plenty of food so there would be no chance of them starving the soldiers or seeing them short of water. The area in front of the wagons was fairly level and there was no cover other than low sage and cactus for almost a hundred yards. He knew there was no way for an attack to be made that would not cost many lives of his friends. He silently cursed the leader of the soldiers that had chosen this spot for a camp. He knew there was only one way to wipe the bluecoats out. He slid back down the hill with Naiche right beside him. Reaching the bottom, the other warriors gathered around him.

"The white man has chosen their camp well," he said. "There is only one way for us to kill them without many of us dying." The braves moved in closer to their leader. "We will wait until after dark and move in close to their camp, crawling on our bellies. With the first sign of dawn, we will attack and be on them before they can defend themselves. We will then have our scalps, guns, and bullets." Nodding of heads and grunts from the warriors told him they agreed with his plan. "Naiche, take two men and see if you can find some meat for us." Naiche nodded, and picking two men left the others, heading away from the white mans camp.

~~~

Sergeant Christian looked around the camp. The wagons had been emptied and turned on their sides to form a barrier. Rocks and dirt had been pushed up to form a wall three feet high that ran right and left of the wagons for ten yards and then circled back to the trees. Spare ammunition had been placed at different places along the wall and behind the wagons as well as canteens. At the first sign of trouble, each man would rush to his spot assigned to him by Christian.

The Cavenders had finished their meal and was preparing for bed when Christian approached them.

"You have the camp looking like a fort, Sergeant," the older Cavender commented.

"It will do," Christian answered. "If trouble comes, Mr. Cavender, take your family behind one of your wagons. Keep them hidden there and don't come out. Do you have pistols for the boys and your wife?"

"Yes. Why?"
~~~

"If our defense gets breached, you and your boys can do a lot of damage with the guns because they will not know you are there until you open fire. It could be the one thing that puts the odds in our favor."

"Do you really think trouble will come?" Mrs. Cavender asked.

"I don't know maam. I know the Apache seem to always know where the soldiers are. If they do come, it will get nasty in a hurry so you and your family do as I said and be prepared to help out if things don't go as planned." He tipped his hat to Mrs. Cavender and nodded to the elder Cavender and the boys. "Ya'll get you some rest now." He left them standing by their small fire and shouted the names of four troopers who came running.

Privates Jensen, Rockford, Maples, and Gregory were gathered around Christian. "You men are the sentries tonight. The order of duty will be Jensen first, and then Rockford, Gregory, and last watch is you," He said pointing to Maples. "Our lives and the lives of that family over there are in each of your hands. If I catch one of you napping, it will be the sorriest day of your miserable lives. UNDERSTOOD?"

"Yes, Sir" came the answer from all four.

"Good. Jensen, you start your watch at ten and then each of you has two hour shifts. Any questions?" The question was followed by silence from the four. "Then, ya'll get you some rest." As they headed for their bedrolls, each man stopped and stared into the darkness as a coyote cut loose with the eerie wailing to the right of the camp and was answered by another from the opposite side. Each man looked at each other thinking the same thing. 'Was it really a coyote or was it the Apache, who could make all kinds of animal calls and sometimes signaled one another that way. They rolled up in their bedrolls, not sleeping, listening for any other sounds.

Christian walked over to where Maples was lying on his bedroll. He kneeled down by the private. "You are the most experienced, Maples, and that is why I have you on the last watch. If trouble comes, it will be just before or at first light. Keep you rifle in your hands so you can fire a warning quickly."

"Yes, Sir, I'll be ready, Sergeant." Christian patted him on the shoulder.

"Get some sleep, Private." He stood up and stretched. 'This business of being in command is damn stressful,' he thought to himself. He made the rounds of the camp, checking everything from canteens being where they were supposed to be, bullets stashed, and even checked the surgeon to make sure he had what he needed out and handy. Satisfied he had done everything he could, he found his bedroll and lay down.

An hour passed and Christian still lay on his bedroll, wide awake. There was no moon and the stars were so bright it was almost as if he could reach up and touch them. Cursing to himself for not being able to go to sleep, he stood up and walked over to the wagons. He saw Jensen get up and walk to the base of the cliff to climb up and relieve the man on sentry duty. He could hear the snoring of Mr. Cavender and a couple of his men. Walking to the wall they had built, he kneeled down to listen. He heard nothing but the usual night sounds…at first. He heard a noise that sounded like a twig snapping. He strained his ears, not even breathing, listening for any sound. Not hearing anything, he relaxed and decided to go back to his bedroll and try to get some sleep. No matter how careful a person was fifty or so men crawling on rocky ground was impossible to be completely quiet, even Apaches. As Christian stood to go to his bedroll, he heard another sound. He knew it was not his imagination this time. He woke each man up, whispered to them what was going on and had each man go to his post quietly. He took his position and settled in to wait for the first sign of the coming dawn…maybe the last one he and his men will ever see.

~~~

Tye had found a spring with good water just before dark, and the column had settled in for the night, bivouacked around it. McClellan had allowed the men small fires for their coffee and biscuits but was to be put out before dark. This small allowance made a big difference in his men's attitude. They were veterans of many patrols but they felt it wasn't right for them to have to endure two nights in a row of a cold camp…at least that's what they thought. They figured it was not necessary to not let the Injuns
~~~

know where they were, since they didn't figure any Apache in his right mind would attack this many soldiers.

Tye, Buff, Dan, and McClellan along with Sergeants Phipps and Arnold, sat around one fire drinking coffee. Sergeant Absher along with Lieutenant Garrison was setting the night sentries in position.

"Wusn't a bad muve, Captain, letting tha men have sum coffee tonight. Seen sum patrols git plum outa hand with angry soldiers because tha didn't have this damn bad coffee," Buff said laughing.

"I might have been one of them," Phipps said jokingly. Everyone laughed when Arnold said "amen to that." All knew that Arnold and Phipps were the epitome of what a soldier should be and were just kidding.

"Just might have had to kill me first captain," Tye added, laughing even harder.

"I didn't realize just a small thing like allowing coffee could make such a difference," McClellan said seriously when things quieted down.

"Seed a kaptain tha refused ta allow his men coffee three days in a row git himself kilt in a charge against sum Blackfut…shot in tha bac," Buff said laughing and slapping McClellan on the shoulder. Everyone laughed including McClellan even though his wasn't as raucous as the others. He wondered if the old scout was serious.

It was almost dark and the order was given to put out the fires. There was rush to refill each man's cups first though.

"Where do you think the Apaches we are trailing are headed, Tye?' McClellan asked just as Garrison and Absher sat down and got the last of the coffee.

"What was all the laughing about over here?" Garrison asked before Tye could answer.

"We were explaining to the captain here just how upset some of you soldiers could get if they had to endure the severity of two nights in a row without their coffee," Tye replied.

"Could get damn serious," Absher said once again bringing laughter from everyone…except McClellan who only half smiled at the remark.

"To answer your question, Sir, I cant' figure out why they are going in the direction they are headed except for following the tracks of two wagons."

"Maybe they just want to kill those people and take what's in the wagon," Lt. Garrison said adding his two bits worth into the conversation.

Tye's scout Dan, emptied what little remained of his coffee. "There's no doubt that's their intentions but why did they pass up some homesteads that were only a little out of the way?"

"Mabee these here Apaches ain't from around here and don't know the area," Buff said. "Tha don't know where tha homesteads are but tha kno there are guns, bullets, and probably a woman or two with those wagons."

"I think you are right, Buff," Tye stated, then added, "And I think we might have a problem, Captain."

"What are you talking about?"

"What if those wagon tracks are the Cavender's and I bet they are, and if so, they are leading the Apaches right to Sergeant Christian." He cursed himself for not figuring that out earlier.

McClellan stood up quickly and stared into the darkness. "How far behind them are we?"

"Four hours, five at the most." Tye stood up. "Are you thinking what I think you are?"

"If what you think about the tracks is true, when would you put the Apaches at Christian's camp?"

Tye thought for a moment. "I figure they are there now and will hit him at first light." He glanced at Dan for his thoughts and received a nod.

McClellan stood with his back to the men, hands clasped behind he back. He turned suddenly and asked. "Tye, do you or your men know a shortcut to the camp and if so, can you find it in the dark?"

Tye looked at Dan and the scout shook his head. "No Captain, we don't. I can find the camp but we will basically follow the tracks of the Apache." He looked at the stars and said "It's about 10:30

now. I'd say we need to leave about midnight to get there by daylight."

"Then it's settled. We will muster the men just before midnight and head out." He turned to Lieutenant Garrison. "You, Phipps, and Arnold pass the word to the troops."

"Yes, Sir."

McClellan stretched out on his bedroll as did the scouts to try and get a little rest.

Chapter Seven

Asay and Naiche lay side by side in the sage, waiting for the moment the sun topped the crest of the hill behind them. With the sun at their backs, it would be a little more difficult for the soldiers to be accurate with their bullets. Asay had put the blue tunic on of a soldier he had killed. .It was of a heavy material and the small rocks did not scratch and cut his arms and elbows as he and the rest moved even closer to the soldier's camp. He lay behind a thick sage and looking through it, he saw he was no more than forty yards from the blue coats camp.

Looking back over his shoulder, he could see the top of the sun coming over the crest. 'Only a few more minutes,' he thought, 'and the victory will be ours.'

He whispered to Naiche, "It looks like they are asleep. I see no one moving about." Naiche nodded in agreement. The light from the sun was already turning the crest of the hill behind the soldiers a light gray and they could see no sentry.

Naiche whispered to his friend, "No guard on the hill. Nah-tanh has killed him." Nah-tanh was a warrior that could sneak upon any animal or man without being seen. It was an amazing feat to behold as he proved his skill to the other warriors time and time again. It had become a game during peace time for him to pick a fellow warrior and sneak up on him and tap him on the shoulder much to the delight of those watching. It was as much an embarrassment to the tricked warrior as it was amusement to the others.

The suns rays struck the camp and Asay knew it was time. He stood up and shouted, "AIIEE," as loud as he could and instantly, sixty or so warriors were up and charging the camp, screaming their war cries and insults to their hated enemy. The soldiers, shocked at first at how close the Indians were to their camp, quickly regained their composure and fired on Christian's command. Several were instantly cut down by the deadly fire from the soldiers but the rest were almost on top of them when a bugle sounded from just over the hill. The Apache stopped their charge and retreated, disappearing like ghost. They mounted their ponies and followed Asay away from the camp. Asay looked back just in time to see a large man in a buckskin shirt on a magnificent horse lead the soldiers in a charge over the hill. He gave a circular motion with his hand and the group of warriors split into three separate groups and headed in different directions. They would meet later at a predetermined spot near a place called Eagle's Nest.

Tye and the column chased the Apache till they split. They halted the chase at that point and headed back to the camp. As they approached the camp, Sergeant Christian came out to meet them along with the rest of the men.

After the saluting and shaking of hands was over, McClellan asked. "Where are the rest?" as he counted only seven men.

"Two dead behind the wall, Sir; and probably another up yonder that was on sentry duty."

"I see six dead Apache, Sergeant. Are they more?"

"Two behind the wall, Sir. They were on us just as the sun came over that cliff yonder," he said nodding to the cliff behind McClellan. The captain turned, and was temporarily blinded by the rays. He immediately realized that it was a miracle they had hit anything and that this Apache leader was no youngster but a seasoned warrior, experienced in the ways of war.

"If you had been another minute, Sir, we would all be dead." Christian said.

Mr. Cavender spoke up from behind Christian. "If the sergeant here had not gotten us up a couple hours ago and to our post…" he didn't need to finish the sentence. McClellan, realizing the situation stepped down from his mount and shook Christian's hand.

"Good job, soldier…good job." He turned to Tye. "Do we pursue the Apache?"

"Yes Sir. That's what we are here to do but let's leave a half dozen more men here first." He turned to Christian. "Sergeant, if I was you, I would have my men clear all that brush away for at least sixty or seventy yards giving you a better killing field."

"Right away, Tye, I'll double the sentries at night also."

"Just stay alert, Sergeant," McClellan said. "The Apache know you are here and could double back so you and your men stay on your toes."

"Yu shore as hell don't have ta wurry about that, Sir," a soldier of maybe fifty said. His remark brought a few 'amens' from the others. They had just learned first hand what could happen and each knew they were alive because of Sergeant Christian having them up and ready and Tye pushing the soldiers to get here. Buff could sense what he already knew. Looking into these men's faces he could see the respect the men had for Tye and they just plain felt safer when he was around.

"We've pushed these horses and men all night, Sir," Tye said turning to McClellan. "I know I said a minute ago that we should chase them but I would suggest we give them a blow for three or four hours, but," he added, "It's only a suggestion."

McClellan turned to Lieutenant Garrison. “Have the men take care of their mounts and then get some rest. We will stay here till noon before heading out.”

Tye nodded to McClellan. “We won’t lose them, Sir. They ain’t going far. They are here for one thing and that’s to kill every white and Mexican on the Border.”

~~~

Asay led his group through a canyon, around arroyos, and over a switchback trail that never ran in a straight line for more than a couple hundred yards. They had pushed their mounts pretty hard and so they slowed them to a walk. Asay twisted his head back to speak to Nah-tanh. “Get a man and go back a short distance. Stay out of sight, and watch for the soldiers. We are meeting the others at where the white man calls Eagle Nest.” Nan-tanh nodded and turned his mount to backtrack and watch. The rest continued making their way to the meeting place.

Naiche guided his mount beside Asay. “I heard one of our men say he heard Gian-nah-tah say he knew this scout that leads the bluecoats. He says that this man big medicine to the Lipan and other Apaches who live here. Say he great warrior and has killed many Apache. Say he track and fight like Apache.”

Asay looked at his friend and smiled. “Tell Gian-nah-tah to come here.” A few seconds later, the man was at his side.
~~~

“What do you know of this scout you say is big medicine that leads the bluecoats and how did you hear of him?” Asay asked.

“My wife’s brother knows a brave that is Lipan. Lipan say this man is like Apache but much bigger,” he said holding his hand a foot over his head. “He much strong and can fight like Apache with knife or tomahawk. They say he like a spirit, one sees him and then he disappears like smoke in the wind. They say he speak Apache. It is said that once he is on your trail, nothing can keep him from finding you. His father was great warrior also but was killed in fight near here several years ago.”

“If his father was killed, then he is flesh and blood like me and you. He will die like the rest of the white invaders.” He turned his head and spit. “He is no spirit and will plead for his life when I catch him. You will see.”

Nothing else was said and as they rode, Asay thought about his past and mulled over in his mind what the future held for him…the Apache as a nation and their way of life. There seemed to be no end of the white man. He would love to live side by side with the white eyes but that was impossible. Besides lying and cheating the Redman, they thought the Indian was less than they and should be killed or placed on reservations. The Apache people could starve for all they cared. ‘The only good Indian is a dead Indian’ was a saying he had heard that they believed.

As he had rode thinking these things, it occurred to him he could not remember ever meeting a white man he felt he could trust, even during the peaceful times. As always when he was brooding like now, he thought of his family…his dead woman, his dead child, and his dead parents all killed by the hand of white soldiers. He had heard they bragged of a great victory. He would not consider killing helpless old men, women, and children a victory. When the Apaches did that, it was called a massacre by the white race, not a great victory for the Indian. As he thought on these things, his mood changed. He would never live with them, he would kill them every chance Ussen, the Creator, allowed him the opportunity to do so.

An hour later, when the sun was directly overhead, they came to Eagle's Nest. It was a deep arroyo that ran north and southwest all the way to the Rio Grande River. It had been carved by rain water over thousands of years. Except after a rain, it was almost always dry. They turned their ponies loose in a small dead end canyon that had an abundance of grass.

Naiche came over and sat beside him. "You look troubled my friend," he said. "Do you worry about this warrior scout that is supposedly after us?"

"I am afraid of no man, especially a white man. What our friend said about this scout is old squaw's tale…made up and not a single thing true except maybe his size. Then," he added, "Size does not matter when a rifle bullet enters the body or a sharp blade slices across one's throat. Even the great buffalo can be brought down with one bullet. This man is no greater than them. He is flesh and blood. You will soon see," he said as the tone of his voice rose in anger. He drew his Bowie from its sheath and violently driving it into the ground, shouting angrily, "HE WILL DIE BY MY KNIFE." The other warriors settled down around their leader to wait on their friends to arrive and all wondered what had caused the sudden, angry outburst from Asay. None asked.

~~~

Less than two hours passed before the first of Asay's men begin to arrive. There was much shouting and greeting of friends. Asay turned to Naiche.

"See if anyone knows of this man who scouts for the bluecoats?" Naiche left his friend for only a few minutes. He returned with a brave named Kol-So and behind him walked Gian-Nah-Tah who had been sent to see if the Pindah-Lickoyee (white eyes) was following.

Asay spoke. "Gian-Nah-Tah, describe this man who leads the bluecoats to Kol-So."

Gian-Nah-Tah spoke. "I have already described to Kol-So. He knows of this white man."

"What do you know?" Asay demanded, looking at Kol-So.

"He is called Watkins," the brave answered. "He big man, maybe a head taller than our tallest warrior; he great warrior. Father
~~~

raised him like Apache father raises his son: teaching to track and fight like Apache warrior; teaching to live off land like Apache; to think like Apache. Many Apache tried to kill him…none has. He is respected for this by all Lipan and other Apache along the Rio Grande. It is also said he, like all Apache, is known to speak from heart…no lie."

Asay took in all this information about this white man and nodded his head to Gian-Nah-Tah and Kol-So. He walked away to think about this man and decide what he would do next. Whatever he decided, he knew his plan would have to allow for this man Watkins being close at hand. He also knew most stories about men made them greater warriors than they actually were. He was glad the bluecoats had this man leading them. He would see to it that they and the Apache would soon find out who the best was…Watkins or himself. His thoughts were interrupted by shouts from his warriors as the third group of braves rode in.

~~~

McClellan had the column moving just before noon. The men were in a good mood and the horses fresh after the four hour rest. Out riders had been assigned on both flanks and Dan and Tye were three hundred yards in front while Buff rode beside McClellan.

"Tell me something, Buff," McClellan said. "I know you have told stories to Tye, O'Malley, Thurston and the rest but I need to know something."
~~~

"Whut's that, Captain?"

"In those mountains back in the twenties, was it really like I have read about?"

"Don't kno whut yu have read but I can tell yu how it really wus. First off, yu had ta be pretty damn tuff ta be a trapper. Not bragging but tha's tha truth. Tha winters got kold, I meen killin kold...twenty ta thirty degrees below zero and yu had no warm house to stay in. Tha ground wus covered by snow frum October to late April...sometimes as early as September and late as May. Seen it thirty fut deep before. Some of the taller mountains peaks were covered year around." He put his hands on the pommel of his saddle stared off into the distance. McClellan noticed the far-a-way look in his eyes.

"Had lots of frens die from that kold and snow. Had more die from starving and grizzles and several frum tha damn Blackfut. A trapper wus lucky to survive mor'n five yeers."

McClellan asked. "Why in God's name did you do it then?"

"Some fur tha money and some, like me, just ta enjoy tha freedom and seeing thangs no white man had seed before. Made a lot a friends during those years...frens like Jim Bridger, Jerome Absher, Jedediah Smith, and my best frend, Ben Watkins,,,Tye's pa. If yu ever saw tha Rockies, yu wud not have ta ask that question, Captain because if yu ever walked thru tha pine trees and drew in that fresh, clean air or saw tha beautiful aspens, yu wud know why.

If yu stood on one of those high peaks and looked across what seemed a hundred miles of mountains, valleys, and green pines, yu wud know. Yu would have ta believe that there was a God too. Only He could have made such a special place."

"I can see why you did it but how in the world did you survive the cold living outside every hour of the day?" McClellan asked.

"Buffalo robes, coffee, and whiskey and not necessarily in that thar order," Buff answered laughing. McClellan chuckled to himself knowing that to survive those conditions one probably did drink a lot of whiskey.

"Tye's coming, Captain." Buff said.

Chapter Eight

Trouble was coming at Major Thurston from every side. Reports of Apache depredations all over the area were coming in from hysterical homesteaders. A dispatch rider from Fort Duncan had arrived earlier and reported trouble in their area also. His commanding officer was asking for Thurston to send some troops to help. Thurston told his orderly to get Captain Langley, his adjutant, to come to his office immediately. In a couple of minutes, boots clicking on the wooden floor announced the arrival of the adjutant.

"Captain," Thurston said, "This corporal from Duncan just brought this dispatch." He handed it to Captain Langley who quickly scanned it.

"Sir," he blurted out, "You are not thinking of sending m… "

"Of course not, Captain," Thurston said cutting him off. "Under any other circumstances I would. Right now, I need to write a dispatch that the corporal here can take back. Then I need to send dispatches out to the commanding officers of Fort Davis, Inge, Stockton, and McKavett."

"Yes, Sir," Langley said taking out his pen and paper. Thurston began dictating to him his message to Fort Duncan.

Major Jacobs

It is with great regret that I am not able to send you any troops. We have the same problem here as you do, maybe worse. I have lost one patrol to the renegades and reports of trouble all over the area are coming hourly from homesteaders wanting protection. I believe this is a planned attack all along the Border with the intentions of spreading us so thin we are vulnerable by not being able to send troops from one fort to another.

A rider from Fort Davis arrived early today with the dispatch stuffed in his mouth. He lay across his saddle with three arrows in his back. I am sending riders to Forts Davis, Stockton, Inge, and McKavett.

I have my best officer and scout pursuing a large number of Apaches north of here that was responsible for the deaths of nine troopers, an officer and a scout. I have patrols west and south of Clark looking for signs of other Apache bands.

Also, the Apache that attacked my patrol was not Lipan, but probably Chiricahua from up in New Mexico. I believe this is a major push by all Apache tribes to rid the country of homesteaders and soldiers.

Again, let me say I deeply regret the situation that prevents me from sending you troops. Good Luck!

Major James Thurston

Commanding officer-Fort Clark, Texas

Thurston signed the dispatch and gave it to the rider from Duncan. He told the man to get him something to eat and a fresh horse would be waiting here for him in one hour. He then dictated to his adjutant, Captain Langely, the dispatches he wanted to send to the other forts. He ordered his orderly to find Master Sergeant O'Malley and have him get four of his best horseman in the saddle with the dispatches quickly.

Thurston sat down behind his desk and buried his head in the palms of his hands, wondering what his next move would be. Trouble was everywhere and he didn't think he had the manpower to handle it. He figured the best move would be to try and get the homesteaders to the fort. He again hollered for his orderly. When he arrived he told him to have O'Malley come to his office immediately.

"But, Sir, I told him to find the riders you asked for."

"I know that, dammit," Thurston said angrily, chomping down hard on his cigar. "Get him here as soon as he gets the riders on their way." The orderly turned tail and scooted out of the office immediately.

A few minutes later, Thurston was standing at the window doing what he always did when he was stressed or worried…puffing on his cigar when he saw the huge man coming across the parade ground. Even at this distance, he knew it to be Sergeant Major O'Malley, the best, most dependable sergeant in the whole damn army. He walked out of his stuffy office and on the porch to wait for him to arrive.

"You send for me, Sir?" A slightly out of breath O'Malley asked while saluting the major.

"Yes, I did," Thurston responded returning the man's salute. "We have a situation here with all the homesteaders wanting protection which I don't have enough men to do the job adequately. I want you to send riders in every direction to the families within a twenty-five mile radius of Clark and tell them what is happening and for their protection, they need to load up what they need in wagons and bring their families to the fort until this problem is taken care of."

"With McClellan and his troops north of here and along with the patrols we have out now, that's going to leave us a little thin here, Sir." O'Malley said.

“I know that, Sergeant, but we are here to protect the families in this area and unless you have another idea, that’s the only way I know to do it.”

“You are right, Sir. I’ll see to it right away. How many do I send?”

“Three in every direction from here; round up your men and bring them to my office and I will have a rough map of the area for each man to cover and a list of the homesteaders living there…at least the ones we know about. Make sure they tell the families to bring what provisions they can with them. Also, make it understood this is for their protection and if they choose to remain, it is at their own risk.”

“Yes, Sir,” O’Malley responded. Saluting the major, he left to carry out the orders. Thurston walked back into his office and sat down behind his desk, wondering if there was anything else he could do.

~~~

Smoke could be seen about two miles ahead of the column. Tye rode up to McClellan telling him what was going on up ahead.

“There is a homestead about where that smoke is, Captain…I believe their names were McCutchen. Dan has ridden ahead to take a look-see.

“Did yu kno’um, Tye?” Buff asked.
~~~

"I met them a couple of times. Last time was at my and Rebecca's wedding. Seemed like good folks. Think they had two small boys, one about eight and the other five or six."

McClellan asked. "Do you think…"?

"Dead, Captain," Tye interrupted. "The parents will be dead. The boys may be captives but unless they are exceptionally strong, they will be killed. An Apache cannot stand weakness, even in children."

"I thought they were gentle with children," McClellan said.

"They are with Apache children and were fairly decent to prisoners until the Mexicans and bluecoats started raiding their camps and killing Apache women and children for no reason a few years ago and they will never forget. They are a good and honorable people that are facing an end to their way of life."

"GOOD!! HONORABLE!!" McClellan said, astonished that those words came from a man who has spent his whole life fighting them. A man whose father was killed by them.

"Yes," Tye said calmly, smiling at the look on his captain's face. "I've said this before to officers, maybe even to you. The Apache is probably the only people that could have adapted to this harsh land and thrived on it. They are tough and resourceful people. They were forced to this land by the Comanche, not because the Comanche were better fighters but because of sheer numbers. The Apache has never had the numbers that other tribes had. When I was young, before all the trouble with the white man began, my best friend was an Apache boy that was about my age. I found him almost dead from a fall from his horse. He had a broken leg, busted head and ribs. My mother took him in and set his leg and doctored his other injuries. The boys' father and several other warriors showed up at our home later that day after trailing me to the homestead. They were angry, figuring I had killed the boy but pa spoke some Apache and knew sign language and managed to get the father to come in and see his son. He did, and turned to my pa, nodded, grunted, and left."

"They just left…that was it?" McClellan asked.

"They returned in a week and took the boy with them, leaving a freshly killed deer to show their appreciation. About a month later, Ke-ah, that was his name, showed up at our home and we visited with pa interpreting for us. Over a period of time he learned some English and I learned some Apache. We were pretty close for three years, until he became old enough to become a warrior. By that time the feelings between the whites and Apache were wearing thin. I've only seen him twice since and that was years ago. I learned a lot about the Apache from him. The warriors are great parents, there is no stealing from another Apache, and there is no such thing as telling a lie. The women are very protective of the children and see to it they are well taken care of. There is no adultery because of the threat of death or banishment. They would like to live in peace but between us and the Mexicans, we are forcing them off their land, taking away their way of life. I would fight too and I'm betting so would you."

"I…I guess I would."

"Ain't no guessing abut it," Buff said. "Tye's right, they are just like the Blackfut, Comanche, Bannocks, and ever uther Injun I ever knu. They are honorable people that are jus fighting fur their way uf life. No sense in hating some wun fur that."

"I understand that…but they are so cruel."

Tye laughed. "I could tell you some stories about cruelty and torture, Captain and they were done to the Apache, not by them. I know they can do terrible things to a prisoner but they have had the same things done to them by Mexicans and Texans, maybe worse." Footsteps from behind caught their attention.

"The man and woman are buried, Sir," Christian said from behind McClellan. McClellan turned toward him.

"And the children?"

"No sign of them, Sir."

Tye placed his hand on McClellan's shoulder. "That means they are alive. We still have a few hours of daylight, Captain so let's try and close the gap some."

"Sergeant Christian," McClellan said. "Get the men mounted and ready to move out." The sergeant shouted the orders and they were moving again.

Chapter Nine

It was late afternoon when Asay and his braves reined their mounts to a halt. He sat on his pony looking over the cliff where the Rio Grande and the Rio Pecos Rivers met about sixty feet below. Naiche rode up beside him.

"We will camp here on our land for the night," Asay said. Asay wondered to himself just how much longer they could consider this land theirs. There seemed to be no end to the white eyes moving into it. This land cradles our families and the spirits of our dead fathers and grandfathers. War? Peace? This question was on his mind when Naiche spoke sweeping his arm across the land before them.

'This land…our fathers land and their fathers before them will be ours alone once we drive these people out. We will be able to start another family and things will be good again," he told Asay. He nodded toward the others. "Some are getting restless for their families. They want to get the whites out quickly so they can join again with their women…their children."

Asay dismounted and sat cross-legged on the edge of the cliff. Naiche sat beside him. Asay said, "I know this to be true of their needs. I, like you, would like again to lay with my woman, hold my children, but that is not possible since the bluecoats killed them. Most of them," he said nodding toward the braves that were preparing camp, "lost their loved ones." He stood up as did Naiche. Asay placed his hand on his friends shoulder. "I will speak with them," he said as he turned to walk toward them. The chatter and laughter stopped as their leader walked into camp and stood among them. Asay stood looking at each man's face. Some he knew by name…others only by their faces. No matter…they all were Apache.

"I know some of you would like to go to your families…lie beside your woman and hold your children. I, as well as Naiche, Nay-tanh, Gian-Nah-Tah, and other among you, would like to do the same but our families are dead, killed by the bluecoats. Right now, the only way that those of you that still have family can live with them again is to live on the reservation and watch your children starve. The only other way is to drive this people from our lands." He looked again at the faces of the men with him. He counted them: tash-ay-ay (one), nah-kee (two), kah-yah (three) all the way to host-kon-tin-yay (sixty) warriors. This was a force he knew to be dealt with. Sixty seasoned Apaches warriors were more than a match for twice or three times that number of enemies, especially the weak bluecoats. “I will not hold anyone here that is not of the mind to kill the white man. Leave us if you do not.” The warriors looked around at their friends to see if any stood up…none did. Asay continued. “In the morning, we will split into three groups. I will lead one, Naiche one, and Nah-tanh the third. We will raid and kill every white man, woman, and child we find. Take no prisoners as they will only slow us down.”

Asay paused for a moment then spoke. “The bluecoats have killed our families.” His voice rose in anger as he spoke. “They have killed our children, even the smallest ones.” He walked over to the two white boys, his body trembling in anger and drawing his knife, cut the ropes that held the boys feet and hands. The boys stood up in front of him, shaking in fear. With a quick flick of his wrist, he slashed both boys’ throats and they fell to the ground, choking on their own blood. Neither made a sound and in a few seconds, both were still. He turned back to the group of warriors. “The white man says the only good Apache is a dead Apache. Now,” he said pointing to the boys, “They are good white men.” The braves stood and shouted Asay’s name and shouted oaths to kill the white settlers and bluecoats. Darkness was settling in as Asay made his way back to the cliff. A lonely coyote howled in the distance. Asay and Naiche looked at each other. Both knew that was not a good sign.

~~~

McClellan had the column stop and told Garrison to have the men camp here for the night. Garrison passed the order to the sergeants who had the men set up camp. There was thirty minutes of daylight left so the troops were told to make their coffee and hot biscuits quickly with small fires that were to be put out before dark. Some of the men started the fires and others took care of their mounts while others were getting the coffee and bacon ready to heat up. Latrines would be dug before dark also. Christian and Phipps was setting the sentry duty roster and Arnold was seeing that the horses were picketed correctly.

The fires were extinguished just before dark and the men settled in drinking their coffee and biscuits. The order had been given to keep a quiet camp so there wasn't much talk. All four sergeants came and sat down by Tye, Buff, McClellan and Garrison. Tye had told Dan to go about two or three miles farther and see if he could see the Apache camp and report back. Tye figured he would be back within an hour or so.

~~~

Dan had traveled about two and a half miles when he stopped. The southeast breeze was in his face and the smell of smoke was carried with it. 'Close,' he thought to himself. "To damn close," he mumbled aloud. He quickly dismounted and tied his mount to a sturdy sage and keeping low to the ground moved slowly forward. He was taking his time, studying every bush and rock before carefully taking the next step.

An experienced fighting man could sometimes feel danger before it occurred. Dan had suddenly gotten that feeling when he had frozen in his tracks, barely breathing, listening for any unusual sound. No sound was to be heard so he took a few more steps then laid down on his belly. Crawling to the top of a hill and looking down, he saw the Apache camp with sixty to seventy warriors moving about. He scooted back down the hill and then in a crouch, ran to his horse. Untying the reins he mounted and started to move back to the soldier's camp when a loud scream cut loose behind him. He lay over his saddle and kicked his horse into an all out run just as a bullet grazed his head and things went black. His mount was running hard and somehow, in his half awake state, Dan managed to hold on to the reins with one hand and his horse's mane with the other. The horse slowed to a walk after about five minutes of running in the dark. The horse shied at a rabbit that jumped up almost under his feet and Dan fell off, hitting the ground hard, but his grip on the reins never loosened. He lay there unconscious, with his fidgety mount stomping and snorting all around his motionless body for ten minutes before Dan, semi-conscious, sat up.

He sat there trying to get his bearings and thinking straight. All he knew at this moment was that his head hurt like hell. Using the reins like a rope, he pulled himself erect and grabbed hold of the pommel of his saddle. He stood beside the horse and lay his head on the seat of the saddle waiting for the fog in his brain to clear and the dizziness to go away. He remembered the Apaches and raising his head looked in all directions but the darkness prevented his from seeing more than a few feet. He heard nothing and his mount, now calmed down, apparently didn't either as he showed no signs of alarm.

Dan struggled to get his foot in the stirrup and when he did, threw his other leg over the saddle and settled his butt in the seat. He reined the horse in the direction of the soldier's camp, at least he hoped it was and not in the direction of the Apache camp. He lay his head on the horse's neck, letting the horse pick his way in the dark, knowing his mount could see better than he could in the darkness.

~~~

When the warrior, that had shot Dan, told Asay about the man escaping in the dark, he was furious. He was not furious with his man but the fact that the army was close because he figured this man was a scout. From the brief description given him, he did not think it was Watkins. But still, the fact they had found his camp enraged him.
~~~

He walked to the edge of the camp and on into the darkness. Naiche followed him and when Asay stopped, walked up beside him. They looked at each other and without saying it, thought the same thing: the coyote's lonely howl.

"The soldiers know where our camp is," Asay said to his friend. "We will split into three groups like I said earlier but we will leave well before daylight."

Naiche grunted and nodded. "Soldiers will be here at daylight, this I know.

With the bluecoats this close, do you think it wise to split our men?"

"Do you know the way to where the rivers meet?" Asay ask.

"The Rio Grande and the Rio Pecos?"

"Yes," Asay answered.

"I know the way," Naiche said.

Asay looked at his friend. "Good. Find Nah-Tanh, and make sure he knows the way. We will meet there in two suns. The bluecoats will probably split the men also, each trailing one of us. When they get to the rivers, we will be waiting," he raised his right fist and smashed it into the palm of his left hand. "We will kill them all."

~~~

A sentry, hearing Dan's horse walking on the rocky ground, shouted a warning. Tye and Buff were the first ones to him just as
~~~

Dan rode into the camp. They carefully took him off his horse. Buff had to pry his fingers from the reins and the horse's mane.

After laying Dan gently on the ground, and after looking at the head wound, Tye searched his body for other wounds. "Thank God," he said. "Someone get me some water." He took off Dan's kerchief and when a trooper brought him a canteen, wetted it and cleaned the wound. He raised Dan's head up and encouraged him to drink some water. Dan coughed and opened his eyes. He saw Tye hovering over him and reached up and grabbed Tye's arm. "Apaches, Tye," he said gasping. "A hell of a lot of Apaches," and he passed out.

"Is he dead, Tye?" McClellan asked hurrying to their side.

"No, Sir, he just passed out. Can't find any other wounds except the scalp wound."

"Will he be okay?"

"I think so. He's gonna have a hell of a headache for a coupled days though."

"Did he say anything?"

"Only Apaches, a hell of a lot of Apaches. They probably know we are behind them so it might be a good idea to double the guard, Sir."

McClellan looked down at Dan and said, "I agree." He turned to Garrison and told to him to double the guards "and tell them they had better stay damn sharp." He had two men carry Dan to his bedroll that Tye had spread and lay him gently down on it. Tye re-wet the kerchief and placed it across Dan's forehead and pulled the blanket up to his chin. He sat on his haunches, looking down at his friend, thankful he was not going to have to tell Dan's wife he had been killed.

"What now," McClellan asked.

"We know they know we are close, or at least think we are. I'm betting that they knew Dan was probably a scout so I'm thinking they will leave well before daylight. I think they will split into two or more groups to make it more difficult to follow them. They will have a meeting place and wherever that is, they will wait for us."

"You mean they will try and ambush us?" McClellan said with a questioning look on his face.

"Tha will meet us, Kaptain," Buff answered. "Tha will be behind every rock and bush when tha do and it will be a sudden attack. Nuthing fancy, just shooting at us standing in tha open whilst they are hidden. Gonna be damn bloody."

Tye looked at Buff and smiled. "Buff's right. They will meet and fight us…and it's our job to make sure it's no surprise." He smiled again at McClellan. "Let's get some rest. I got me a feeling the next two or three days are gonna be the longest of our lives."

The three of them started toward their bedrolls. McClellan wondered how in hell a man could smile when he's facing what they are fixing to do. Hell, he was nervous as hell just thinking about it.

In fact, he needed to relieve his bladder. He smiled and thought that maybe the old saying of getting the piss scared out of you, just might be true. He retraced his steps and made the rounds checking on the sentries. He found Christian and Arnold sitting on a large flat rock, talking.

"Is it true what Tye said about things getting rough?" Christian asked. Christian was a good sergeant and hell on wheels in a fight, but he tended to get uptight worrying about things.

"Tye said things might…just might get that way Sergeant. He did not say they would."

"I have been with Tye on many patrols, Sir and his feelings usually come true. Never in my life have I ever seen a man that could feel and smell trouble before it comes like he can," Arnold said.

"He's good," McClellan added, "And we have a lot of good men here to try and keep those things from happening."

"Well, if it does come, you know what the Indian says; it's a good day to die."

"Just what in hell does that mean?" Arnold questioned.

Christian laughed. "Don't ask me…ask Tye. He told me that once while we were chasing Yancey and his gang and he came up with a idea that he, Lieutenant Garrison, and myself were gonna surprise that whole damn gang of cutthroats. I asked him if he thought it would work and that was his answer, 'if it doesn't, it's a good day to die. He just laughed and walked off and left me and the lieutenant looking at each other and scratching our heads trying to figure that one out."

"We will take things as they come," McClellan said. "It's late so let's get some shut eye."

Chapter Ten

Sleep would not come to Asay this night as his mind would not rest. He tried but the thought of the bluecoats being this close and his not knowing it bothered him. This scout named Watkins was on his mind also. He missed lying with his woman and holding his children. He missed his father and his grandfather's stories of the old days when the Apache ruled this land. He missed his mother and grandmother and their tender hands nursing him when he had been wounded in battle. He missed…he missed all this because the bluecoats had killed them. He clutched his Bowie, squeezing the handle till his knuckles turned white.

He relaxed, and shutting his eyes, prayed to the Creator of all things, Ussen, to give him strength, to give him wisdom to lead his men to victory against the white eyes, these invaders of his land. He prayed for the chance to revenge the deaths of his family. He prayed for the chance to kill this White Apache called Watkins. He was mumbling…Watkins…Watkins …when he fell into a deep sleep.

A white horse appeared before him. On this magnificent animal rode this mighty warrior holding a rifle in one hand above his head and a bloody bluecoat flag in the other. The warrior came closer and Asay was shocked…it was his grandfather. He recognized him even though this warrior on the horse was a young man. Asay had never seen his grandfather when he was a warrior, only as the old man whom he loved. He was a splendid looking man, broad-shouldered, flat belly, and huge, muscled arms. He had a red bandana around his head and his long raven hair hung loosely to his shoulders. A single white strip of paint ran from his left cheek, across his nose to his right cheek. His chest had a white bolt of lightning across it and his only clothing was a breech cloth and knee high moccasins.

The white horse with black lightning streaks painted on both sides of his neck and feathers dangling from his mane and tail was prancing back and forth. The warriors sacred hoop with its four eagle feathers dangled from the horses mane, tied to the long hair with rawhide strips. The hoop had magical powers and would protect the warrior from harm. The rider looked up at the darkening sky raising his arms with the rifle and flag in his hands to the heavens. Lightning suddenly streaked across the sky and thunder roared from the clouds. The warrior lowered his arms and head and Asay could feel the man's eyes on him, could feel the man's strength flowing into his own body.

Horse and rider seemed to float in the air to the edge of a cliff and Asay, as if he was now on the horse looking through the warrior's eyes, looked down from the cliff. Below, between two canyon walls flowed a small river. All around the floor of the canyon and floating in the stream were the bloody bodies of blue coated soldiers. So many bodies floated the water in the stream was turning pink. Looking to his right he saw a small trail that ran down the side of the far cliff. This is the trail the soldiers had come down to reach the floor of the canyon and forded the shallow water to this side of the cliff directly below where Asay was. Looking to the left, he could see where the soldiers were heading. A trail led from the floor up to the top of the canyon. The small stream ran into a river which he knew to be the Rio Grande.

Suddenly he was out of the warrior's body and looking at his grandfather again. Words from his grandfather reached his ears even though he could see his grandfather's lips were closed. He was telling him not to fight the bluecoats until he found the canyon and then crush them. His grandfather nodded to him and then was gone, like a puff of smoke in the wind. Asay woke up and even though the night was cool, he was sweating, his heart racing as he sat up and looked around the camp. All were asleep in their blankets as he stood up. As silent as he was though, the slight noise of dropping his blanket to the ground woke Naiche who watched his friend move among the sleeping warriors, the moccasins on his feet moving silently on the rocky ground. Naiche stood up and followed his friend who had walked just outside camp.

"What is on my friend's mind that he can't sleep," he asked? "Is it the soldiers or maybe the scout, Watkins?"

Asay looked at his friend and placed his hand on Naiche's shoulder. "I have thought of both, the soldiers and of this scout but that is not why I am awake. I had a dream or maybe a vision."

"You had a vision?" Naiche asked excitedly knowing that only a select few ever received one from the spirits.

Asay sat down on a flat rock and Naiche sat next to him, waiting to hear of this vision.

"My grandfather appeared on a white horse," Asay began. "He was a young man and a powerful warrior. He spoke to me but his lips did not move." Naiche was excited as he asked.

"What did he say?

"Do not fight the soldiers yet." He paused for a few seconds and looked in his friends eyes. "Do you know of a place where there is a deep canyon with a small stream that meets the Rio Grande?"

"No. Why?"

"My grandfather showed me such a place and that is where we will kill the bluecoats. I will recognize the place in my vision when I see it. There is a trail leading down from one side and one leading up the other side. The walls of the canyon are much to steep for escape." He clasped his hands together and held them. "We will have them trapped and we will kill them all."

"Let me get Gian-Nah-Tah. He may have heard of such a place," Naiche said rising up from the rock and walking back into the camp. He returned in a moment with Gian-Nah-Tah.

Asay repeated his vision to the warrior. Gian-Nah-Tah though for a moment. "There is such a place," he said. "About a half days ride from where we stand. It is a place where a stream called the Rio Pecos by the whites meets the Rio Grande."

"Can you find it and can you give directions to another so they can find it," Asay questioned? Gian-Nah-Tah nodded his head. "Good," Asay said. He looked at the stars and knew dawn was approaching. "Wake the others and bring them here," he said to the two men.

When the men were around Asay he said. "We will split into two groups instead of three. Gian-Nah-Tah will lead the large group and I will take the smaller. We will meet where the Rio Grande is met by what I think is called the Rio Pecos by the white eyes. There, where the two meet, we will trap the soldiers.

~~~

Tye and Buff were up and saddling their mounts when the camp started coming alive. Men were getting out of their bedrolls and pulling their boots on, standing up grumbling, stretching and scratching. Some headed for the latrine while others rolled up their
~~~

bedrolls and walked to the picket lines to find their horses. After saddling their mounts, they pulled biscuits and jerky from their saddle bags. They stood beside their mounts chewing their breakfast, waiting for the order to mount up.

McClellan, Lieutenant Garrison and Sergeants Arnold and Absher walked up to Buff and Tye who were sitting on their mounts. "Ready to go, Captain," Tye asked?

"Ready," McClellan said as a soldier handed him the reins of his mount. He forked the saddle and turned to Garrison.

"Lieutenant, have the men mount and we will move out two abreast." Garrison turned and shouted.

"Prepare to Mount." The men scrambled to the side of their horses and placed their foot in the stirrups. "MOUNT," and instantly the men were in their saddles. "C Troop on me here," he shouted. "A Troop will follow and then F Troop." The soldiers reined their mounts where they should be. "BY THE TWO'S…YO," he said raising and dropping his right arm. The column moved out with C Troop's guidon waving above them. A Troop followed with Absher leading them and bringing up the rear, Sergeant Arnold and F Troop. Dan lay on a travois that Tye had made and was being dragged behind Sergeant Phipp's mount to the side of the column, away from the dust the troops would raise. Out riders were assigned to each side of the column to prevent a surprise attack.

Up front, McClellan rode with Buff beside him. Tye was at least two hundred yards in front and barely visible in the gray light of approaching dawn. He could barely make out the tracks of Dan's horse in the dim light. Every few steps he would rein in Sandy and take a long look in all directions, keeping an eye on Sandy for any sign the big horse saw, smelled, or heard. Not paying attention to one's horse's actions could get a man killed out here. A horse can see and hear better than a man. He can also smell a strange horse from a good distance if the wind is right. In the last few months, Sandy had saved Tye's hide more than once with a sudden snort or twitching of the ears warning Tye.

Just as the sun broke over the hills, Tye found the Apache camp…or what was the camp. He motioned for McClellan to hold the troops back while he looked around before everything was messed up with the soldiers mounts milling around. Buff rode on into the camp and reined in beside Tye.

"Pretty large camp, Buff," Tye said looking around. Buff nodded and spit a stream of tobacco juice to the ground. He had been around enough Indian camps to know what Tye said was true. He had passed where the pony herd had been held.

"From the number of ponies that was over there," he said nodding to his right, "I would say fifty, maybe sixty warriors."

Tye nodded in agreement with his friend. "About what I figured," as he glanced around at the remains of four fires that were still smoldering and the many places that the grass was still laying down where the men had slept. "Figure they left about two, maybe three hours ago," he added. Buff, dismounting, walked over to where the horses had been. He picked up a twig and finding the freshest pile of manure, stuck the stick in and pulled it out. Looking at the condition of the dung on the stick, he knew it was no more than three hours old. "Three hours at the most," he hollered at Tye.

Tye motioned for McClellan to come into the camp. Arriving, McClellan raised his arm and the column stopped behind him. "What do you two think?" He asked looking at Tye and then Buff. He had been around Buff long enough to know his skills were damn near as good as Tyes, something he figured he would never see. He would listen to him as quick as he would Tye.

"About fifty or so warriors, Sir. They had their horse herd over there," Tye said pointing to the right of the camp. "They left, heading southwest…in a hurry."

"Running from us?" the captain questioned.

Tye and Buff both laughed at the same time. When Tye quit laughing, he reached across and put his hand on the captain's shoulder. "Don't intend on making fun of you, Captain, but you know Apaches well enough to know that they have no fear of the white man. Fifty or so of them sure as hell would not be running except for a reason."

"And just what would that reason be?" McClellan asked, a little rankled at what had just happened in front of his men.

"Ambush, Captain!" Buff mumbled. "Hurrying to set up an ambush."

A sudden shout came from where the Apache ponies had been held. "CAPTAIN…OVER HERE," shouted Sergeant Absher. The four of them, McClellan, Tye, Buff, and Garrison hurried over to where the sergeant stood. He pointed behind some sage where two bodies lay, young boy's bodies.

"MY GOD," McClellan uttered. Tye and Buff were quickly beside the bodies of the two boys. "No injuries to either except their throats being cut," Buff said.

"Why in God's name would they do that?" Garrison asked? Tye stood up with one of the small boys in his arms, and turned his back to the officers so they would not see his grief. Buff had the other and they carried them a ways from the rest of the men and lay them gently on the ground.

"Bring two blankest and shovels," Tye said not looking back. He remembered these two boys from his and Rebecca's wedding party. They came up to him, eyes as big as saucers, and said they wanted to be like him, helping people. "You're in God's hands now, boys…rest in peace," he whispered, his voice cracking. He patted each on the forehead and stood up. Buff could see Tye was upset and said nothing. When the men arrived with the blankets, he took them and wrapped each boy carefully. Two soldiers were scraping out two graves as best they could in the rocky ground.

Tye turned around and walked through the men past McClellan and Garrison to where Sandy stood. The men had stepped aside as Tye walked through them and none could miss the look of anger on his face…a look they had not seen before. Buff walked over to Garrison and McClellan. "Leave him alone fur a few minutes. He remembered those two boys and he's a little more than upset."

"From the look on his face, I would have to agree," Garrison said.

"Yu asked a few minutes ago why tha did that to tha boys," Buff said. "Wun uf two reesons. Ferst, tha were slowing them down or mabee showed sum weakness by crying; second, it wus a lesson ta tha uther braves showing tha wure taking no captives and tha wure here ta kill every white man tha kud find. Sorta an example ta get their blood boiling."

"Lets git tha men mounted Lootenant, and go with him," Buff said nodding toward Tye who was already a hundred yards in front of them. Buff mounted and galloped his mount to Tye's side.

"Yu okay," he asked Tye. Tye did not reply. "You know the first rule in scouting, Tye. Don't let thangs like anger kloud yur judgment and make you do thangs yu wud not normally do?" He rode beside Tye, not saying anything else. After a couple of minutes, Tye turned toward Buff and Buff could see the anger, the set of his jaw was not what it was a few minutes ago. Tye reached over and patted Buff on the shoulder.

"I'm okay, now. Sometimes I get a little worked up at things I see out here and it sets me off for a few minutes till I calm down." He reined Sandy down to a walk. "Let's get back to work."

Chapter Eleven

Back at Fort Clark, Major Thurston continued to have his hands full…full of trouble. Seems every hour some frantic homesteader came in reporting more Apache trouble. No time before had there been so many reports of hostile attacks over such a wide area. He was in a quandary because there was no way he could send troops to every reported incident. He simply did not have enough men to do that. With the numbers of Apaches being reported he was afraid to send the usual ten or twelve men patrols. Also, Tye, his Chief of Scouts, as well as two more experience scouts were on patrol to the north tracking down a large group of hostiles with his most reliable and experienced officers. Not only did he not have enough men but was short of scouts and experienced officers as well. He paced the floor in his office, puffing on his ever present cigar, trying to figure out what to do. He had already sent riders to warn the homesteaders and try to convince them to come to the fort.

Everyone has perfect hindsight and he was no different. He wished he had not sent so many men, especially his most experienced scouts and officers, all on one patrol.

"God, I wish Tye and McClellan was here," he mumbled under his breath. He hollered for his orderly. "CORPORAL JENKINS…GET IN HERE." He heard a chair fall over the sound of boots hurrying to his door. Swinging the door open, Jenkins stepped in.

"Sir?" he said saluting.

"Have someone find the scout named Mankins and get him here pronto."

"Yes, Sir," Jenkins said turning on his heels to leave, then turned back and saluted, which Thurston returned quickly, without looking up from his desk.

~~~

The column had been moving at a fast pace for about two hours when McClellan call for a short break. As usual, the men took care of their mounts needs before their own by loosening the saddle girths and feeding them a little grain.

"Have the men check and clean their weapons, Lieutenant."

Garrison stood up, "Yes, Sir." He walked to where Sergeants Christian and Absher were sitting and repeated the captain's order to them which they repeated to their men. After a little minor grumbling the men did as they were ordered. Breaking the breech
~~~

open on their Sharps model 1863 rifle and removing the .54 caliber shell, they began cleaning their guns. There were several models of the Sharps but the cavalry used the model with the shorter barrel which was twenty-two inches long instead of a thirty inch barrel like the infantry used. The shorter barrel was easier to handle from the back of a horse plus it was lighter.

Up ahead, Tye was cursing the Apache they were after. They had split into two groups, one slightly larger than the other. He stepped down from the saddle and squatted on his heels staring into the hills ahead of him. He took the makings out of his pocket and rolled himself a smoke and then lighting it, sat there pondering why the hell they split. He turned to look over his shoulder when he heard hooves striking the rocky ground. Buff was coming to where he was.

"Whut's trubling yu, Tye? Frum the luk on yur face yore shore koncerned abut sumthang."

"Trying to figure out this," Tye said pointing to the ground. Buff looked at the tracks, stood up in his stirrups and turning his head, spit a black wad of tobacco juice.

"Luks kike they done split up." He commented. "Why do yu thank tha did that?"

"That's what I'm concerned about," Tye said. "Why?" Tye stood and dropped his cigarette to the ground, stepping on it to put it out. He looked back in the direction Buff came from. He should have been able to see McClellan. "McClellan delay up the troops?"

Buff laughed. "Yep, has them thar boys cleaning their guns too. Tha wurn't to happy abuts it since that cut into thar resting time." Tye smiled because he knew why McClellan had them cleaning their guns. He had been adamant on several patrols he was leading for McClellan that the captain has the men keep their equipment in good working order. This lesson had been pounded into Tye's head by his father over his early years. "Ben would say it doesn't matter if you have the best equipment there is, it ain't worth squat if it don't work proper."

His mind reached back to all the stories his pa had told him about his time in the mountains fighting Indians. He tried to remember any lesson his father had taught him that might explain why the Apaches split into two groups, both smaller than the number of soldiers he was sure they knew was chasing them. That fact did not make any sense to him. Most of the time, he could figure out the Apache's plans ahead of time but this leader had him more than a little concerned. Tye wasn't sure if this Apache was sly like a fox or dumber than a piece of wood. Then again, he had never known an Apache leader that was dumb.

"I don't know, Buff. I can't figure what this Apache plans to do."

"I don't kno either but I can tell yu wun thang. Whutever his plans are, it has sumthang ta do with killing soldiers." Tye nodded and mounted Sandy.

"Let's go back and see McClellan,' he said.

~~~

Asay stood on the rim of the canyon and studied the river below and the opposite canyon wall. Looking right he could see the Rio Grande and below, what he figured was the Rio Pecos. He was standing on the east rim and he could see a trail from the west rim down to the banks of the Pecos. To the left there was a narrow trail leading from the Rio Pecos up to the rim on the side he was standing on. He shut his eyes to visualize what the place he had seen in the vision from Ussen. He quickly realized this was the exact place in his vision. He turned to Naiche, "Send a man along this rim up the Rio Pecos and see if there is another crossing. Send another to see where the bluecoats are."

He rode down the trail from his side of the rim to study the walls for places of concealment for the ambush. He could see a large, deep recess in the east wall that would probably hold maybe twenty braves. He looked to the rim where his braves stood and saw that whoever was in the recess could not be seen from above. He smiled. The Rio Pecos was fairly shallow and not very wide and could be crossed just about anywhere.
~~~

He turned his mount back toward the Rio Grande to see what he would find there. Again he could see where men could hide and remain unseen from above. This was the perfect place to kill the bluecoats. Once in the canyon of the Rio Pecos they would have guns on them from the east wall, and if they break for the Rio Grande and the trail up the east wall, the guns of the men hidden along the rim by the trial would cut them down. He would wait for the brave to report if there is another way out of the canyon up the Rio Pecos to make the final plans. He rode up the trail to the camp and waited.

~~~

By the time Tye and Buff had returned to the column, and reported to McClellan, they were ready to move out. There had been a meeting of the officers, Sergeants Phipps, Arnold, Christian, Absher, and the two scouts. Tye told them this was a different Apache than they had encountered before. He was either the dumbest or the smartest Apache he had encountered and he had not figured out which he was yet, but if he was guessing, he would be smart, experienced, and a vicious warrior.

"Both Buff and me figure this is going to be the biggest, bloodiest encounter any of you have ever seen. There is over sixty blood-thirsty, white hating, warriors waiting for us somewhere." As somber as he could be he added, "There will be lot of empty saddles when this is over. Tell your men they had better damn well stay
~~~

alert and ready for anything. All of you know how quick the Apache can strike. This group is three or four times the size we normally encounter. So be ready."

The column formed again and moved out. Tye had checked on Dan who was resting comfortable in the travois. He still had a head ache and became dizzy if he stood up. Tye told him the situation and he had no idea what the Apache had in mind either.

"This here Apache is wun meen bastard," Buff said to Tye. "Seed a Blackfut wun time like this. He killed everwun-men, women, children…made him no difference."

They were following the larger of the two groups. McClellan did not want to split his forces which Tye figured was the smart thing to do.

By late afternoon, Tye had figured out where they were headed and he cursed to himself. They were heading to the junction of the Rio Grande and the Pecos rivers. The Apache knew we had to follow if we were going to stop them. Tye knew this place well. It was there he had almost met his death at the hands of the Yancey gang. If there ever was a better place to trap soldiers, that was the place.

"I know where he is going, Buff."

"Didn't figure it wud take yu long."

"He is taking us to the junction of the Rio Grande and Pecos River. If we want to pursue them, you have to go into the canyon or go two days around." They rode for another minute before Tye said. "Well, he ain't dumb."

"How fer are we frum tha place?"

"Maybe two hours, three at the most. It will be dark in less than an hour, let's wait here for McClellan and see if he wants to make camp."

Chapter Twelve

Meanwhile at Fort Clark, Major Thurston had spent most of the day making arrangements for places for the people coming in for protection, to camp. Later in the afternoon, he turned that responsibility over to O'Malley so he could concentrate on other things. He had sent Mankins, one of Tye's scouts, to find McClellan and the column. He needed to know what was going on. Mankins said he was familiar with the area where Braddock's patrol had been wiped out. He wanted to travel alone saying he could travel faster and quieter by himself. His orders were to find McClellan, tell him what was going on all along the Border with the Apache. Find out what the situation was with the group they were chasing and last, bring Lieutenant Garrison and Sergeant Arnold back to the fort. He needed an experienced officer and a reliable non-com for leading another patrol. It had been a long day and as the sun was setting, he lit the lamp on his desk knowing it would be a long night.

~~~

Asay sat on his blankets smiling at the news his scout brought to him. The man had ridden for two hours looking for a way down the cliffs to cross the river. He found none that would be safe for a horse and rider.

He would now wait on the rider he had sent to find the bluecoats before making any more plans. He already had an idea where he would place his men. All his plans depended on two things, when would the bluecoats arrive and when the other group of his men would arrive. The second part was answered a few minutes later when the sound of horses coming reached the camp. Excited cries from his men on the other side of camp told him it was the other group of warriors arriving.

Gian-Nah-Tah stepped down from his pony and came to where Asay sat. Asay motioned with his hand to sit on his blanket with him and Naiche. From the excitement of the braves arriving and the ones that were already in camp told Asay something good had happened.

Gian-Nah-Tah spoke. "We came across two homes of the white men and killed all of them. We killed one soldier as he rode away from one of the homes."

Asay grunted his approval. "This is good news. Did you lose any men?"

"None," Gian-Nah-Tah said boastfully. "Not even a wound."
~~~

Asay grunted his approval again. "Gian-Nah-Tah is a great warrior and leader." Gian-Nah-Tah sat up straighter, chest swelling and shoulders square, pleased with himself. If he had been standing he would be strutting like a proud peacock.

"Has Asay made the final plans for tomorrow," he asked?

"I am waiting on the rider to come back with a report where the bluecoats are. We will talk some more then." He motioned with his hand, "Go to your blankets and get some rest until the rider comes back."

~~~

McClellan had arrived where Tye and Buff waited and had decided to bivouac there. Horses were picketed, latrines dug, and small fires were lit for coffee and to heat the biscuits and bacon. The fires were again to be put out by dark. Sergeant Christian had set sentry duty and Phipps set the guards for the horses. With the Apaches close and probably knowing where they were camped, the sentries and men watching the picket lines were doubled. Hobbles on the horses were double checked also. The worse thing that could happen would be to lose the horses.

With the fires out and men settling in for the night, Tye, Buff, McClellan, Garrison, Phipps and Arnold had a get-together. Tye wanted to tell them what was happening tomorrow. Dan came also being helped by one of the troops. "Just wanted to know what was going on and what our plans are," he said.
~~~

"Good to see you on your feet, Dan," Tye said. "Take a seat."

They were unaware that an Apache was within fifty feet of the camp. He watched the men going to their blankets and saw the officers meeting with the scouts. He watched a few more minutes and then, silently moved away from the camp, mounted his pony and rode away.

In a low voice, Tye broke the dreaded news. "I have a good idea of where the Apaches are taking us. Up ahead, maybe two or so hours, is where the Rio Pecos meets the Rio Grande. Dan, you know the spot." Dan nodded and Tye continued. "The canyon of the Rio Pecos is deep, maybe sixty foot walls in most places. The walls are almost vertical and can not be traversed with a horse. To go around the canyon would take two or more days. The Apache leader is smart and he knows we won't waste two days so he'll be ready for us there. There's a trail down from the east side and one trail up the west side…that's it. You will have Apaches on the rim, on the floor, and by the trial leading out on the other side." He looked at the men's faces and could see fear in almost every one of them. "I know it sounds bad…and it is, but there may be a way we can turn the cards in our favor." The men looked at each other. Tye always had a plan. That's the reason they respected him, he was always ahead of the Apache.

Tye continued. "It is a risky plan at best but there is no other way and there will be casualties…maybe a lot of casualties." The bright faces darkened some and most looked at the ground. Tye noticed this. "You are soldiers," he said, "And your duty is to protect this area from Apaches and bandits: It is to protect and care for your fellow soldiers: It is to follow orders at all times without question. It will be your responsibility to remind your troops of this. If everyone does his duty as ordered, we can keep the casualties to a minimum, but if one fails to do what he is told, it could be a damn disaster."

McClellan spoke up. "Tye, Buff, Dan, and Garrison will meet with me here shortly, and you'll be told what each of your responsibilities will be…that's all." The sergeants stood up and walked to their bedrolls whispering among themselves.

McClellan sat down with Garrison and the scouts. "Are you sure that's where they're taking us," Dan asked Tye.

"As sure as I can be, Dan, but you know the Apaches as well as I do, and you can never be sure about anything they will do. You have to go with your gut feeling and be prepared for anything."

McClellan said. "You said you had a plan?"

Tye motioned for everyone to move a little closer. There was just enough light from the half moon and stars to see what he was drawing on the ground. He had two crooked lines that ran parallel to each other and then one turned and met the other.

"The one here is the Rio Pecos and where the two lines meet is the Rio Grande." He drew an x on each side of the line representing the Rio Pecos. "The trail going down is here," he said pointing to the x closest to the Rio Grande. "That is where we will enter the canyon and the other mark is where we will exit the canyon. There is less than a quarter mile from here to here," he said pointing to the two marks. "It will be easy to get in the canyon but it will be bloody hell getting out."

"Is your plan just to go charging down the trail and running the gauntlet to the trail leading out?" Garrison asked.

Tye smiled, "Just about but with a couple of twists. The Apache know we will be leery of entering the canyon chasing them without looking it over real well. With this in mind they will hide their men on the side we will be entering from."

"How do you know that," McClellan asked?

"If we are on this side of the canyon looking down we could spot any Apaches hidden on the other side while we cannot see directly below us. That is where I believe they will be hidden, on this side. They will be on our right when we are on the floor. They will be spread all along the wall with several across from the trail leading out and leading in. They won't give away their positions until all our men are on the bottom of the canyon and walking their horses along the Rio Pecos. I propose we have ten men, on foot, climb down the cliff and cross the Rio Pecos here," he said marking a spot about a mile up the Pecos. "They'll work their way up the other side and move to a point where they are opposite from where we are now. They can quickly move to the west rim when the first shot is fired. They will be looking down on the Apaches from there and should be able to throw some devastating lead their way. We can place four men where they can shoot anything that comes up the trails trying to escape. The trails are narrow and only two riders at a time can navigate them. Four men that are good shots should be able to keep most from escaping. That's my idea, Captain. You have the final say."

McClellan looked around. "Do any of you have a better idea?" No one said anything. "Okay, we'll do it Tye's way. Garrison, make a list of your best shots. I want them on the rim and by the trail exits."

"Yes, Sir."

"Who's going to lead the men into the canyon?" McClellan asked Tye.

"Me," Tye said. "Buff, do you think you can lead the men down and up the cliffs to get in position on the rim across from us? Sergeant Christian has been here before and he can go with you."

"Konsider it done, Tye." Buff answered.

"Anything else Tye," McClellan asked. Tye shook his head. McClellan continued, "Let's get some sleep then."

Each man stood and headed to their bedrolls. Sitting down, Tye rolled a smoke, covered the flare of the match with his hand and touched the flame to the cigarette. He inhaled deeply enjoying the flavor of the tobacco and then exhaled slowly. Sergeant Absher's bedroll was next to his and he sat up.

He spoke to Tye in a low voice, almost a whisper. "Is it going to be as bad as you said tomorrow?"

"You never know about the Apache," Tye whispered back. "They may or may not be there but I'm betting they will be. They know we are chasing them and figure we will not lose two days going out of our way to bypass the canyon. If we did that it would give them those two days to kill more of the homesteaders. If they are there, it will be a bloody mess for both sides." Absher lay back down wishing he had not asked.

Tye lay down after taking a few more puffs and putting the cigarette out. He had a lot of thinking to do before going to sleep. Plans to make and plans to dismiss that would not work. A lot of lives would depend on what plans he and McClellan came up with.

~~~~

It was midnight when the rider sent to find the bluecoats returned to the Apache camp. He reported that the number of soldiers were five times the number of fingers on both hands. He told Asay they were two hours away. This, Asay figured, would mean the soldiers would be here two maybe three hours after daylight. Satisfied, Asay lay back down on his blanket and fell asleep with the thought that tomorrow would be a great day.
~~~~

Chapter Thirteen

A few hours earlier and fifty miles south of where Tye and McClellan were, a twelve man patrol led by a young Lieutenant Morton was in serious trouble with some Apaches. Having left Fort Clark before word of Apache trouble everywhere, they rode into a canyon unaware there was any trouble. Two men were dead and the rest were penned down, unable to escape the trap. Worse of all, their horses had ran off with most of their water and spare ammunition. Things had gone bad and were soon to get worse. The only thing in their favor was the temperature. It was not very hot during the day this time of the year so they could get by on less water.

Morton had been on patrols before, even led a few, but this was the first time he had encountered any Apaches. "Sergeant Carver," he yelled.

"Over here, Sir," came the reply from his right, maybe twenty feet away and from behind a large boulder.

"Gather the canteens and get me a count of what ammunition we have. You'll also be responsible for rationing the water."

"Yes, Sir," The sergeant replied and started collecting the canteens.

Morton took time to look around for the first time, studying the defensive position they were in. He was surprised it was as good as it was. There was no way, with the gigantic boulders behind them that the Apaches could shoot down on them from behind. The boulders were large enough so the men could stand and fire with only their head and shoulders exposed for whatever time it took for them to pull the trigger. They could drop down out of sight while reloading the single shot Sharps with another .52 caliber shell. The Apaches were bunched about two hundred yards away. They had to cross open ground to attack the soldiers.

"Lieutenant Morton!" Carver said trying to get Morton's attention.

"Sergeant."

"We have seven canteens, all only about three quarters full," Carver reported. "We have one hundred fifty-four .52 caliber rounds for the rifles and about fifteen rounds per man for their Colts."

"Leave the rounds for the colts with whatever each man has on him. Gather the .52 caliber shells then divided them evenly. There will be no firing unless I give the order. Is that understood?"

"YES, SIR," the sergeant replied.

Morton spoke to his men to try and calm their fears somewhat. He hoped he could speak without the nervousness showing in his own voice. "Men, I know things look bad but there are some positives. We are in a good position to fend off any attacks. We have enough water for maybe three days if we are careful. There are maybe twenty-five or thirty Apaches out there and we have one hundred fifty rounds for our Sharps plus our side arms. We were due back to Clark this afternoon and Thurston knew our route. I figure he will have a relief patrol on its way late tomorrow. I figure we are about five hours from Clark, so we need to make it till help arrives which I think will be day after tomorrow at the latest. When the Apache attack, shoot with your Sharps when I give the order. Do not try and reload. Lay your rifles down and use your Colts and fire at will. Any questions?"

There was dead silence. "Sergeant, make sure there are two men watching at all times, and four after dark. The others need to rest." The last words barley had come out of his mouth when the thundering sound of hooves and screaming Apaches reached their ears. "GET READY, MEN." Morton shouted. "HOLD YOUR FIRE!"

The Apaches were 100 yards out and spreading out, running their ponies all out and each brave lay low over their pony's neck. "HOLD," Morton hollered. "HOLD."

At fifty yards he screamed "FIRE," and ten rifles spoke as one spewing a deadly wall of lead at the charging horde. Four of the warriors cart wheeled off the rear of their ponies, dead before they hit the ground. Two more were hit hard but managed to stay astride their ponies and three horses were hit, throwing their riders hard into the rocky ground.

The soldiers were firing their Colts and dodging the bullets that were coming in and ricocheting off the rocks, sending cutting splinters of rocks into the soldiers.

The attack broke off with three horses down, six or so Apaches on the ground and at lest three barely hanging onto their pony's mane. One stopped and raised his rifle and fired a last shot. Lieutenant Morton felt like someone slugged him in the shoulder with their fist and the force spun him half way around. He did not realize he had been shot for a few seconds and then a searing pain racked his body. He got control of himself and hollered for Sergeant Carver.

"Get me a casualty report, Sergeant."

"Yes, Sir," A few seconds later he reported to Morton. "One dead, one wounded and several with minor cuts from rock fragments.

"Who is dead?"

"Private Jansen, Sir."

"Have someone move him deeper into the rocks and cover him with a blanket and see what you can do for the wounded man. Give each man a swallow of water, no more."

"Yes, Sir," Carver noticed the blood on Morton's shoulder. "You're hit, Sir."

"Take care of the men then we'll see what you can do for me." Morton sat down and winced as a sharp pain racked his body. He had a bullet hole in his left shoulder that luckily had gone through without hitting bone. It was hurting and he knew it would hurt like hell for a few days. The next two days, if he lived that long, was going to be the longest of his life. It was getting dark by the time the Sergeant had taken care of the wounded man and given each man their drink. He had four men rotating sentry duty including him. Each man knew that Apaches did not like to fight at night but they would sneak into a camp and kill if they felt safe in doing so. Morton and his troops settled in for what they knew was going to be a long night.

What neither he nor any of the patrol knew was that Private Decker had been an observer of the battle earlier. He was one of the riders sent by O'Malley to round up the homesteaders. He had heard the sound of a hell of a lot of guns being fired and decided to investigate. He saw the pickle the patrol was in and watched as they fought off the last charge by the Apaches. He was well on his way to Clark by dark.

~~~

Rebecca, having closed the curtains and locking the door, stepped into the hot bath she had poured for herself. Today had been another monotonous day for her which was not unusual when her Tye was away on patrol. She had visited Mrs. O'Malley and a couple other officers' wives during the morning and spent the afternoon cleaning the house for the third time since Tye had left. She lay back and let the hot water relax her body. She loved to soak and did a lot of thinking and planning when in the tub.

She had a lot to think about this particular day. She was sure she was pregnant and was thinking of how and when to tell Tye. How would he react? Would he be happy or unhappy? Probably not unhappy she figured, but worried about supporting a wife and child. She studied the ring on her finger and then closed her eyes in deep meditation. Nope, she realized, forget all those worries because she knew Tye well and he would be more excited about it than she was, if that was possible.

Stepping out of the tub, she dried herself off and stood naked in front of a mirror. She studied her body for telltale signs. There was no bump on her flat stomach as of yet and no swelling in her breast. Her body looked no different than it had six months ago, yet she knew there were changes going on inside…she just knew it. She put her night clothes on and then put her robe on. She picked up the pistol that was by the door and stepped out on the porch and sat on
~~~

the top step. Tye insisted she have the pistol with her when he was gone. He had shown her how to use it and she had become a fairly decent shot.

She loved sitting on the porch at night looking at the stars and listening to the gurgling sound of rushing water over the rocks of Los Moras Creek which was only a few feet away. She loved looking for various constellations in the heavens that Tye had taught her to recognize. Even though Tye was gone a lot and she spent a lot of time alone, she loved her life. She loved Tye more than life itself and felt secure in knowing he felt the same of her. She would stay here a few more minutes listening to the night sounds and then go to bed. She would hug Tye's pillow tight to her breast, and go to sleep thinking of Tye holding her tight to his chest.

Chapter Fourteen

One hour after full daylight Tye and Buff sat on a knoll about a half mile from the junction of the Rio Pecos and the Rio Grande. Looking through binoculars, he caught a glimpse of an Apache just as he disappeared down the trail into the canyon. "They're there Buff. They are there and you can bet your last dollar…waiting." He turned in the saddle and saw the tops of the column's banners and the Flag of the United States of American appearing over the top of a hill a quarter mile off. In another minute, he could hear the hooves striking rocks, the jingle of sabers and the squeaking of saddles. He figured that fifty cavalrymen made more noise than a thousand Apaches.

Tye lifted the binoculars again and looked a little to the left of where he saw the Apache. He saw a sight that brought back memories…real bad memories. He was looking at the burned remains of the Freeman's homestead. A few months earlier the outlaw gang led by Yancey Cates had murdered the whole Freeman family. The Freeman's where only one of several families the murdering bunch killed before Tye along with Lieutenant Garrison and then Private Christian managed to corral and kill most of them. Yancey was the only surviving gang member and was hung a couple months ago after escaping once with Tye having to track him down again. Tye shivered remembering the night he had crept close to the gang's camp and overheard their laughing and bragging of killing and raping Freeman's daughters. He also remembered it was the night he was captured by the gang and only the fast action of Garrison and Christian saved him from torture and possibly death. He placed the glasses back in their case and placed them back in his saddle bags. He glanced over his shoulder and saw McClellan and Garrison were almost to where he and Buff were.

"We need a parley, Sir," Tye said to McClellan when he arrived. The four of them dismounted. "I've got a plan I would like to go over with you and see what you think, Sir." They all kneeled on the ground. Tye picked up a stick.

"They are there waiting on us. I saw an Apache just as Buff and I topped this knoll so I know they are there. Captain, May I suggest you get the sergeants here. Let's go over this thoroughly because if anyone doesn't know what's going on it can get a lot of men killed."

McClellan nodded his agreement. "Take care of it Lieutenant." Garrison left and returned quickly with Sergeants Phipps, Christian, Arnold, and Absher. They all gathered around Tye. "Maybe some of you or your men were hoping the Apache were not here.

Well…they are there. I want to make sure everyone understands what is going to come down because if anyone doesn't, they can get themselves and others killed."

"The Captain and I have come up with this plan to try and turn the tables on the Apaches." McClellan knew this was one of the many traits that the officers liked about Tye. He would always involve the officers in his plan and let them share in the credit if it worked out even though the officer had no idea what was going to happen.

"Do we have the sharpshooters picked out?" Tye asked.

"Yes, Sir I do." Garrison responded. "Fifteen of them, I know you said ten but I thought you might need more."

"Good thinking, Garrison. They will go with Buff up the Pecos. You will go about a mile up river and find a way down from the rim and up the other side on foot. We will send some men with you to bring your horses back. Make your way to the opposite rim from where we are now. Stay back from the rim so the Apache cannot see you and then come running to the edge with the first shot. Put five of your men close to the trail that comes out of the canyon on your side. I figure they will have several of their warriors bunched there to try and keep us from making it up the trail. Spread the others out along the rim. No talking and no noise. Sound carries in these canyons." He paused for a second before continuing.

"Now here comes the nasty part. The rest of us will go into the trap they have planned." A look of surprise could be seen on the faces of the men. "I know it is against the so called army manual to do this, but hear me out before you start cussing and calling me names." He smiled and continued. "I don't figure they will show themselves till we are all on the canyon floor. When they do, I need Phipps to take his men left, toward the Rio Grande. Stop after fifty feet or so, lay your mounts down, get behind them, and prevent any Apaches from getting up the trail we just came down. I figure they will figure out real quick the table has been turned and they will make a bee line for the trail to escape. You need to have half the men firing while the other half is re-loading so you have a continuous fire."

"I will be in front with the Captain. Phipps, you bring up the rear and as soon as your horse hits the canyon floor, fire your pistol and you take your men as planned to the Rio Grande. Arnold, you and Absher have you men lay over their mounts necks and kick your mounts to an all out run up the canyon. Now all hell is going to break loose after the shot by Phipps. Explain to your men exactly what to expect. It will be scary as hell and I don't want anyone to be surprised and freeze up. If he does he is a dead man and maybe some of the men behind him too. Hopefully, the men on the rim can do enough damage and cause enough confusion that we can make it up the trail and on the rim where we can shoot down on the Apache."

Sergeant Phipps spoke up. "What if the Apache head up the canyon instead toward us at the mouth?"

"The Apache know if he heads up the river we can kill all of them by following them and firing from both rims. He will head left and try to get to his horses which I figure are being held a little ways up the Rio Grande. Are there any more questions?" No one said anything for a moment then Arnold spoke up.

"Let's get it done. It's time we trapped those red bastards instead of the other way around. Let's do it for our friends this sonofabitch killed a couple days ago." The men's spirit picked up and Tye was grateful for his friend speaking up.

Sergeant Christian was staring at the homestead. "Tye, ain't that the Freeman's place where…"

"That's the place, Sergeant," Tye interrupted. McClellan and every man in the column knew of the fight there that Garrison, Christian and Tye had with the Yancey gang. As the word was passed among the troops they all managed to take a look. They could see the graves of the Freeman family.

"Buff, you and Christian take your men and get started. We will wait until you are on the other side." Buff left with Christian to get the sharpshooters and head up river. "Phipps, you, Absher, and Arnold get to your men and carefully explain what the plan is.

Remember one thing though. All of you have been in fights before and you know that even though things are planned to the last detail, when the first shot is fired things go crazy. Try to stick with the plan. Good luck." He shook each mans hand as they left. Tye turned to McClellan. "It's time for us to make our appearance."

"Appearance? What appearance?"

"The Apache are going to wonder where we are and if we are coming or not. We need to let them see us so they will not get impatient. We need four or five men to go with us." McClellan got the men and they fell in behind Tye, walking instead of on their horses. "If you men see an Apache, do not say anything or let it be known you saw them. Understood?"

"We understand, Tye."

They reached the trail leading down and walked down it about twenty yards to a point Tye felt sure they could be seen. He stopped the men and walked farther by himself appearing to whoever was watching that he was looking the canyon over. He saw two Apaches on the east wall like he figured. He turned back to the men and said "take a break here, on the trail; talk and act like everything is normal. Just don't let the Apaches know you know they are there." He and McClellan walked back up the trail and when they were on the rim, the captain spoke up.

"Sweet Jesus, I was scared to death, Tye. I felt like I had a big bull's eye on my chest."

"I know how you feel. A scout always feels like he has a bull's eye on him when he's in front leading a patrol."

"How in hell can you do it day after day?"

"It's a living, Captain…it's a living." Tye answered laughing. McClellan watched him walk ahead of him and shook his head and mumbled to himself, "He's got to be crazy to go through that all the time…damn crazy." He caught up with Tye and everyone settled down to wait for Buff and the others to appear on the opposite rim. The men arrived back with the horses of Buff and the sharpshooters. The waiting game had started. The plan had been explained to all the men. There was no talk as each man was lost in his own thoughts. Some could be seen praying, others writing letters. Almost all were smoking or chewing, and all had that nervous stomach that one gets when they are going into a situation where men are going to die. This is the worse part of going into battle…waiting for it to begin.

~~~

With the thundering of hooves and screams from the Apaches, Lieutenant Morton and his men faced the Apache charge just as the sun broke the horizon. Morton could not believe his eyes. More warriors had joined the original bunch and now numbered more than fifty warriors.

"HOLD," he screamed. At fifty yards again he screamed the order, "FIRE."
~~~

Nine Sharps fired as one, the .52 caliber pieces of lead tearing into the charging warriors. Two horses reared, throwing their riders hard to the ground. Four left their ponies as if a rope had been tied around them, jerking them backwards. They hit the ground like rag dolls and one could tell they were dead simply by the way they hit. What seemed like a thousand bullets were splattering the rocks around the troops. The colts were being used now at close range with deadly effect. More ponies with no riders were milling around. The noise was deafening with the colts being fired, screams of wounded and dying men, whinnying of injured horses, and Apache war cries. Add to this, the hooves of thirty or more horse's running back and forth on the rocky ground and a man could not hear his own screaming.

It was impossible to see very far because of the smoke from the guns and the dust raised by the horses. Morton had emptied his pistol and was swinging his saber like a mad man with his good arm. Other men were doing the same, fighting for their lives. Each man was living a soldier's nightmare… hand to hand combat with an Apache warrior.

Suddenly, when Morton figured all was lost, the Apaches retreated out of the rocks and finding their mounts started running as fast as they could away from the troops. Then Morton and the beleaguered soldiers in the rocks saw the most beautiful sight they have ever seen or heard…a bugle sounding charge and a line of blue clad cavalryman charging the Indians. Whooping, hollering and waving their arms, the soldiers that could still walk came out of the rocks. Morton looked around and counted four men standing besides him and not a one that was not injured. He walked past the men who were laughing and happy as only a man could be that had been jerked from the jaws of death could be. The scene behind the rocks sobered him quickly. He saw soldiers lying on their backs with two or three dead Apaches on top of each of them. It was apparent even to a green trooper like himself that every one of them had fought with ever ounce of strength they could muster against overwhelming odds. Later they would find not a single trooper had a wound in his back, they all died fighting their assailants head on.

Senior Master Sergeant O'Malley reined his mount up to Lieutenant Morton, dismounted and saluted the officer. "We got here as fast as we could Lieutenant." Looking past the officer he added, "Looks like we were almost too late."

"You got here just fine Sergeant but how...how did you get here so quick? I thought maybe it would be tomorrow at the earliest."

"Private Decker here was rounding up homesteaders when he heard the shots yesterday. He saw what was going on and headed for help. Thank him, not me."

Morton went over and shook Decker's hand and then embraced him with his good arm. The other men came to him offering their thanks also.

When the wounded were attended to and the dead wrapped in blankets, they started their trek back to Fort Clark. There were seven dead troopers laid across the saddles and twenty-three dead Apaches left in the rocks. This would go down in the report as a remarkable feat of courage by the troops in Morton's patrol.

Morton was feeling a little low about losing men under his command. This was the first time. O'Malley sensed this and maneuvered his mount beside the lieutenant's and thought a minute before speaking.

"I know how you feel, Lieutenant… about the dead soldiers." Morton looked at him as if he hadn't been aware that the sergeant had moved next to him.

"And just how do I feel, Sergeant?"

"That you failed your men; that you could have done more; that you should have not done something you did and you didn't do something you should have." O'Malley said and spit a trail of tobacco juice at a flat rock. "Losing men is part of war, Lieutenant. The men understand that and so do the officers. From what I have heard, you done real well and that's what counts with them. There's not a one of them that wouldn't go on patrol with you again and that's about the highest praise you are going to get from these men."

Morton sat a little taller in the saddle and looked O'Malley square in the eyes. A slight smile slowly formed and he reached between the horses and shook O'Malley's hand.

"Thanks, Sergeant. I suppose I was feeling a little sorry for myself." The next day Thurston, after listening to the sergeant and enlisted men's account of the battle in the rocks, was satisfied he had himself another dependable officer in Lieutenant Morton.

~~~

Asay watched the soldiers sitting on the trail. He had his men well hidden all along the wall behind boulders and brush. He had walked earlier along the floor and looked; making sure none could be seen. Now, if only his men would wait until he gives the signal to open fire, the soldiers would be easy targets. But, as other Apache leaders had learned, the Apache warrior sometimes got over zealous and did not follow instructions.

He had made his way back to his spot and had just sat down when the soldiers appeared. His heart raced when he saw the scout which he knew had to be Watkins. He could not figure out why the bluecoats had sat down while the scout and officer left, but with the ones on the trail being left there, he knew the others would be coming. He praised the life giver, Ussen, for giving him this chance for such a victory. He also praised The Gans, the Apache Mountain Spirits. His friend Naiche sat beside him behind the huge boulder and whispered, "Why do the bluecoats wait?"
~~~

Asay answered. “This, I do not know but they have left soldiers so they will come my friend. They will come and then…they will die.” He looked his friend in the face. “Did you see the big scout?” Naiche nodded. “That has to be the so called great warrior Watkins. He will die first. My signal shot will be aimed at him. Then you and all the rest will see he is just a man.” Asay smiled and leaned back against the rock wall behind him. “Just wait my friend…just wait.”

Chapter Fifteen

An hour before high noon, Tye saw Buff and his troops with him on the west rim of the canyon. They were well back from the edge of the cliff so the Apache couldn't see them. He walked over to McClellan.

"Buff and the men are in place, Sir." McClellan stood up and looked across the canyon.

"All right, Tye. Get the men ready, Lieutenant," he said turning to Garrison.

"Yes, Sir."

Tye walked to where Sandy was picketed, mounted him and prepared to start down the trail, a trail that he knew was going to a bloody. For the tenth time, he checked his Colt and the Henry repeater he had picked up from one of Yancey's men he had killed three months earlier. He took the good luck charm from his saddle bags that he had carried since his pa gave it to him before he was killed. He held the silver cross in the palm of his hand, remembering the last few minutes he had spent with Ben after he had been shot by an Apache. It didn't seem like years ago and he remembered every word; every detail of those last minutes. Tye recalled Ben telling him how much he loved him, how much he loved Tye's mother, Lori. He made Tye promise to take care of her, to make sure she never wanted for anything.

Tye tried to keep his promise but his mother died two years later. The doctor said there was nothing wrong except she just did not have the will to live anymore. Tye knew this was true because the day her Ben died, a part of her died also. They now lay side by side at the old homestead about forty miles southwest of Fort Clark. Whenever Tye was on patrol in that area he stopped by and removed the weeds and trash from the graves and kept the old place in fair shape.

"We're ready, Tye." McClellan said bringing Tye back from the past to the present.

Tye rode back, past each man speaking to them four or five at a time, making sure they understand what they were to do. One private spoke to him.

"Sir, I'm so dammed scared I can't even get enough moisture in my mouth to spit. My hands are shaking so I don't think I can shoot a gun, much less hit anything." Tye put his hand on the young man's shoulder.

"Do you think any man here isn't scared?"

"Not you, Tye?"

Tye spoke in a voice to the young man loud enough for all to hear. "I'm no different than you or any of you. Any man who says he is not scared going into a fight where men are going to be killed is a damn liar. It's how each of you handles that fear that separates the man, the soldier, from the coward. I know every one of you are men and I know each of you are soldiers and you will act as such. Do what you are supposed to do and you will be fine." He reined up in front of Phipps. "Fire that gun as soon as you touch the bottom of the canyon."

"Don't you worry none, Tye. I'll take care of it." Tye rode back to the front letting Sandy have free rein as he started down the trail with McClelland following him. He was thinking how in hell Tye did this thing he does. Everyone knows that the first shot from the Apache will be aimed at him. He shook his head in total amazement. He didn't know what Tye made in salary for being a scout but he did know one thing…it sure as hell wasn't enough.

Sandy's hooves hit the canyon floor and the hair on the back of Tye's neck stood up like the quills on the back of an enraged porcupine. The extra sense he possessed that told him of impending danger, made him feel there was a hundred eyes on him. Sweat trickled down his face and left a salty taste on his lips. He slowly took his feet out of the stirrups so if anything happen to Sandy and he went down, his feet would not be caught up in them. He looked back and saw that Phipps was a couple steps from reaching the canyon floor and before he could turn back around, Phipps fired his pistol and all hell broke loose.

Chapter Sixteen

Asay was livid. One second he had the scouts head in his sights and in the next instant, he was no longer there. The instant the first shot was fired, the horse under Tye jumped about ten feet, or so it seemed to the warrior. His shot burned thru the empty space where Tye's head had been an instant before. His warriors were firing as fast as they could. A few had the repeating rifles, and there was a lot of lead being thrown in the direction of the blue coats who lay low in the saddle with their mounts running all out up the canyon.

Two braves to his left and one to the right were hit and tumbled out of the rocks. He saw no soldier from the running horses firing their guns. He was confused as to who had shot the men. "Up there," Naiche screamed. "They are above us." Asay looked and instantly knew he had been outsmarted by the scout. Smoke from several rifles could be seen coming from the opposite rim. He knew they had to get out of the canyon quickly. He gave a signal and headed for the opening of the canyon with his men coming out of the rocks and following him. So confident of their trap, they had their horse herd about three hundred yards up the Rio Grande from the canyon opening. They had to get to them but the distance they had to cover could now be their downfall. With warriors dropping all around him he spotted the bluecoats at the mouth of the canyon firing from behind their mounts that lay on the ground. He led his men in a charge to over run them.

Tye reached the trail going up the west wall and he reined Sandy to a halt, jumped to the ground motioning the others to get up the trail. He dropped behind a boulder and began to give covering fire with his thirteen shot Henry. There were probably fifteen Apaches still in the rocks and were being fairly accurate with their fire. Tye was bumped from behind and turned to see a trooper that had been hit and after falling from his horse rolled down the trail into Tye. Tye checked the soldier to see if he was injured or dead…he was dead. Turning back around he saw an Apache that stood up to fire at the soldiers. Tye quickly raised his Henry and fired an instant after the Apache fired. The warrior dropped his rifle and grabbed at his chest before falling over the boulder he was behind and tumbling down to the floor of the canyon.

About half of the troopers had started up the trail. Tye could see four or five soldiers scattered along the banks of the shallow river and two lay in the water. Sergeant Absher jumped off his mount as he led his men up the trail and moved into the rocks by Tye.

"Nice day, huh Sergeant?" Tye said with that ever present smile. Absher looked at him like he was crazy and then fired his Colt at the Apache across the canyon. It was sixty or seventy yards and at that distance very few men were accurate with a revolver. He was no different but it did help keep some of the Apaches heads down so they weren't shooting at his men.

At the mouth of the canyon, Sergeant Phipps and his men were in deep trouble. About thirty Apaches were charging them desperately trying to get past them to their horses. Asay was among these men and was in front, leading the charge.

Phipps immediately saw they were going to be overrun and ordered his men to move close together instead of spread out and use their empty rifles as clubs. Each had managed a shot or two from their revolvers after firing their Sharps and had knocked down seven or eight of the warriors, but now, it was going to be hand to hand combat, knives, war clubs, and rifles being used as clubs. The only sound was the grunting of fighting men, a few screams from men being stabbed or clubbed. Phipps was a wild man, swinging his rifle till he broke the stock splitting open an Apache's head. He reached down to grab the dead warriors club when he was struck in the back of his head and things went black. It was total chaos for a few seconds and then the Apaches, the ones that were able, broke through to make it to their ponies. Asay and Naiche were among the ones that had made it.

Buff and the men on the rim were taking a heavy toll on the Apaches that remained in the rocks. The warriors left in the rocks suddenly jumped up and made a dash for the canyon opening where they had seen Asay and his men over run the soldiers. They were making it difficult for the soldiers as they were running in a zig zag pattern. About fifteen Apaches that were still able, left the rocks, six made it out the other end.

Tye and Absher stood up and as the smoke begin to clear saw a sight that shook a man to his boots. Men, both Apache and soldiers; lay everywhere. The shallow stream, normally fairly clear, was becoming stained with blood from the dead and injured.

Some of the soldiers came back down the trail and were walking among the men lying in the sand along the Rio Pecos. They were helping the wounded soldiers and an occasional shot was heard when they found a wounded Indian. McClellan came back down and stood beside Tye, shaking his head.

"We took some heavy losses, Tye…real heavy."

Tye nodded his head. "I know, Captain, but we hurt them bad…real bad. Let's hurry out to Phipps and his men. I'm sure they were hit hard." They moved quickly to the mouth of the canyon, waded across the Rio Pecos to where Phipps and his men made their stand. They could see no one moving.

"Oh, God," McClellan said as they came to the small area where the terrific struggle took place. Dead troopers along with dead Apaches were stacked like cordwood. Groans from the center of the bloody mess got their attention. They rushed to where the sound came from. Not knowing if soldiers or Apaches were making the sound, they had their pistols out and cocked.

The moans were coming from under some dead Apaches. Throwing the bodies aside, Tye found Phipps and two privates still alive. One private had a knife high in the right side of his chest and a nasty cut above his left ear while the other had caught a war club in the side of the face. His jaw was broken and his cheek bones looked crushed. Tye knew he was in bad shape and it would be a miracle if he lived. Sergeant Phipps was alive but unconscious. Tye sat down and placed his friends head in his lap. "Get me some water," he said to no one in particular but a canteen appeared almost immediately. He poured a little water on Phipps's face and washed his wound on the back of his head. He did not appear to have a busted skull, but had a nasty looking gash just above his hair line. He would be okay but was going to have one hell of a head ache for awhile.

"Phipps opened his eyes and looked into Tye's face. "Got any whiskey?" Tye and the others had to laugh a little in spite of the situation. Tye was just happy his friend was okay. He considered all the soldiers his friend but a few, like Arnold and Phipps, were special to him. They had been on many patrols together and shared many a campfire.

"Good to see you, Phipps and no, I don't have any whiskey…just water."

Phipps looked at the men standing over him. "Any of you got a bottle on you?" No one said anything. Phipps shut his eyes and mumbled, "Water…damn." McClellan, who had been kneeling beside the sergeant, stood up and told Garrison to get him a casualty report, also how much food was left and how the ammunition was holding up. He turned to some of the men who had followed them out here.

"You men pile the dead Apaches over there by those rocks. Find some blankets and wrap up these men and carry them to the mouth of the canyon with the other dead soldiers."

Tye and McClellan helped Phipps stand up. He wobbled for a few seconds before he got his legs under him. With one on each side, they walked him to the canyon.

Lieutenant Garrison was there with the casualty report. "Thirteen dead, Sir and eighteen wounded. Four of the wounded may not make it till nightfall. Of the other fourteen wounded, all but four can continue the patrol."

"Thank you Lieutenant; how about the food and ammunition?"

"I should have that information shortly, Sir."

McClellan looked where the men were stacking the dead Apaches. "How many of them did we kill?"

"Thirty-one that we have found, Sir, the number of wounded would just be a guess but I would say it was high."

"I would agree with you, Lieutenant." Tye said. "If we killed thirty-one you can probably figure close to that number wounded. At least that's been my experience over the years." He turned to the Captain. "Sir, we need to get a man up the trail we came down and bring Dan down here."

"My mistake, Tye, in all this," he swept his right arm in front of him, "I forgot about Dan." He dispatched a private to go up and get him. "Lieutenant, as soon as you have the other information I need, have the men set up a temporary camp. We need to take care of the wounded and also rest the horses and the men for awhile." Tye, Buff, and McClellan walked off to the side. "Was the death of thirteen good men worth it, Tye?"

"I always hate to see men die, Sir, but that's a price one sometimes has to pay out here. Tomorrow it may be me or you or Garrison over there that makes that sacrifice. The men took an oath when they joined the army and sometimes that oath requires men to die. To answer your question; yes, it was worth it. We killed probably close to half of them and God knows how many are hurting right now. Yeah, it was worth it because they probably won't be anxious to fight anyone right now and that includes the homesteaders. It takes years for a dead Apache warrior to be replaced. They cannot bring in more because there are none. They have to wait on a youngster to grow into a warrior and that time is figured in years. Life is precious to them and they will never lose men unnecessarily if it can be helped. We hurt them bad today and it took some of the sting out of their stingers. They will lay low for awhile."

"But what a price…what a price," McClellan sighed. "Thirteen dead troopers," he said shaking his head. Tye put his arm on the captain's shoulder and walked him away from the men. When they were out of hearing, Tye spoke to him.

"Get hold of yourself, Captain." Tye said getting in McClellan's face. "What did you think coming out here, leading men against the Apache was going to be, a friendly excursion, a damn vacation. This is a hard land, Captain, and it requires hard men to help tame it and make it a home. It requires hard work and sometimes sacrifices to accomplish that dream. From previous patrols with you I thought you had the mettle to handle this…maybe I was wrong." He turned to walk away from McClellan but the captain grabbed him by the shoulder.

"Wait, Tye?" He said. "I guess I was just feeling sorry for myself. What you said…you're right…thanks."

Tye smiled and replied, "Maybe I was out of line in saying …"

"No you weren't," McClellan interrupted. "That's twice in the last six months you have had to straighten my head out. I appreciate it and it will not happen again no matter what happens." He stuck out his hand and Tye gladly took it.

"Now let's get back to work." Tye said. McClellan nodded and hollered for Sergeant Arnold to find Lieutenant Garrison. They sat down on the ground and both took the makings out and rolled a smoke. There was no conversation, both just enjoying the tobacco. Within a minute, Garrison appeared.

"Yes, Sir."

"Get the dead wrapped in their blankets and tied on horses. Tye and Buff will help you make a travois for the injured that cannot continue. Have four of the lesser injured but who can still ride and two non-injured take them directly back to where Christian and the surgeons are camped. Have Sergeants Arnold and Absher assemble the men and prepare to move out immediately."

"Right away, Sir."

Tye walked over to where Sergeant Phipps lay and knelt down beside him. "How's the head soldier?"

"It would feel a hell of lot better if I had some good whiskey instead of this damnable water." Tye laughed then turned as he heard footsteps behind him. It was Buff. Buff knelt down on the other side of Phipps and looked all around to see where the captain and Garrison were.

"Got yu sum medicine here. Sergeant." He stuck the small bottle of whiskey on Phipps's lips and let him have a couple good sips. The sergeants eyes opened wide, he gasped and then coughed.

"Buff, what in God's name is that?" he asked between gasps. Buff reared back, his face toward the sky and burst out laughing. He was laughing so hard that Tye begin to laugh and Arnold looked at both of them like they were crazy. He thought, 'here I am, helpless with a busted head and that old codger done poisoned me…damn.' A minute later, when the two of them quit snickering, Buff looked down at Arnold and in a jovial tone said to him.

"Tha thar was genuine mountain man whesky. Been savin it fer an occasion like this when sum wun might really need it."

"What do you mean need it?" Tye asked.

"I'll tell you what he means," Phipps said propping him self up on his elbows. 'That damn rot gut will make you forget whatever the hell is hurting because your throat and belly are burning like the fires of hell." He looked at Buff and smiled. "I'm suffering a lot; so let me have another sip."

"Better put it up, Buff," Tye suggested. "McClellan's coming." The captain walked over to where they were and squatted beside Tye. He looked at Phipps.

"How is it going Sergeant?"

"Just slap a bandage on my head and let's go," Phipps replied.

"I don't think bouncing on a horse would do your head any good."

"Just get me on a horse and let me worry about that. From what I hear there are other wounded that will still be chasing them heathens." McClellan looked questionably at Tye.

Tye looked at Phipps and then at McClellan and bobbed his head. "I know him well, Sir. He will make it okay."

McClellan stood up. "It's up to you Sergeant but I can't afford to send any more men back with the wounded. If you want to go…it's all the way. Understood?"

"Yes, Sir. Thank you, Sir."

Buff stood up and nodded toward the canyon. "Heer cums tha lootenant." Buff and Tye stood up as Garrison walked up to them. He saluted McClellan and handed him the report. McClellan studied it for only a couple seconds. "Our ammunition is sufficient and if we are careful, our supplies will last three, maybe four days." He looked at Garrison. "Are the wounded and the deceased ready to head back to the base camp?" Garrison answered they were. "I have this dispatch to Major Thurston explaining the fight, number of casualties on both sides, and that we were pursuing those that escaped our trap. Have one of the men continue on back to Clark with it after dropping off the wounded." He handed it to the lieutenant. "Give it to one of the men and report back here. We will be moving out shortly. Please remind the men to stay alert for trouble. The Apaches we are chasing are headed a little more southwest than the patrol will be traveling but they could change their direction of travel and stumble into our men. Make sure they have secured the dead to the horses in case they have to make a run for it."

"What about the injured on the travois?"

"Cut the travois from each man's horse and set him in the saddle with a healthy trooper. They will just have to hang on and hope they make it. You might consider giving each man riding some rope so if attacked, they can tie the wounded man to him so he won't fall off."

"Yes, Sir." Garrison answered."

Chapter Seventeen

Who's that coming down tha trail"? Buff asked pointing to the rider making his way down the trail they had just come down from the east side of the rim.

Tye took his hat off and held it so that it shaded his eyes. "Hell, that's my scout Alex Mankins! What's he doing out here?" They watched Mankins reach the bottom of the trail and after speaking with a couple of soldiers, headed toward where Tye and McClellan waited. When he arrived he stepped down from his horse and shook hands with Tye and McClellan.

"What in the world are you doing out here, Alex?" Tye asked.

"Got a dispatch here for the Captain," he said as he handed it to McClellan. McClellan took the dispatch and walked a few feet away to read it.

Mankins looked around and saw the dead Apaches. He had seen the blankets draped over several horses as he came down the trail and knew what they were. "What the hell happened, Tye?"

Tye explained everything in detail because he figured his scout would be returning to the fort to bring Thurston up to date on everything. Garrison walked up at that time and shook hands with Mankins. He knew the scout fairly well and he knew Tye thought a lot of him. McClellan returned and the men could tell from his expression something was wrong.

"Mr., Garrison," he said, "Would you Tye and Buff walk over here with me. When they were out of hearing from the others he handed the dispatch to Tye.

Captain McClellan:

You need to know that Apache attacks all over the area are now being reported. I have over a hundred homesteaders' who have come in for protection. I know Fort Duncan is being overwhelmed with Apache problems also. I need to send a troop southwest but I have no experienced field officer here that I trust. I do not know your situation but I need for Lieutenant Garrison and Sergeant Arnold to come back to the fort with Mankins.

If all the reports I have received are true, there are several bands of Apaches roaming the area and they are not the usual fifteen or so but thirty warriors or more in each band. I wanted you to be aware that the group you are after are not the only ones.

Send me a report back with Garrison.

Good Luck

Major James Thurston

Tye handed the report back to McClellan who stuck it in the pocket of his tunic. “Lieutenant, just give Thurston the report I gave you a few minutes ago for one of the men to carry.” He shook hands with Garrison and added, “Take Sergeant Arnold with you. He’s dependable and will help you.” Garrison nodded his understanding and McClellan walked away toward the river to wash some of the dust and sweat from his face.

“Things looked like they were pretty sticky here,” Mankins commented to Tye.

“It could have been worse,” Tye said. “We killed a lot of them,” he nodded toward the stack of dead warriors. “There are a lot more that’s hurting right now.”

“Did you get their leader?”

“Don’t know for sure but I don’t think so. I saw one with a soldier’s blue tunic on that led them from the rocks and into Phipps men. He could have been the leader. I didn’t see a dead Indian with a tunic on so I figured if he was the leader, he got away.” He turned to Garrison. “You will be leading a troop into some dangerous situations. I think Thurston will have Alex here scouting for you. He’s a good man so listen to him before you make any decisions and you will have a lot of help with Arnold riding beside you. He’s a damn good soldier and you can count on him when things go bad.

Hope to see you in a few days at Clark. If you have time before you leave on patrol, drop in on Rebecca and see how she is and tell her I was thinking of her." They shook hands and Tye and Buff walked to where McClellan was leaving Garrison and Arnold with Mankins. The three of them mounted their horses and headed up the trail back to Fort Clark. They rode past the soldiers leading the dead and wounded who were headed to the base camp.

Tye and Buff kneeled beside McClellan on the banks of the Rio Grande and washed their faces and necks. "Think it's time to go, Captain?" Tye asked in a questioning tone.

McClellan stood up and hollered at a private to go find Sergeant Absher. He could see Sergeant Phipps downstream about thirty yards. He had his head in the water up to his shoulders. 'I hope he makes it,' he thought to himself. 'I'm going to need him before this is over.' Tye and Buff were finished washing and stood up just as Absher arrived.

"Sergeant," McClellan said, "Get the men ready. We will pull out in ten minutes."

"Yes, Sir," replied Absher and turned to leave and carry out the Captains orders. He stopped when McClellan spoke again.

"You did well back there in the canyon. I saw you drop beside Tye and give the covering fire for the men."

"Thank you, Sir. Is that all, Sir?"

"Yes. Carry on Sergeant." McClellan turned to Tye and Buff. "You two ready?"

"Waiting on yu," Buff said.

~~~

Asay and Naiche along with the remaining braves of his war party were camped about seven miles down river from where the patrol was preparing to move out. There was no celebrating, no Apache screams of victory, no scalps…just quite. He had, counting Naiche and himself, about thirty five braves and half of them had at least one wound. Two braves were sure to not see the sunrise in the morning. He was still trying to figure out what happened. He turned to Naiche. "Where do you think those soldiers on the west rim came from?"

"They had to go up the Rio Pecos and cross over. I think it was the scout's doing."

"If I knew the brother who fired that shot before I fired, I would shoot him myself." He held his rifle against his shoulder and sighted down the barrel. "I had Watkins head in my sights when the shot was fired, then he was gone."

"I think one of the soldiers fired the shot," Naiche said.

"Why you say this?'

"It looked like it was planed because even before the sound had gone away the soldiers split, some for the opening of the canyon and the rest toward the trail out of the canyon." Asay shut his eyes,
~~~

trying to bring back what things looked like after the shot. He saw the soldiers lay over the pony's necks running to the trail on the west wall. They did not return fire and at the time he thought that was strange and then some of his men started tumbling from the rocks from shots. He realized, after Naiche spoke up, the shots were coming from the opposite rim. The scout and a couple other bluecoats lay covering fire from the rocks beside the trail. He thought about it for a moment longer and nodded.

"You are right. It was a signal shot and I'm sure the scout had planned the trap. The bluecoat officers are stupid and would be dead now if not for him."

"Him part Apache maybe," Naiche said.

Asay spit on the ground in contempt. "He is no Apache but he is smart in Apache ways. We must think how we can trap and kill him."

"It is hard to trap an Apache," Naiche said.

"He just trapped us my friend, and if he had put more men at the opening of the canyon none of us would have escaped. No, he is not Apache but he knows Apache ways, the way an Apache thinks and fights." This day had taught Asay two things: one, this scout is better than any scout he has fought and second, the bluecoats were warriors. He had led the charge against those men in the mouth of the Rio Pecos and not one bluecoat turned his back in fear but fought like Apache fights.

He was sure this scout would be on their trail quickly. "Have our warriors prepare to leave," he said to his friend. "This scout will be on our trail very quick and we must stay ahead until the time comes again to fight." The Rio Grande was very wide but shallow where they were. Asay led them into the water. They would travel as far as they could in the water and make this Watkins work hard and slow to find their tracks. They were headed downstream so what mud their pony's hooves stirred up in the water would stay ahead of them leaving no trace for the bluecoats coming behind them.

As Asay rode he thought of this scout. He had lost some status among his men after the defeat at the mouth of the canyon. 'Canyon of the dead' is the name given to it by his followers and would be remember for a long time by that name. He thought maybe this scout was special. That appealed to him because that would make him even more important if he could kill this scout.

As they walked their ponies in the river they passed a large cave. The cave only went back in the cliff maybe fifty feet but he could see from the blackened roof that this cave had sheltered many people over a long time. Strange markings were on the walls, paintings of animals he had never seen before. He wondered who the people were that had painted them and what happened to them.

The canyon, the river ran through, was about a quarter mile wide at the widest and maybe a hundred yards at the narrowest.

Asay's eyes were always watching the rim on the left, the Texas side. For some unknown reason, the bluecoats would not cross the Rio Grande which would put them in Mexico. As soon as he found a way up the rim on the right side he would take his men into Mexico and rest a few days. He would go away from the others and build a sweat lodge. He would not eat or drink and would smoke the ceremonial pipe and wait for a vision. He would then know what to do.

Chapter Eighteen

Tye and Buff had been looking for tracks on both sides of the Rio Grande. Tye was on the Mexican side because he figured the Apaches left Texas to lick their wounds. There was a second reason also, he did not want Buff in any more danger than he already was and by being on the Mexican side of the river, he was definitely a target. Beads of sweat rolled down his face getting in his eyes and making them burn. He only occasionally glanced at the ground keeping his eyes on the canyon rim and the rocks along the face of the cliff. Thirty or so horses would make enough tracks that a blind scout could find so watching every inch of the mud on the banks was not that important…watching for a shooter was.

Tye saw the trail up the cliff a hundred yards before he reached it. He knew this was where he would find the tracks. He waved at Buff until he got the old mountain man's attention, motioned him to come over to the Mexican side. Buff led his mount into the water which was only three foot deep at the deepest and reined in beside Tye.

"Here's where they left the river." Buff looked up the trail and saw the tracks that had been made recently, probably in the last two hours.

"We gonna follur them thar tracks?" Tye stood in the stirrups for a moment resting his butt from the saddle.

"Don't know, Buff. We'll let McClellan make that decision." He looked back up river and saw the column approaching about two hundred yards away. "Let's get to the other side and wait." When on the Texas side, they stepped from the saddle and loosened the girths of their saddles to let their horses breathe a little better. They allowed them to drink their fill and then both men begin scratching their mounts between the ears. Sandy rubbed his nose against Tye and whinnied causing a smile to cross Tye's face. He loved this horse. "Guess I have sort of been ignoring you lately old boy haven't I," he said. Sandy whinnied again and nodded her head up and down bringing a bigger smile to Tye's face.

"I swear tha thar horse understands ever' wurd yu say." Buff mumbled.

Tye laughed. "Seems so." McClellan arrived and looked up the trail across the river.

"Is that where they crossed?" he asked.

"Yes, Sir, they are in Mexico."

“Why do you suppose they went there instead of killing more homesteaders over here?” the captain asked.

“We hurt them back there and they’ve gone to lick their wounds for awhile. They will be back in a week or so.” McClellan took off his hat and scratched his head.

“What do you think, Tye?”

“That blue uniform cannot go into Mexico…I can.”

“What do you mean by that?”

“I would like to know how much we did hurt them instead of guessing. It would be information Thurston needs to know.”

“Going by yourself?”

“No, Buff would go with me. I don’t figure they went far. They know the army won’t chase them into Mexico so they won’t be that careful.” Tye looked at the midday sun. “We will be back before sundown.” He waited for an answer. McClellan looked both men in the eye and nodded.

“We’ll wait here. I’ll get some men up on the cliff on this side to keep an eye for you coming back.” Tye nodded and the two shook hands. Buff had cinched the saddle girth on both horses. They mounted up, crossed the river and headed up the trail into Mexico.

“Keep your eyes on the tracks Buff and I’ll keep an eye out for Apaches.” They trotted their mounts making good time because the tracks were plain as day. After about twenty minutes it was obvious they were getting close by looking at the tracks and manure. They dismounted and followed on foot. Five minutes later they were on their bellies, crawling from cactus to cactus and sage bush to sage bush. Finally, they were within fifty yards of the camp. They were surprised to find the number of warriors walking around, obviously unhurt. They could see four or five lying on blankets. All together there were about thirty-five still left to fight another day which was ten or fifteen more than Tye had expected…or had at least hoped for. He looked at Buff and motioned with his head to go back. They begin to crawl slowly back the way they had come until they felt they could stand and run to the horses. Just as they reached them and settled in the saddles, both men felt it at the same time…they were being watched.

~~~

The wounded and dead soldiers arrived at base camp. The wounded were being tended to and the two healthy soldiers that brought them there took the dead on to Fort Clark. Sergeant Christian was appalled at the number of casualties that had been inflicted on the troops. The troops with him had been bored to death after cleaning the area in front of brush. There was nothing to do but stand watch. The sight of their friends wrapped in blankets had a sobering effect on each man and they were complaining no more about standing guard and doing nothing else. Christian didn't know
~~~

how long they would stay alert and not bitching twenty-four hours a day, but for now, it was nice.

Laverne Cavender was an angel sent from above as far as the wounded men were concerned. Not only was she a comfort to the men but she knew a lot about doctoring.

Jarrod and his oldest had ventured out early this morning and killed a large doe which was now roasting on a spit. Fresh meat tonight would also raise the men's spirits some.

Sergeant Lance Christian had been in the army for three years. After helping Tye and Lieutenant Garrison corral the Yancey Cates Gang three or four months ago, he was promoted to sergeant and was proving to be a good one. He was a little young compared to sergeants Arnold and Phipps, but all the men respected him. He had been stationed at Clark for over a year having come from San Antonio. He loved the army and he loved this country regardless of how it looked to others.

He was impressed with the Cavenders and knew they would make a go of it out here. They were God fearing people and they were tough and determined like most of the settlers he had met out here. They were what he and the army were fighting for in this land. He had become well acquainted with the Cavender family and liked them a lot. He understood why Tye becomes infuriated when a family he knew like this one was murdered. Christian had come across a lot of families that had been totally wiped out and he felt bad for them but they were just bodies with no names. He felt he would feel a little different from now on.

~~~

Tye looked at the Apaches and then where the river and the soldiers were about a half mile or so away. There were about fifty Apaches on the hill and now they were charging.

"IT'S GOING TO BE CLOSE, BUFF," he screamed as he kicked Sandy into an all out run with Buff on his heels. He glanced at the Apaches who were angling toward the river intending on cutting them off and preventing them from reaching the cliff and the trail down to the river. He took out his Colt and fired two quick rounds in the air. He hoped the shots would alert McClellan and he would have the soldiers ready to help them.

McClellan, hearing the shots, was shouting orders to the men on the cliff to be ready and had the rest kneeling on the east bank ready to fire. Tye was calculating the time and distance and it wasn't coming out good. Four or five Apaches were well out in front of the others and they were going to get to the trail down the cliff first.

"We'll have to fight our way through," Tye hollered. Buff pulled his sidearm and kicked his horse to get an extra spurt and pulled up beside Sandy.

The main group of warriors was still over a hundred yards away but the others were at the edge of the rim where the path was to keep the two white men from getting through. The only problem
~~~

with their plan was they did not see the soldiers until a volley from across the river tore into them, killing three of them. The other two lay flat on the ground and fired their rifles at Tye and Buff. Tye felt a bullet cut the air by his head. Both men fired their colts as their horses jumped over the two prone Apaches. Tye's bullet caught one square between the shoulder blades, exploding his heart. Buff missed but between the bullet and the horse jumping over him the Apache could do nothing and the two men scrambled down the trail just as the main body arrived. There was a tremendous volley of shots fired from both sides of the canyon. Neither man was looking back until their horse's hooves hit the east bank. The water around looked like they were in a thick hailstorm with all the splashes from the Apache bullets hitting all around them. When they reached the bank and looked back, no Apaches were to be seen and all the shooting had ceased.

"Damn Tye," Buff said smiling. "Do yu always hav this much fun on these heer patrols.

Tye exhaled and smiled. "Not always but a little excitement is good."

"Wal, yu can have all this type you want."

"You two okay?" McClellan asked running over to them. Both men nodded.

"What happened?"

Tye shook his head. "We found the bunch we were chasing but I don't know about the others that showed up."

"You mean those were not the ones we fought earlier?"

"Yes, Sir." He answered "I don't know where in hell those Apaches that almost got us come from. There must have been fifty of them." He said shaking his head.

"What about the ones we were after? Did you see them?"

"We saw them. There's about thirty-five of them left and only four or five that were on blankets. You take them and add the others and we got real problems." He stepped down and scratched Sandy under the chin. "Thanks old boy," he said.

"What do you think we should do?" McClellan asked

"It's up to you Sir. We can go back to the fort. We only have a couple days' rations left plus the men and horses are exhausted. If you like, we can rest here and watch that trail until our rations are exhausted but there are probably a dozen trails leading from Mexico in this area. We're only about five hours from Clark. The decision is yours and neither is wrong."

McClellan took off his hat and scratched his head which he always does before making a decision. He took a long look at the trail and then at Sergeant Absher. "Get the men ready to move out, Sergeant. We are going to Clark." Tye watched the smiles spread across the men's faces as Absher moved among them passing along the orders. They quickly retrieved their mounts and prepared to leave.

"Buff can find Christian and the base camp and get them to Clark, if that is okay with you Captain?"

"That's fine, Tye."

Tye asked the captain. "Can you find your way to the fort?"

"I think so…why?"

"Thurston needs to find out what we are dealing with. I need to get back into Mexico and find out what's going on."

Buff looked at Tye. "Do yu thank that's a gud idea?"

Tye smiled. "Not really but it needs to be done."

"I don't know, Tye. The odds of you getting through all those Apaches are pretty slim," McClellan said.

"Are you ordering me not to go?"

"Well…no. I just don't think it's a good idea."

"Is there anything in that manual at the Point about knowing your enemy?"

"Well. Yes there is but…"

"Thurston needs to know if there is a hundred, a thousand or somewhere in between before he puts men's lives in danger by sending out patrols that are too small and have them get overwhelmed."

"Take someone with you then." McClellan stated.

"This is a one man job. I can move quieter by myself and not have the burden of worrying about another man's safety. Just give me enough biscuits and jerky for two or three days and an extra canteen or so."

"I think it's a bad idea but I know you will go anyway. Get your rations and get out of here." He said shaking Tye's hand.

Tye turned to Buff. "Tell Rebecca I will see her in a couple of days…three at the most." Buff and Tye shook hands.

"Be karful Tye. Thar's a hell uf a lot uf Apaches out thar that wud love ta have yur scalp. I'll see ya in a kuple days."

The patrol moved out with Tye riding with them for about a mile before he found another path up the cliff on the Mexico side. He said his goodbyes and Sandy scrambled up the trail to the top. He watched the column until they disappeared. He knew Buff would have them out of the river bed the first trail he saw on the Texas side.

He turned his attention to the business at hand. He knew that this would be the most dangerous scout he had ever made because of the number of Apaches in the area and he might not have seen them all. He checked his Spencer and then his Navy Colt to make sure they were loaded and in good order. He placed his Spencer back in the scabbard and checked his Henry in the other scabbard to make sure it was loaded with the thirteen rounds. Besides extra water and rations, one of his saddle bags held extra ammunition. He took a drink of water and reined Sandy around and headed into Mexico. He pulled the Henry back out and held it in his right hand where it would be handy if needed.

He had not gone a hundred yards before he came across a large number of unshod pony tracks. Stepping down, he kneeled and looked at the tracks from close range. He traced one print with his finger and figured they were no more than an hour old. It was impossible to tell how many but he knew it was a large group. It could have been the ones that jumped him and Buff but on the other hand, it could be another group. That's what he had to find out; how many Apaches they were dealing with.

Chapter Nineteen

Major Thurston was doing what he had been doing all day…pacing the floor and puffing his cigars. He had sent for Senior Master Sergeant O'Malley a few minutes ago. He valued the old Sergeant's opinion on every issue and he sure as hell needed some help now. He felt naked and helpless as a new born baby and had no idea what to do for the first time in his military career. He had been overwhelmed by the number of families coming to him for protection. He had lost one patrol and almost lost another. He had fifty men and scouts northwest of the fort and he did not know what was happening with them. Until Garrison arrives, if he's not a casualty, he has no real experienced officers that he could depend on. He has O'Malley of course but he was hesitating to send him in the field. It was not that he was afraid O'Malley could not handle any situation because he knew he could…he had for his whole military career which went back before the War Between the States. His reasoning went back a few months when Tye brought in two kids whose parents had been killed by the Apache. Tye tracked down the Apaches and rescued the kids along with some others. The parents and grandparents of the kids were dear friends of Tye. O'Malley and his wife adopted them. Tye and Thurston made a pact that the kids lost one set of parents and grandparents and did not need to lose them again. It would take an extreme emergency for him to send O'Malley in the field.

"Sergeant O'Malley is here, Sir," the orderly said.

"Send him in…send him in."

"Sir," O'Malley said saluting.

"At ease, Sergeant," Thurston said. "Take a seat." The old sergeant eased his butt down in the wooden, straight back chair, hands flat on his thighs.

"I need your advice, Sergeant."

"My advice, Sir?" Thurston nodded his head.

"We have Apache problems like never before." He walked to the wall map showing in detail the area that surrounded Fort Clark for about forty-five miles in every direction. He started pointing to all the places Apache trouble had been reported. All this area to cover and almost one third of my command is out on patrols now. I need men here and here," he said pointing to different places that had a pin stuck representing reported trouble.

"You need more men…Right."

"Yes, I need more men but there are none. I can't send men to help the other forts and they can't send men to me." Thurston sounded disheartened as he collapsed in his chair, elbows on his desk and his face buried in his palms. He sat up, looked at O'Malley. "For the first time in my military career, I don't have a clue which way to turn. With the number of Apache bands and the reported size of them, it would be suicidal to send several small patrols out because they'd be overwhelmed. I have to keep a good number here to protect the fort."

"You have the men, Sir. You just don't know it."

"Men! What men are you talking about?"

"The settlers…we must have seventy-five to a hundred families here and there is a husband, a father, for every one," O'Malley said smiling. Some have boys old enough to handle guns.

Thurston looked dumbfounded. "I'm afraid I don't understand where you are headed."

O'Malley smiled. "Swear them in as soldiers. They can help defend the fort if trouble comes. You can then send out three patrols with twenty or twenty five men each."

Thurston looked at O'Malley like the sergeant had lost his mind. "I can't swear in civilians…it cannot be done. Besides, they wouldn't fight and sure as hell wouldn't follow orders."

"Sir, these men aren't your drunks, outlaws, trappers, or buffalo hunters. They are not politicians or lawyers either. These men are honest, God fearing, family loving men who want to make a go out here. They will do what it takes to protect their family and to fulfill their dreams. If becoming a soldier for a short time will make that dream come true, I bet my career that ever damn man will volunteer." Thurston did not know what to say. He just stared at the craggily old face of the sergeant. After a moment he found his voice.

"It's not legal. I don't know that it's ever been done in peacetime."

"First of all, we are at war, Sir. It may be a small war, but none the less, its war. I guarantee none of these men know whether it's legal or not and they don't give a tinkers damn if doing it will save their families. I believe somewhere in that manual it should say something about adapting to circumstances."

Thurston laughed in spite of himself and the situation. "Yes it does, Sergeant. Yes it does." He stood up and walked to the window and stared out over the parade ground. "Saying I agree to this crazy idea of yours, how will they be disciplined enough to fight if necessary."

O'Malley stood up, walked over to the window and stood next to the major. "Let me pick five men to help me and I guarantee you they will be able to fight as soldiers in one or two days. Not as good as experienced soldiers, but well enough. That would allow you to put close to one hundred men out in the field."

"Let me think about it for awhile. In the meantime why don't you mingle with the civilians and get a feel to see if what you suggest could happen. I'll see you later today."

"Yes, Sir, Major". He saluted, turned and walked out of the office. Thurston shook his head as he looked at the broad back of the old sergeant as he exited his office. Never would he in a million years have ever thought of such a hair brained idea. But if it would work it would allow him to put two large patrols together instead of three smaller ones and would be a hell of lot safer for the men.

~~~

Tye walked, leading Sandy along the side of the hills as he moved deeper into Mexico. He didn't want to be in the bottom of the canyons and he sure didn't want to be sky-lined by walking or riding along the crest of the hills. It was simple to see a man, especially a man on a horse, standing or moving on top of a hill outlined against the background of blue sky.

He had come maybe two miles in the last hour and he had come across two more sets of tracks of large numbers of unshod ponies. He stopped and took one of the canteens from his saddle and poured some water in his hat and gave Sandy a good drink. He took a swallow himself, swishing the water around in his mouth and then spitting it out. "Looks like we have a whole lot of Apaches in the area, Sandy," he said scratching his horse under the chin while he looked in all directions for trouble. All of the tracks so far where
~~~

going in the same direction, southwest and parallel to the river leading him to believe they were all different groups. "If that's true old boy, we have at least one hundred fifty or so warriors in the area and there may be more." Sandy nickered causing Tye to quickly close his hands on his horse's nose. "No noise, Sandy," he whispered.

A lot of men Tye had known that spent a good deal of time alone talked to their horses. Their horse was their best friend and the best part of the relationship was the horse never talked back. Tye had been known to sing a song or two and Sandy never complained about his being off key. Tye always said a man has to talk to let off pressure or he might just explode. But right now, talking was not an option…being as quite as possible was. Sound carried a long ways in this country and letting people know where you were could get a man planted prematurely.

Tye was stopping every few minutes to listen, sniff the air for smoke, and searching every conceivable hiding place. It was at one such stop that he smelled the pungent, never to be forgotten, odor of burned flesh. He stood perfectly still holding Sandy's nose, his eyes searching the terrain ahead of him for any sign of trouble. Hearing and seeing nothing he walked cautiously ahead leading Sandy. He had the Henry cocked and ready. He checked his Bowie in his right boot and made sure his Army Colt was loose in the holster. Suddenly, he stopped, listening. He had heard something but could not identify it. Then he heard it again; the sound of a man moaning and he wasn't very far away. He tied Sandy's reins loosely to a sage and in a crouch, warily moved toward the sound. He had the Henry in his left hand and the cocked Navy Colt in his right.

"Damn," he mumbled under his breath as he saw the man a few feet ahead of him. The Mexican was spread eagled on the ground, hands and feet tied with rawhide to stakes. The coals in his upturned palms were still smoldering as was the coals between his legs. Tye knew the man was suffering horribly. He dropped to one knee and studied the surrounding area. No matter the situation in this country, a man was a fool to rush into it without thinking and looking first. He slowly stood up and took a cautious step forward…and all hell broke loose.

Chapter Twenty

Lieutenant Garrison, Sergeant Arnold, and scout Mankins arrived at the fort about two hours before sunset and headed directly to Thurston's office. Major Thurston saw them coming and met them on the porch. "Good to see you Lieutenant…Sergeant Arnold," he said returning the salutes of the two soldiers. "Come into my office and fill me in on what's going on in the field."

Upon entering Thurston's office, Garrison took out the dispatch and handed it to the major. "Captain McClellan asked me to give this to you, Sir." Thurston took the paper and sat down at his desk and quickly unfolded it.

Major Thurston:

We have encountered the Apaches twice. We inflicted heavy damages to them but we suffered thirteen dead and several wounded. The dead and wounded will be coming to the fort with Sergeant Christian and the medical personnel. We will continue to follow the Apaches and try to eliminate them or have them surrender. We have supplies for three or four more days.

Your obedient servant

Captain McClellan

A frown crossed Thurston's face. He stood up and walked to the wall map with all the pins stuck in it. "What are the pins for, Sir?" Garrison asked.

"Marking the reports of Apache trouble," Thurston answered.

Garrison walked quickly to the map. "All of these mark different places the Apaches have struck?" Garrison questioned.

"Reported problems, Lieutenant. We haven't verified any of them because of being short on men and officers." Garrison looked at the map, disbelief on his face. "We are facing the largest Indian problem we've ever had on the Border. From what we hear, there must be several bands of Apaches and they may total over two hundred warriors, maybe as high as three hundred."

Garrison sat down in the chair. "Three hundred warriors…damn," he said. "What about McClellan and the troops. They are down to about thirty men; thirty men that could be wiped out completely if they get ambushed by that many Indians."

"Hopefully Tye and Buff can keep that from happening," Thurston said. "I want you to get cleaned up and get a good night's sleep. You will lead a patrol out in the morning." He looked at Arnold. "Tye thinks a lot of you as a man and a soldier and so do I. I'm doing something that goes against all the rules; you will lead a patrol also. I want you to cover the area to the south and southwest of Fort Clark all the way to the Rio Grande and up to the Old Mail Road. Lieutenant, you'll cover the area due west of Clark to the Rio Grande and then up river for twenty miles or so. Mr. Mankins, you'll go with Sergeant Arnold and I will have another scout that will go with you lieutenant. You will leave before daylight. Now get cleaned up and get some rest."

"Sir," Garrison said. "How can you send that many men in the field and still protect the fort."

"I have that covered, Lieutenant, but don't ask how," Thurston answered smiling as the men turned to leave. Thurston started the paperwork for supplies.

~~~

An Apache came out of the sand almost at Tye's feet and he instantly knew he had stupidly walked into a trap. In the instant he saw the Apache at his feet he saw at least two more rise from the sand a few feet away. Instinct, and years of living on the edge had honed his reflexes to a razor's edge. Without even thinking, he swung the heavy Army Colt like a club and struck the nearest Apache across the nose. You could hear the bones crunch and the Apache dropped like a rock. The other two were on Tye quickly,
~~~

one swinging his war club at Tye's head and the other trying to gut him with a Bowie. Tye blocked the war club with his Henry and was lucky the warrior with the knife misjudged the distance as his blade only scratched his belly. Another inch and he would have been gutted. It was not deep but stung like hell and there was some blood.

Before the Apache could make another try, Tye kicked him in the groin doubling the man over. He raised the barrel of the Colt and shot from the waist. The warrior with the club was knocked backwards by the slug striking him in the chest. Tye heard Sandy whinnying and looking in that direction was startled to see two more Apache warriors only ten feet away and coming fast and one was in the process of releasing a lance. Tye threw his body to the left hitting on his shoulder on the ground, rolled, and coming up on his feet quickly. He fired his Colt as he came up and hit the one who had thrown the lance in the thigh taking him out of the fight, at least temporarily. The other brave swung his club and struck Tye on the right wrist. Pain shot up his arm and his hand went numb. The Colt fell to the sand. Tye swung the Henry with his left hand at the Apache that had struck him. The warrior ducked the blow and swung his club at Tye's legs. Tye jumped back and swung the rifle again catching the brave in the ribs, doubling him over. Tye struck him hard in the face with a vicious kick, snapping the man's head back and he crumbled to the ground unconscious.

Breathing hard, Tye stooped and picked up his Colt and stumbled toward the Apache he shot in the leg. The Apache scrambled to his feet and pulled his knife out holding it in his right hand, his left on his thigh trying to stem the flow of blood. He took a clumsy step toward Tye but stopped when he saw the Colt in the white man's hand pointed at his chest. Tye didn't want to fire another shot and he did not want to kill a man who was injured and helpless…at least as helpless as an Apache can be. Tye spoke to him in Apache. "Go…get out of here. We will meet another day." He knew he had to get away fast because the shots would draw Apaches like bees to honey. His hand hurt like hell and the gash in his stomach was bleeding. The Apache looked at him and then backed off a ways, turned and stumbled away from him.

Tye received his second shock when he saw Sandy was gone. He quickly scanned the area and was sure this was where he left him. Then he saw the dead Apache who had obviously tried to take Sandy and got stomped for his efforts. "At least he is not in some damn Apache hands," Tye mumbled to himself. Maybe he will find me or vice versa he thought. He sat down and looked at his stomach. The cut was still bleeding a little but was not as serious as he had previously thought. He looked at his hand and wiggled his fingers and rotated his wrist. Satisfied it was just badly bruised and not broken he stood up, looked around again. "Damn," he cursed. He reloaded his Army colt and checked his rifle and only then realized he was thirsty and his canteens were on Sandy. "Damn again," he cursed. He knew a man in this country was in trouble without a horse and you could double that trouble when he was in the middle of a bunch of Apaches. Chances were that man was as good as dead.

He walked to where the Mexican lay and saw he had died, the man's face contorted showing the agony he had been in. "Any other time," he said, "I would bury you proper but not this time." He walked as fast as he could away from the scene and toward the river. He was trying his best to cover his trail. Fortunately, his moccasin boots left little to be seen as far as tracks is concerned. Taking no chances he stayed on rocky ground as much as possible being careful not to over turn any of the rocks that would betray his passing. He knew even being as careful as he was it would only slow them some. An Apache could track a lizard over rocks.

It was not too long until the sun would be going down. He figured he needed a place to hole up till full dark, and then make his way to the river. He found a place a couple minutes later. There were a great number of huge boulders just ahead that would offer a place to hide and if worse came to worse, a defendable position. He was moving toward them when he was startled by a voice. "Where you go white man?" Tye quickly turned in the direction of the voice and was startled to see five Apaches watching him. He also saw Sandy being held by one of them. He stood looking at them as they sat on their ponies watching his every move. Thoughts of Rebecca flashed across his mind and he knew he would never see her again. He swallowed the lump in his throat at that thought. There was just no way out of this, not against five Apache warriors that had him dead to rights.

For what seemed an eternity, they watched each other, neither wanting to make the first move because all knew that some one was going to die…maybe more than one. The Apaches knew this man was a warrior because of what they found back on the trail where the fight took place a few minutes ago. Sweat rolled down Tye's face as he dropped into a crouch and was bringing the Henry up when he received the shock of his life.

He heard his name, "Tye Watkins," from the throat of a very large, muscular brave. Tye hesitated and stood straight up trying to figure out what was going on. The man who had spoke raised his hand, palm forward in the peace sign. Tye lowered his rifle a little as the brave dismounted and slowly walked toward him. Tye stood there still confused as what the hell was going on because he knew he should be dead by now.

The Apache walking toward him was a splendid example of an Apache warrior. He was a little taller than the average Apache but was muscular beyond anything Tye had ever seen before. He stopped five feet from Tye and stood there staring. Somehow he looked familiar to Tye and he was trying to remember where he had met him before.

"Picked up any more Apache boys that were hurt?" the warrior asked. Tye was startled as he realized who this was.

"Ke-ah, is that you," he asked as he dropped his rifle barrel, pointing it to the ground.

"It is I, my friend," and he extended his hand which Tye took with his left after laying the rifle down.

"Ke-ah, my friend, I cannot believe it is you." He looked past his friend toward the other Apaches. He could tell by the look on their faces that he was not their friend and they did not approve of this meeting of old friends.

"Let us talk," his friend said and motioned for Tye to sit. He sat on his heels facing Tye, his back to the other braves. "It has been long time, my friend." Tye nodded in agreement.

"Too long my red brother."

"Much has happened since we were young," Ke-ah said. "There is much unrest among my people. Some want to live with the white man in peace. These are mostly the old ones." He motioned with his head toward the others. "The young wants to hunt and live free like their fathers. To do this they think they must kill all the white men on our land."

"How does my friend feel about it?"

Ke-Ah looked past Tye at some unknown object in the distance and shrugged his massive shoulders. "I have killed many white men. You have killed many Apache. You are big medicine to my people. Those with me want to kill you...want to torture you to see how tough this white man with such a reputation really is. They saw what you did back there so they are more curious than anything else. They never believed a white man could do that to four Apache warriors."

"What is going on along the Rio Grande?" Tye asked. "There are many Apache warriors in the land."

"Apache believe that the only way to live like Apache is to kill white man and run them from our land. Many Apache from different tribes are here to do this."

"How many?" Tye asked.

"Many," he said. "Maybe more than too-ooh-asht-tin-yay." Tye, remembering his Apache, knew that was one hundred and fifty or more and that was big trouble.

"What do we do now?" Tye asked nodding toward Ke-ah's fellow warriors.

"You save my life once. I now return that favor and we are even." He stood up and spoke in Apache where the others could understand. Tye understood most of what. Ke-ah said.

"This man saved my life once and now I have saved his. Once he is away from us, he like all white man, and we will kill him next time we meet." His words were received with grunts and nods. The brave holding Sandy's reins nudged his pony toward them leading Sandy. Glaring like only an Apache with hate in his heart can, he dropped the reins in front of the scout. Sandy immediately stepped to Tye and rubbed his nose on Tye's chest. Tye scratched him between the ears with his good hand.

Ke-ah said. "We will ride with you to the river. From there you are on your own." Nothing else was said as Tye mounted Sandy. He rode beside his friend with the others trailing behind them. Tye was a little uptight not knowing for sure how much control Ke-ah had over the others. He rode expecting a knife or a bullet in the back any second.

~~~

After cleaning up, Lieutenant Garrison made his way to Tye's home. It was almost dark and he was hurrying. It would not be proper for him to be seen at the house of a married woman whose husband was away at night. He knocked on the door and it was quickly opened and Rebecca stood there, a pistol in her hand.

"Oh, Lieutenant Garrison," she said obviously embarrassed holding the gun. She put the gun on a table beside the door and stepped out on the porch. "I thought you were on patrol with Tye." At that thought she felt coldness inside her. "Is...Is Tye okay?"

Garrison smiled. "Last time I saw him he was fine."
~~~

"Then," she asked smiling, "What brings you here at this time of day?"

"Tye asked me to drop by and see if you were okay and to tell you he was thinking of you." Rebecca felt relieved.

"That's mighty sweet of you, Lieutenant. I appreciate you going to the effort of coming over. You must be exhausted."

"I am a little tired. I need to get a little food and rest. I'm leading another patrol out in the morning."

"What's happening with Tye and Buff?"

"We ran into a large band of Apaches. There were heavy casualties on both sides with thirteen soldiers killed and several wounded."

"Thirteen dead!" Rebecca said in disbelief. Garrison nodded. "My God," she added.

"Tye said he would see you in two or three days." Rebecca nodded. "Thank you again Lieutenant for coming by." She shut the door and Garrison walked away wondering how in hell a man could leave a woman that beautiful to go off chasing Apaches. 'Only that crazy sonofabitch, Watkins,' he thought to himself and laughed. He shook his head and headed to his quarters.

~~~

Captain McClellan, Buff and what was left of the original fifty men rode into the fort about two hours after dark. The blue uniforms that were clean when they left were now filthy and the
~~~

men, heads down and shoulders hunched, were tuckered out. Even the horse's heads hung down with weariness. McClellan and Buff headed for headquarters hoping Thurston was still there. They could see the light through the window in his office. It was the only light in the building.

Thurston jumped up from his chair when they walked into his office. "Captain…Buff, God it's good to see you." He rushed over and shook both men's hands ignoring McClellan's salute. "Sit down…sit down," he said turning the two chairs where the men could sit. When they were seated he said. "Where is Tye?" he asked fearing the worse.

"He left us and went into Mexico. He said you needed to know exactly what we are up against."

"Alone?"

Buff spoke up. "Yu kno Tye, Major. He thinks he can muve quicker and quiter by himself. He didn't want no wun ta go with him." Thurston nodded. He knew Tye and most of the time he liked to do things by himself.

"I know both of you are tired and need some rest but I need you to head out again tomorrow if you are up to it. I have almost one hundred families camped all over the fort and we need to rid this land quickly of the Apache where they can go home."

"That may take awhile, Sir," McClellan said. "There are more Apaches in the area than we could have ever imagined."

"I figured as much. I think your dispatch you sent with Lieutenant Garrison pretty well filled me in on what happened. Do you have anything to add?"

"No, Sir."

"Then get yourselves cleaned up, something to eat and then get some rest. I'll see you early tomorrow." The two men left and Thurston blew out the lamp, shut the door and left for his quarters. It had been another long, stressful day and he was glad it was over with.

Rebecca was startled when she heard the knock on the door. She picked up the pistol and walked to the door. "Who is it?"

"It's me Rebecca...Buff." The door flew open and Buff found himself being hugged and kissed on the cheek. He was totally embarrassed. Rebecca pulled back and looked past Buff.

"Where's Tye?" she asked, "Is he okay?" she asked, her voice betraying her fear.

"Tye is fine Rebecca. He went into Mexico ta see if he kud find out how manee Apaches we are facing. It wus infurmation Majur Thurston needed ta kno, he said. He shud be heer by late tomorrow or tha next. I need ta klean up sum then we can talk sum more."

"I'll warm up some water."

"Don't yu go ta tha trouble. I can wash up in the creek."

"In case you haven't noticed it's still a little nippy outside. You would catch a fever if I let you do that. You just wait a minute and I will have you a bath." She set a bucket of water on the pot bellied stove. Buff took a bucket and walked to the creek and filled it and dumped it into the tub in the center of the room. In a few minutes the water on the stove was hot and she poured it into the tub. "I'll go outside and you take your bath, Buff. We will talk some more when you are through."

Chapter Twenty One

Reaching the river, Tye and Ke-ah sat side by side each waiting on the other to speak. It had been twenty years ago that their lives became entwined. Their friendship ended suddenly about sixteen years ago when Ke-ah had become old enough for warrior status. There were a thousand questions Tye wanted to ask about the years since they parted.

Ke-ah's voice broke the silence between them. "I must leave you my friend. Go in peace but remember one thing: you are white and I am Apache. The next time we meet, one will die." He reached over and put his hand on Tye's shoulder. "I know you are not like other white men. You do not hate the Apache, you understand them. It is known among my people that of all white men, you are only one who can be trusted. This is good my friend…you are like white Apache. You be careful Tye Watkins. Your scalp would bring much status to a warrior." He quickly reined his great white horse around and with the others, left in a cloud of dust and once again, out of Tye's life.

"I hope we don't meet again my friend," Tye said out loud knowing what it would mean if they did. He started down the trail to the river and toward Texas anxious to see something he feared he would never see again a short time ago…Rebecca.

~~~

Ke-ah reined in his pony and turned to look back at his friend. The others continued on their way to their camp. Ke-ah saw Tye disappear down the trail to the river. He was glad he was with the others when they came across Tye because his friend would have been dead otherwise. He sat on his pony for a moment and thought of his childhood when things were simpler and Tye was his friend. He was welcome in Tye's home and Tye was welcome in his parent's wickiup. They had many good times together. Over time, he had learned to speak English from Tye and Tye learned the Apache language from him. They were best friends and went hunting together, played games together and had mock war games where they fought each other. Who would have thought their war games were now going to become real.

Ke-ah was a powerful man in his band, not just in strength but in fighting ability and leadership. He was thirty winters old and in the prime of his life as a warrior with no equal in battle. He had a wife and son and life had been good until the white man started
~~~

coming in large numbers two winters ago. Since that time, the Apache never stayed in one place more than a few days. They were always on the move and fighting the white man was becoming more and more of a reality. Finally, the people had enough and begin to strike back at the invaders of their country.

Two winters of small raids had now come to this. One hundred and fifty or more warriors were here preparing themselves to wipe the white man from their land. He looked wistfully at where his friend had disappeared. He would do his best to not have an encounter in the days to come with his friend. "I have no wish to kill you my friend," he said loudly and then turned and headed into the semi-darkness following his friends.

~~~

Asay sat naked in the sweat lodge he had constructed. Hot rocks were in the center and he poured water on them. Steam filled the lodge and the air grew very hot quickly. He sat cross-legged and chewed peyote, a powerful stimulant drug from the buttons of the mescal cactus. He had not eaten nor taken water in hours and he would not until he received a vision. He had his magical hoop with him and he shut his eyes and begins to chant so Ussen, The Creator, would appear to him. He repeated over and over his prayer, "hey ya ya hey ya ya hey," while waiting for the magical appearance of The Creator. He stopped chanting long enough to chew more peyote and then resumed his prayer. His eyes were shut and sweat rolled down
~~~

his face and chest as he continued his monotonous chanting. "Hey ya ya Hey ya ya Hey ya ya."

Two hours later, exhausted he fell into a deep sleep. He saw the horizon was on fire and from it rode a magnificent warrior on a white horse. The horse's eyes were as red as burning coals and fire came from his mouth when he breathed. On the stallion sat a warrior of great physique. He was naked from the waist up and had two white stripes of war paint across his nose and cheeks. Asay knew this man was a leader and a great warrior. The man said nothing but Asay could feel his eyes burning into his inner soul and his unspoken words were clear to Asay. "Come…follow me and we will kill all the white eyes." The great white stallion pranced back and forth and then reared up on his hind legs, the warrior remained seated on the horses back as if he was part of the stallion. Coming down, the stallion turned and walked away from Asay and the warrior, looking over his shoulder, bided Asay to follow.

Asay awoke from the sleep and shook his head trying to get his thoughts straight. He stepped outside of the now cold sweat lodge into the darkness of night. He put his clothes back on and walked down the hill to the camp where his waiting braves stood up, anxious to hear if their leader had received a vision or not. Asay walked to the fire and removed a piece of venison and chewed on it while his braves waited, and waited. He swallowed the venison and took a long drink of water.

He stood up and faced his men. “I had a vision…” Before he could continue the braves were shouting and shaking their rifles above their heads. Asay held up his hands and the warriors became quite. “A warrior of great physique appeared to me on a great white horse. He came from what appeared to be fire. He said nothing yet I understood what he wanted. I was to join him in the fight for our land, our way of life and we would wipe out the white man.” It was so quite in the camp you could hear the breathing of the men. No one said anything nor moved. This was a magical moment in the lives of the Apache when a man received a vision.

“Who is this man?” Asay’s friend, Naiche asked.

“This I do not know,” Asay answered. “I will sleep on it tonight and we will speak of it in the morning.” With that said he went to his blankets, lay down and was immediately asleep.

~~~

Tye had traveled hard for the last three hours finally stopping to give Sandy a rest. He dismounted, loosened the saddle girth and gave his horse a good drink. He sat on a rock with a canteen and a piece of jerky. While chewing the tasteless jerky, he thought back on the meeting with Ke-ah. He had been fortunate it had been his friend instead of other warriors or he would probably be a meal for the buzzards and coyotes by now. In truth, the meeting was a melancholy experience for him. He had been thrilled to see his old friend again but sad that when they parted, it was the last time it was
~~~

to be that way. He hoped it would not come down to a life or death situation between him and his friend.

He mounted Sandy again, took his kerchief and made a sling around his neck and placed his throbbing right hand through it. The wrist was swollen and turning black and blue. He headed toward the fort which was no more than an hour or so away. He knew this part of the country well so he kicked Sandy into an easy lope keeping him going in the general direction of Clark but letting him pick his way since a horse could see better at night than a man. He wasn't worried now about stumbling onto Apaches. He didn't figure they would be this close to the fort.

He had come across three homesteads that were burned but could find no bodies. He figured the word had spread about the uprising and he hoped each family had abandoned their homes temporarily. They could always rebuild but lives could never be replaced. He patted Sandy on the neck; "We'll be home soon old boy." He figured to be there just before sunrise.

~~~

Thirty miles behind Tye, Asay was up and watching a lightning storm to the west of them. It was coming toward them and would be here within an hour or so. Lightning was magical to the Apache and was to be avoided at all times if possible. They did everything in their power to dodge or get away from the fiery arrows of the Thunder People. They would sit in their wickiup during a storm
~~~

refusing to eat because they believed to do so during the storm would cause ones teeth to fall out. Asay and his braves broke camp and headed south hoping to get around the storm. Naiche, already mounted walked his pony to where Asay stood.

"We need to leave now or we will catch the fiery bolts from the sky." Asay swung himself onto the pony Naiche held. They galloped their ponies to try to get away from the storm which was getting closer and closer. The lightning kept the still darken skies lit almost constantly and the low rumbling of constant thunder could be heard. It reminded Asay of the buffalo herds that use to run through this country in uncountable numbers when he was young.

One brave pulled alongside of Asay and Naiche, an excited look on his face talking so fast neither could understand him. They reined in and looked where the man was pointing. On a hill, maybe a hundred yards away was a very large band of Apaches but this was not what the excited man was jabbering about. Sitting in the middle of the group, with the lightning illuminating the sky behind them, sat a man on a horse, a white horse. The band rode toward Asay's band and they all knew at the same time what was happening. The Apache on the great white horse was a very muscular man and the lightning behind him made him appear to be coming from fire. Asay and Naiche looked at each other. Asay's vision was coming true and there was much excitement, jabbering and pointing as the band closed in on them. Asay knew they were Lipan Apache before the man on the white horse spoke. He had white paint on his face.

"I am Ke-ah, Lipan Apache."

"I am Asay from the mountains north of here. We are Chiricahua."

Ke-ah saw some of braves were wounded. "You have fought the Bluecoats?" Asay nodded.

"We had a trap for them yesterday but their scout was smarter than I thought and he almost trapped us. We killed many soldiers but we lost almost half my men."

"You know this scout?"

"He big man, maybe head taller than me. Name is Watkins." Ke-ah nodded.

"I thought so. I know this man well. He big medicine among my people." He dismounted and said. "Let us talk." Asay and Naiche dismounted and sat on the ground with Ke-ah, this man from Asay's vision. He had their undivided attention.

"I would ask you and your warriors join me and my warriors in the fight against the white eyes. Together no bluecoat soldiers could stand against us. To-ooh (100) braves is too many for even twice that number of bluecoats. No one can stop us if we fight together. It is known that the Chiricahua are one of the best fighters among all Apaches." Naiche and Asay's chest swelled with pride at the compliment. "It would be a great honor to have such men fight beside me." What else could Asay say accept yes to this man from his vision and who has such respect for the Chiricahua. Asay stood up and faced his men.

"We will fight with the Lipan." The two groups merged and there was much shouting and celebrating. A tremendous clap of thunder startled everyone. They turned and looked toward the clouds and were amazed at the sight. The clouds were dispersing and the storm was no longer threatening the group. The warriors were speechless at this and considered it a sign that Ussen was favoring them for their fight against the invaders. All mounted their ponies and followed the warrior on the white stallion as the rising sun broke over the hills.

Chapter Twenty Two

Thurston was roused from his quarters before daylight with news that Tye was back and at the hospital. Arriving at the hospital he saw Rebecca running there. He waited for her opening the door and held it while she rushed past him. Tye was lying on a table, shirt pulled up and the surgeon cleaning his stomach wound. His hand had already been doctored and wrapped.

Rebecca, tears streaming down her face, rushed to Tye and kissed him, as she threw her arms around him. Tye kissed her back and wrapped his good arm around her holding her tightly to his chest. Thurston smiled at the sight as the surgeon, obviously unperturbed by the two lovers, continued cleansing Tye's wound.

"I guess you are okay, Tye," the major said. Tye raised his head just now aware of Thurston's presence.

"Yes, Sir, Just a little banged up but otherwise I'm fine." Thurston looked at the beautiful Rebecca.

“I can see that.” He tipped his hat to her. “Can you excuse us for a moment Rebecca? I need to speak to Tye. You can have him in a few minutes.” She smiled, stood up and went outside.

“What did you find?”

“A hell of lot of Apaches, Major, probably one hundred fifty warriors or more are out there just waiting on the army.”

“One hundred and fifty…my God, did you see them?”

“No, Sir I didn’t.”

“Then how do you know?”

Tye told him the story of meeting Ke-ah and him saving Tye’s life. He told him everything his friend had told him.

“Do you think there is a way we can come up with a plan of peace?”

Tye laughed. “Any peace parley would end up in a disaster. The Apache have been down that road before and were tricked and ambushed at these peace parleys. No, Sir, there’s not a snowball’s chance in hell of peace until there has been a lot of dying…on both sides and maybe peace would come as a last resort but not before. They are dead set on killing every white man, woman, and child on the Border.”

Thurston shook his head. “I figured as much. There have been too many lies, too many broken promises by the army for them to trust us.” He sat down in a chair and looked at Tye. “I need you in the field Tye. Do you think you may be able to go tomorrow?”

"I may be a little sore and will be one-handed for a couple days but I'll be ready."

A look of relief was apparent on the major's face. "I have got to send two patrols out tomorrow, Tye. We need to end this thing quickly." Tye nodded.

"Yes, Sir, I agree but don't get your hopes up of a quick ending." He got up off the table and walked outside where Rebecca was.

"Are you alright, honey," she asked hugging him.

"Nothing wrong that a little loving care won't cure," he replied.

She laughed and said. "The first thing we will do is get you a bath then we'll see about the other," she said slapping him on the butt.

"Tye," Thurston hollered at him. "I forgot to give you this." He handed Tye a letter. "It's from the governor."

"What is it?" Tye asked. Thurston shook his head and walked off toward his office. 'Whatever it is, it's probably good news for Tye and bad for me and the army,' Thurston thought.

"Buff get back?" he asked Rebecca

"Last night just a little after dark. I made him take a hot bath," she said laughing.

"I bet he pitched a fit over that," Tye said joining her in laughing.

They made it to their home and Tye, while having his bath, told Buff what happened.

"Sounds ta me like yu wure damn lucky tha thar Apache friend uf yurs wus thar." Tye just nodded his head and lay back in the hot water. "Wal, I'd better git muving. I'm supposed to leave on patrol with Garrison."

"You be careful, Buff. There's a lot of Apaches running loose out there.

~~~

Christian arrived at the fort about mid-morning with the dead and wounded. Upon reporting to Thurston he was ordered to join Tye and McClellan on patrol leaving in the morning. He was told Garrison had left this morning with Buff and Mankins scouting for him. He had forty men with him including Sergeants Arnold and O'Leary and a new second lieutenant by the name of Williams.

"Get some food and rest and be ready at daylight," Thurston said.

"Yes, Sir, I'll be ready."

Tye lay on his back in bed with Rebecca snuggled up next to him. She had decided to wait until the Apache problem was over with before she told Tye she was pregnant. She did not want anything else on his mind while out there. Early morning sun rays filtered through the window curtains in their bedroom.

"What was in the letter Thurston gave you?"
~~~

"I haven't read it yet. Been sort of busy you know," he said kissing her. She giggled and snuggled closer, her breast crushed against his chest.

"Maybe you should. It was from the governor you know," she said as her left hand tickled the hair on his chest.

"The damn letter can wait…" Tye said pulling her on top of him.

~~~

Thurston sat in his office with Sergeant O'Malley. "I want fifty men, Sergeant, fifty good men to go with McClellan to leave this afternoon."

"Yes, Sir, but I thought they were leaving in the morning?"

"They were but there has been a change in plans. Please get the men but first get Tye and ask him to come see me."

O'Malley rushed to the Watkins home. He knocked on the door and had to wait a couple minutes for Tye to answer his knock.

"Come in Sergeant," he said. Tye had only his pants on so O'Malley reluctantly took one step in not wanting to intrude any longer than necessary. He knew the two lovebirds had been apart for awhile and he could remember back in the past when he had come in off patrol anxious to see his wife. "Major Thurston wants to see you, Tye."

"Now?" Tye asked.
~~~

"As soon as you can." O'Malley looked at the bedroom and winked. Tye smiled and O'Malley left.

"Wonder what the major wants?" Rebecca asked.

"Don't have a clue, honey. He pulled his boots on and started out the door when he noticed the letter lying on the table. He picked it up and opened it.

Mr. Tye Watkins

% of Fort Clark, Texas

Mr. Watkins:

I have become aware over the last few months of your exploits along the Border dealing with bandits and the Apache. I know you were at one time a Ranger before you begin scouting. I know you made an officer in a short time with them.

With the State's growing population we have had an influx of thieves, gamblers, and murderers come in with them. Our crime rate is three times what it was right after the War and becoming worse every day. There are not enough officers of the law to control it and keep it from becoming worse.

We are sorely short of men like you who can take care of themselves and can track these men down and bring them to justice.

I am offering you the position of U.S. Marshall for the area west of San Antonio to the Border, south to the Gulf of Mexico and north on a line running from Fort Davis east to Fort Stockton.

Your pay would be one hundred per month starting out and fifty cents per day you are on assignment for using your own horse. You will have an expense account for meals, staples, ammunition, and whatever other expense you incur while on assignment.

Please consider this offer and let me hear from you as soon as possible.

Yours Truly

Elisha M. Pease

Governor of the State Of Texas

He handed the letter to Rebecca. After reading it she asked. "It sounds exciting Tye. What will you do?"

"Don't know yet, honey but we will discuss it. It has to be something we both will be happy with. I have to see the major and we will talk about it when I get back." He put his shirt on and left.

Rebecca put water on the stove to heat so she could wash his socks and buckskin pants and shirt. She would sew up the shirt where the knife had cut it and wait for his return. The stitches in the shirt would be one of many. The shirt had belonged to Tye's father who had been shot while wearing it and Tye had been wounded several times since he had begin wearing it. It was his fathers and Tye would not leave on patrol without it.

Chapter Twenty Three

Major Thurston had his head buried in paper work when Tye walked into his office. Ever since Tye had been at Clark, the orderly had never failed to be outside Thurston's office to announce him. His sudden entrance startled Thurston for a second. He quickly stood up and motioned for Tye to come in and sit.

"Tye, I need your opinion on a plan I have. I'm thinking about having the patrol you are leading leaving this afternoon instead of in the morning."

"Yes, Sir. Could I ask the reason for it?"

"I have a feeling that the Apaches, sooner or later, will hit Garrison's troops in full force. When they do the troops led by you and McClellan, who will be following Garrison's troops will hit them and maybe catch them with their pants down, or maybe I should say breechcloths." Despite his problems he smiled at his joke. Tye wasn't smiling.

"I don't know Major. I don't feel right about using a bunch of soldiers as bait. A lot of them could get killed."

"If we don't end this pretty quick, there may not be any soldiers, homesteaders or anyone else out here except the Apaches."

Tye could not argue that reasoning. One hundred or more Apaches are trouble for the army…a hell of lot of trouble. In fact, knowing what he knew about the Apache warrior he wasn't a hundred per cent sure that the number of soldiers at Clark could handle them. From what he had seen, at least half of the warriors had rifles, repeating rifles. The damn army was still stuck on using the breech loading single shot Sharps. It was a great rifle but not up against the Henry repeater. The only advantage the Sharps had was the distance that it could kill was far greater than the Henry.

"Do you plan to let Garrison in on the plan?"

"Of course I would. I would never put soldiers in harms way without them knowing what was going on."

"I didn't figure you would major but I wanted to hear you say it. I don't particularly care for your plan because I don't like to go into something blind."

Thurston looked at him. "What do you mean…blind?"

"In this situation, you probably won't know ahead of time when the Apache will strike. That eliminates you picking your ground and there is no chance to have a plan since you don't know how, when or where it will happen. You are the boss and I will do what you say, but you asked my opinion. I do have a suggestion though if you are insistent on doing it this way."

"This is why I wanted you here…for your opinion. What is your suggestion?"

"Let me catch up with Garrison and scout for him. Let Buff come back and take McClellan and follow. I can let Garrison know the plan and he will slow down enough for the two groups to get close enough to help each other. If they are too far apart and it takes too long for one to help, it could be a disaster. Mankins is a good scout but he's young. I've been up the river and around the bend a lot more times than he has. Maybe I can figure out ahead of time what, when and where."

Thurston sat back down and spread some of the papers on his desk pretending to look at them. A minute later he stopped shuffling them and looked up at Tye. "When can you leave?"

"As soon as we can meet with McClellan and go over the plan with him. I can go over the plan with Garrison. There's always the chance the Apaches could hit McClellan instead of Garrison. Everyone needs to know what's expected of them."

Thurston nodded his approval and stood up. "It's settled then. I will have McClellan here in two hours." Tye nodded and left headquarters heading home. He knew Rebecca wasn't going to be happy when he told her he was leaving again so soon.

Arriving at his house he saw his clothes hanging out to dry. He smiled when he thought of her holding her nose before she washed them. There weren't too many opportunities for a man to bathe out here or wash his clothes while on patrol. Smoke from campfires, sweat, horse smell, and sometimes blood is pretty much what a man's clothes smelled of when he came in off a patrol. He told her of his having to leave.

"Why do you have to leave today? You said it was tomorrow."

"I know honey, but the major came up with a plan that is just crazy enough to work and I have to leave to catch up with Garrison and his patrol to let them in on the plan."

She stood there, arms crossed across her breast, staring a hole through Tye.

"So, when do you leave?"

"In about two hours." She turned and started toward the bedroom.

"Then we had better hurry."

"Hurry! Hurry for what?"

She looked over her shoulder and smiled, winked and threw off her blouse. Tye stood there for a minute before a smile crossed his face. "Oh," is all he could say then followed her into the room, a big smile on his face.

Tye, Buff, and McClellan all sat around Thurston's desk. Thurston explained what his plan was. There was no response from anyone for a moment then Buff spoke up. "Kud be yur hangin out sum soldiers fur a possible massacre. If wun hundred or more Apache hit either wun uf tha patrols and tha uther can't get thar quick…in kud be bad."

Thurston nodded. “I know that and that’s why it will be up to you and Tye to keep the two patrols close enough to help but far enough apart the Apaches won’t know both are there.” Buff and Tye looked at each other questionably.

“Major,” Tye said. “There’s not a lot that goes on in this country that the Apaches don’t know about. I’ve sometimes wondered if the hawks that are everywhere speak to the Apache and let them know where their enemies are. This plan might work but it’s going to take a hell of lot of pure luck.”

“Does anyone of you have a better one?” Thurston asked. Complete silence followed his question. “Then we will proceed with this one.”

“I have a suggestion, Sir,” Tye said. “Send some civilian clothes with some of the soldiers.”

“Civilian clothes!” Thurston said. “Why in God’s name do we want to send Civilian clothes?”

“If you plan does work there is no way all the Apaches will be taken or killed. You can bet they will head for Mexico. If you want to end this, we can follow them and stay on them not giving them time to eat or sleep until they stand and fight… or give up.”

Thurston took the ever present cigar out of his mouth realizing what Tye was saying. Soldiers caught out of uniform would be shot as spies by the Mexican Federales and no telling what political consequences could follow. “That coul…”

"Be the end of your career," Tye interrupted. "Then again, it could endure you and the army to a whole country of people whose lives you just saved. Besides, it wouldn't be the first time you sent men into Mexico."

"I know that," Thurston said remembering when he sent Tye and three men into Mexico after the bandit, Alex Vasquez.

"That worked out just fine didn't it?" Tye asked.

Thurston nodded, "But that was just four men. We are talking about a lot more this time. How would you explain that many men to the Federales?"

"Same plan you are using here. Split the men into three groups and stay a mile or so apart. I would scout for one, Buff for one and Mankins the other. The three of us can keep the groups close enough to help each other but far enough that if the Federales show up they won't know about the other two…at least that's the way it's suppose to work."

Thurston put the cigar back in his mouth, rolled it from the left side of his mouth to the right and then clamped his teeth down on it. "Do you think it will work?" he asked looking at Tye.

"Who knows Major? If things go right, yes it will, just like your plan will…if things go right." Tye answered smiling.

Thurston stood up and leaned forward, both hands flat on his desk, the cigar firmly clamped in his teeth. "I pray your plan won't be necessary."

"So do I, Major. So do I."

"I'll add more supplies than normal just in case, along with the clothes." Thurston said. The men left to get their personal things together and left assigning the men for the patrol to Senior Master Sergeant O'Malley. They knew he would get the best and the best is what they were going to need.

Chapter Twenty Four

The troops crossed the Los Moras Creek Bridge shortly after two p.m. on this, the 6th day of April, 1869. With two columns of more than fifty men in the field it was the largest campaign against the Apache so far along the Border. Eighty per cent of the troops at Fort Clark were in the field. Both had two wagons filled with medical supplies, food, grain for the horses, barrels of water, and of course ammunition. A surgeon and an assistant were with each column.

Tye rode beside McClellan, Buff, and Sergeant Christian. "I think we need to add one little change in Thurston's plan. The more I thought about it the more I thought it might work. It is imperative that one troop can get to the other quickly, within five to ten minutes or it could be a disaster. What I am afraid of is if the two get more than a mile or so apart, depending on the breeze, the battle might not be heard by the other till it's too late to help. Let me assure you that one hundred Apaches can do a hell of a lot of damage in five minutes." He turned in the saddle and faced Buff and spoke a little louder so each of the four men could hear clearly.

"Buff, you are the key to this. I want you to stay half way in between the two groups so you can hear any gunfire from either one and can get McClellan to Garrison or Garrison to McClellan. This way, whichever one the Apache strikes, the other will know immediately." He looked at McClellan. "What do you think, Sir?"

"I wondered about one being to far to hear the other. This should work. Yeah, I feel a lot better about the plan if we do it this way."

"It's settled then. I'm going ahead to catch up with Garrison." He shook each man's hand. Buff's was the last and Tye held the shake. "You take care of yourself old friend."

"Yu too Tye. We'll be thare when yu need us." Tye nodded, turned Sandy and headed out to catch up with Garrison. The men watched him disappear in the distance.

No one spoke and the only sound was the squeaking of saddles, nickering and snorting of the horses and their hooves striking rocks.

Sergeant Christian broke the silence. "That's what I love about Tye. I would not have thought about using Buff that way. He just thinks of all the problems that could come up and does something to prevent them."

"His pa wus tha way too," Buff said. "Ole Jim Bridger wus great at strategy but Ben wud always ask 'what if' and it wud be sumthang Jim hadn't figured on. Use ta make Bridger so damn mad," Buff added laughing.

"I only know one thing," McClellan said. "I and every damn soldier in the fort feel a lot better when he's around."

Buff nudged his horse with his heels and rode ahead about a hundred yards. He knew there was no Indians close but out of habit, he was watching the hills, brush, and arroyos for signs of trouble. A blind man could follow the tracks of the two wagons that were with Garrison and he found where they left the Old Mail Road and headed northwest. He reined in and waited on the men to catch up.

~~~

Tye caught up with Garrison just as the sun was setting. They had camped on a hill and had several campfires going. Garrison had also put out several sentries that would be replaced every two hours. The horses were picketed in a stand of sage. Tye took all this in immediately. 'Garrison has learned quickly,' Tye thought to himself. He remembered about a year ago when Garrison was so green that he had to be told when to go relieve his bladder and knew absolutely nothing about the Apache or fighting them. After several patrols with him, Tye was proud of his progress and called him his friend. In fact, when he was captured by the Yancey Cates gang, Garrison's quick thinking had saved his hide.

Garrison was sitting by one of the fires with Mankins and Sergeants Arnold and Absher when one of the sentries hollered that
~~~

Tye was coming in. Garrison jumped up. “Tye, what are you doing here?” Tye stepped down from Sandy and shook hands with Garrison and the rest of the men around the fire.

“Figured you boys might need some babysitting,” Tye said laughing.

“No reflection on Mankins here,” Arnold said, “but I for one sure am glad to see your sorry ass.”

“No offense taken, Sergeant,” Mankins said. “I’m glad he’s here too.”

“But why are you here?” Garrison asked offering Tye some hot bicuits, jerky, and a cup of coffee.

“The major came up with a crazy plan to try and catch the Apaches in a trap.” He sat down as did the rest of the men. “He has another column a few hours behind you. We are to stay within a mile or two of each other and if the Apaches attack one, the other will come running and hopefully surprise them.”

“That’s it…that’s the plan?” Garrison questioned.

Mankins spoke up. “What if the shots cannot be heard because of distance or the wind?”

“Buff will be in-between the groups. He will be close enough to hear shots and he will get help immediately from the other column. I figure help will be coming in five minutes, ten at the most.”

Garrison nodded his head in approval. "So one of us is the bait?"

Tye laughed. "I guess that's a simple way to put it. Let's keep the fires going after dark and see if we can't attract some Apaches."

"That's something different…wanting to attract Apaches," Absher said. They all laughed but it was a hollow laugh as each wondered if they were already being watched.

"Alex, you will need to ride back in the morning to help Buff. I figure the two of you working together will insure the trap works. At least, I will feel a lot better with two scouts between the two columns instead of one." Mankins nodded and said he would leave before first light.

~~~

Three miles away, sitting on a hill, Asay and Ke-ah watched the fires of the soldiers "Something wrong," Ke-ah said. "Soldiers don't have fires after dark."

"It is strange unless it new leader and he don't know Apache very well."

Ke-ah nodded. "But men with him should know better. Again, I say something is wrong."

Asay said, "It almost like they want to be attacked." He turned to Ke-ah. "We should send someone to see the camp…see what going on." Ke-ah agreed. Asay stood up and walked away to find Naiche. Finding him he told him to get another and find the
~~~

bluecoat camp and see what he could find out. After watching Naiche leave he walked back to where Ke-ah was and sat down beside him.

He spoke to Ke-ah. "You said earlier you knew the scout Watkins."

Ke-ah answered. "That was many years ago. I knew his mother and father also. I ate many meals with them and Tye ate many meals in my wickiup with my mother and father."

"How did this happen…how were you friends?" A bewildered Asay asked.

"I fell off horse when I was nine summers old. I was hurt pretty bad. Tye found me and took me to his home. His mother doctored me and that was the beginning of our friendship. We hunted, played war games, camped out together for four or five summers. Then more white men started coming into our land and my people forbid me to see him again. He saved my life. Yesterday, I saved his. We both know we are even and the next time we meet it will be as Apache and white man."

"Why is he such big medicine to the Lipan Apache?" Asay asked.

"He fights like Apache. He thinks like Apache. He tracks better than most Apache. He smart and seem always to be ready for whatever the Lipan plan to do. He killed many Lipan warriors. But it is known he only white man Apache can trust. He like Apache in he speaks from heart…he no lie. If he Apache, he would be a great chief."

"If you and he meet in battle, can you kill him?"

"We both know that as much as we not like it, we are no longer brothers. Yes, I could kill him and he could and kill me."

Asay put his hand on the massive shoulders of Ke-ah and said. "Maybe the Creator, Ussen will not let that happen."

"Maybe," Ke-ah replied. "Maybe he get killed by other Apache or maybe I get killed by bluecoats. What will happen, will happen."

~~~

McClellan pushed his troops till almost full dark. He instructed Sergeants Christian and the sore-headed Phipps to tell the men there would be no unnecessary noise and no fires. He was impressed with Phipps because his head had to still be hurting from the war club but he was a soldier's soldier and he was doing his job. McClellan knew the men respected the sergeant before and sure as hell even more now.

They had covered a lot of ground having taken only one rest period but he was not sure exactly how far behind Garrison he was. Maybe Buff would know when he came in. That thought had just come to him when one of the sentries hollered "Buffs coming in." McClellan stood up and walked to the edge of the camp. He saw Buff dismounting and walking his way. McClellan walked toward him speaking before they reached each other.
~~~

"Do you know how far we are behind Garrison?"

"Seed their kampfires on a hill mabee five miles or so away."

"They had campfires?" An astonished McClellan asked.

"Shor tha did. How else wud yu tell tha Apache whar yu wure?"

McClellan shook his head in agreement with that. "It makes sense, I guess." He turned to his sergeants. "Tell the men we will head out an hour earlier than normal to make up ground in case they are attacked at dawn."

Both sergeants saluted and left to pass the word to their men. Buff stuck a piece of jerky in his mouth. His horse had been taken by a private to picket and feed. He dropped his saddle and blanket on the ground. He spread his blanket out and sat down to think about tomorrow. He was tired and didn't really want to talk to anyone. He needed his rest because he was going to be all alone tomorrow and he would be a good ways from either column if anything happens. If he wanted to stay alive he had better be sharp. If something happened to him and the Apaches attacked either column, it would be a disaster.

Chapter Twenty Five

Naiche came back to the Apache camp about midnight. He woke both Asay and Ke-ah. "We found the soldier camp. There are many bluecoats, maybe ten times the fingers on my hand. They have two wagons with them. The scout you call Watkins is there."

Ke-ah looked at Naiche. "Are you sure Watkins is there? He was injured the last time I saw him."

"It was Watkins." He held out his hand. "His hand is wrapped."

Ke-ah looked away. He was hoping there would not be an encounter but now there was a good chance there would be. "It makes no difference. He will die with the rest." He placed his hand on the shoulder of Naiche. "Get some rest." He turned to Asay. "We will lead the bluecoats on a chase and hit them quickly and disappear before hitting them again. We will do this until they are tired and then we will trap them." He raised his hand and closed his hand. "We will trap them," he repeated. "Let us get some rest my friend. Tomorrow is going to be a great victory for our people or…it will be a good day to die."

~~~

The night passed quietly in the McClellan camp and for the soldier on patrol, always too quickly. They were mounted and on the move two hours before daylight intending to close the gap between the two columns of soldiers. McClellan knew Tye would have the other column starting a little later than normal in order for this to happen. He just prayed the Apaches did not attack.

When it was light enough to see fairly well, Buff moved out in front of the column about a half mile. The country was condusive to ambush everywhere a man looked. Hills, arroyos, thick brush, and huge boulders were everywhere that an Apache, or a hell of a lot of Apaches, could remain unseen till the last second before they attacked. The sun wasn't full up yet, but Buff was already sweating. He took his kerchief out and wiped the sweat from his eyes. The hair was standing up on the back of his neck and he felt like a thousand eyes were on him. He rode with his Spencer cocked, butt resting on his thigh and his finger on the trigger. He also paid close attention to his horse looking for ears twitching or a quick turn of the head.

His horse jumped sideways suddenly almost unseating him. A huge rattlesnake was coiled right between the wagon tracks. He guided the skittish horse around him and watched the snake. If there
~~~

was one thing in the world he hated, it was snakes. A chill went up his spine when he figured the monster must be six or seven feet long with a head wider than his foot. He looked over his shoulder as he passed by and the snake was stilled coiled ready to strike, his head turning and watching Buff. Buff knew that rattlers have poor vision but was sensitive to heat and vibrations. He was following Buff because of the vibrations from the hooves of the horse. "Not enough tha I have ta watch fer Injuns but fer damn snakes too," he mumbled out loud. He shivered again and continued on.

~~~

Tye and Garrison were not in any hurry to put their butts in the saddle. They were delaying for a while to let McClellan catch up. Tye figured this was a good time to have a meeting of the officers and sergeants. He passed his suggestion to Garrison and the lieutenant had the men together in a couple minutes. They were away from the other men.

Tye said, "As you know we are facing the possibility of meeting at least one hundred and maybe more Apaches. Now I know all of you have fought the Apache before, except you Arnold." Tye laughed as did the rest. They all knew that Arnold had been in many skirmishes and was hell on wheels in a fight. "What I am saying is that each of you knows the ability of an Apache warrior and until now, we usually only meet fifteen to thirty at a time and that's trouble enough. The possibility of a hundred warriors, hell maybe
~~~

two hundred is a serious situation and one mistake could lead to a massacre." He picked up a stick and started making marks on the ground. "This is the way Lieutenant Garrison and I want to handle things. The Apache are up here somewhere," he put an X in the sand, "and from tracks I have observed, not very far. We are here," he put an X on the ground, "and back here is McClellan." He put another X on the ground. "Somewhere in between is Buff. Now it is imperative the men in the back of our column be alert to any gun shots coming from behind them. If they hear some, they are to notify Lieutenant Garrison immediately." He paused for a moment and then stood up.

"This is important Lieutenant. I think we will be hit but if they hit McClellan instead and I'm out in front of you somewhere send a man to get me and you take the troops back to help McClellan. Do not wait for me. I will catch up with you. One other thing and this is most important to remember. Have your bugler put his bugle away. If he blows that damn thing the way sound carries out here the Apache will be gone before you get there. The whole idea is to have them so engrossed in killing McClellan and his men or killing us they won't see the other group coming till it's too late to escape." He looked at the men. "Any questions?" No one said anything.

Garrison stood up and said to the sergeants, "Get the men mounted and ready to move out. Sergeant Arnold, get Corporal Smitherson and you two take F troop and bring up the rear.

Sergeant Absher, get Corporal O'Riley and you two take C troop and be on mine and Lieutenant Williams' heels. Explain to your men what Tye said. Dismissed." He returned the salute of the sergeants and turned to Tye.

"How far do you think they are ahead of us?"

Tye shrugged his shoulders, "Hell, Lieutenant, one could have you in his sights right now for all I know." Garrison unconsciously quickly looked around and then figured out Tye was fooling around with him.

He thought to himself, 'Only man I know that in any situation, no matter how bad can find a way to joke around with you. Maybe that's the secret thing about him that endears him to everyone. They know no matter what happens they can count on him to be calm and bring them through safely.' He and Williams mounted their horses that had been brought to them and watched the two scouts disappear over the hill.

~~~

Ke-ah and Asay rode quietly while listening intently to the two braves that had been watching the movement of the bluecoats. The white eyes were about an hour behind them and moving slowly. This bothered Ke-ah because he knew in the past the bluecoats moved quickly. 'Why,' he wondered. He turned to Asay. "We must be careful with our plans because of Watkins. He will think
~~~

like us and will know when and where we are going to strike. We have to change…trick him somehow."

"Do you have a plan?"

"Not yet, but I will." With that said he kicked his heels in his pony's flanks and was quickly at a gallop with the others right behind him. His eyes were searching for a place that would not be obvious to the eyes of the scouts but usable as a place for ambush. He was looking for a simple place that Watkins would not expect trouble from.

A half hour later he found it. An arroyo about ten foot deep and twenty foot wide ran parallel to their tracks the soldiers would be following. Unless Watkins was extremely lucky, he would never see it. The land was mostly gently rolling hills and with sage and cactus covering the ground made the arroyo hard to see. Ke-ah thought it would be perfect. He could leave a few men to harass the bluecoats. They could fire a few shots and then be on their ponies and escape down the arroyo. He mentioned his plan to Asay.

Asay asked. "Why do we not hit them quickly with all our braves?"

"That is what Watkins would expect. There is a reason my people have never trapped him; he is Apache…a white Apache and we must treat him as such. We will change our ways. We will do things Apache does not normally do." Naiche was left with twenty warriors hidden in the arroyo to wait for the bluecoats. They were instructed to fire two shots each quickly and then mount their ponies and escape and catch up with the main group.

~~~

Tye and Mankins were well ahead of Garrison when they decided to hold up and wait. They were exactly where Ke-ah and the rest had stopped, discussing the trap. Tye was studying the tracks. It was obvious to both, the Apache had stopped and had been milling around as if looking for something.

"What do you think?" Mankins asked.

"They are discussing something. Maybe they are trying to decide where to ambush us or simply run to Mexico rather than fight fifty soldiers. I doubt it is the latter." He stood up in his stirrups, looking in all directions for something. Hell, he didn't know really what he was looking for just hoping something would catch his eye.

Suddenly the hairs stood up on the back of Tye's neck and at the same time, Sandy nickered and twitched his ears. This was a warning from Sandy that Tye had seen many times. He turned to Private Jacobs who had come with him.

"Something is wrong. Go back and tell Lieutenant Garrison to come on quickly and have their rifles ready." Jacobs reined his mount around and galloped back the way they had come. Tye sat on Sandy, sweat running down his collar, looking for trouble hiding somewhere. Sandy was staring at the brush to his right, ears twitching, sniffing the air.
~~~

Garrison reined in and raised his hand to stop the troops behind him when he saw Jacobs coming. He moved his mount a few steps toward the incoming rider.

"What's wrong?" he asked when the two met.

"Not sure Lieutenant but Tye said come to where he was and be ready with your guns out."

Garrison turned to Sergeant Absher. "Pass the word for the men to have their guns out and be ready for trouble." He turned back to Jacobs. "What do you think we are facing?"

"You know Tye, Sir. When he gets those feelings something usually happens. The Apaches had stopped for some reason and Tye suddenly got the feeling something was wrong. That's all I know." Garrison pumped his arm and the men were off at a trot.

~~~

Tye still sat on Sandy staring in the direction he had been looking. He knew something was there that had Sandy's attention but what. If it was Apaches and not knowing if it was one or fifty, Tye did not want to find them by himself so he just sat there, waiting for Garrison.

He heard the patrol before he saw them and reined Sandy around to go meet them.

"What do we have, Tye?" Garrison asked as they met.

Tye, looking back over his shoulder where he had been waiting, answered. "Not sure, Lieutenant. I got a feeling though
~~~

there's trouble just ahead." Garrison had a perplexed look on his face when Tye looked back at him. "I had one of those feelings I get every once in a while and Sandy was nervous about something. May be nothing Lieutenant, but with the number of Apaches we are chasing, it's best to be a little on the cautious side."

Garrison nodded and studied the surrounding terrain. He turned to Sergeant Absher.

"Have the men stay where they are and stay alert." He reined his mount around to face Jacobs. "Find a way up that hill a see what's down there." Jacobs dismounted and walked toward the hill. "Be quiet and don't get spotted." Jacobs looked over his shoulder at the lieutenant with this incredulous look on his face, stopped and spit a wad of tobacco juice that hit the lieutenant's horse's hoof. He shook his head and headed toward the high ground. Garrison heard Tye laugh and turned to him.

"What's so damn funny?"

Tye quit laughing and smiling, replied. "The look on Jacobs' face when you told him to be quiet and not be seen."

"What's so damn funny about that?"

"Jacobs was an old trapper and buffalo hunter before joining the army. He's been out here for ten years. It just sorta ruffled his feathers some when you felt like it was necessary to remind him to be careful."

Garrison realized how stupid it was to say that. "I'll apologize to him."

"Just let things be, Sir. I'll smooth his feelings." They both took a quick sip of water from their canteens. Garrison looked back the way they had come.

"Do you figure McClellan is close?"

Tye looked where the lieutenant was staring. "Count on it. He's a good officer and with Buff and Mankins out there, they are close." Sergeant Absher moved to where Garrison and Tye were.

"Jacobs is coming back, Sir." Tye and Garrison watched as the old private hurried over to where they were.

He stopped and spit a juicy wad of tobacco at Garrison's feet, a couple drops hitting his dusty boot and dribbled off leaving a trail. "Good thing you got one of those feelings Tye. There's about twenty to twenty-five warriors hid along that draw just below the rim waiting to ambush us."

Garrison had seen those feelings before that Tye gets. About six months ago when he was with Tye chasing the outlaw Alex Vasquez in Mexico, Tye put one of the bandits they had captured in front with Tye's hat and buckskin jacket on. He figured it was about time for Alex to get tired of being chased. Five minutes later, the Mexican was knocked backwards off his horse, a hole in his forehead and his brains blown out the back of his skull. He had seen it before so he didn't act surprised this time. He looked at Tye.

“How do we handle this? If there’s a lot of shooting, McClellan is going to come charging in and ruining the surprise for the main bunch.”

“We’ll have to take a chance that they don’t have someone watching besides the ones in the ravine. Pass the word back to the end of the column to Sergeant Arnold. Have him detach one man to go back and find Buff and tell him not to come running when he hears the shooting this time.”

Garrison said. “Sergeant Absher, pass the word to Sergeant Arnold what Tye just said.” He turned back to Tye. “How do we handle this?”

“I’m working on that, Lieutenant.” Tye was trying to figure out how they could surprise the Apaches who were waiting to surprise them without getting a lot of soldiers killed.

~~~

Buff saw the soldier coming a long time before he was seen by Private Jameson. He sat on his horse waiting, chewing his tobacco and wondering what was going on. He knew it had to be important for Tye to risk the Apache seeing a man leave the column and start back tracking. The Apaches would send a brave to follow and see where he was going and that would put the whole plan in jeopardy if he saw McClellan and his men.

“Whut’s goin on private?” he asked when Jameson arrived.
~~~

Jameson, taking a second to remember exactly what he was told to say before he spoke; "Lieutenant Garrison said there was going to be some shooting in a few minutes and you were not to come running in with McClellan."

"Tell me whut is going on and why thar is going to be sum shuting."

"Tye done found sum Apaches that was gong to ambush us. He and Garrison are trying to figure out how to turn the tables on them. There will probably be some shooting and they did not want you and McClellan to come and let the Apaches see both columns of soldiers. If they did, the major's plan would be worthless."

Buff spit a wad of juice that splattered on a flat rock about ten feet away. "Yu git yur ass bac to Tye. I'll make shur tha the captain and me don't cum running in and spoil tha partee fur yu." He slapped the private's horse on the rump and yelled, "NOW GIT."
The horse jumped and the private barely stayed in the saddle. He got his balance and his butt back in the saddle, turned and waved at Buff and was gone. Buff waited on McClellan to tell him what was going on.

~~~

Naiche took a chance and raised his head just enough over the rim to see what the soldiers were doing. He was hidden by a huge sage bush. He could not see very well but well enough to know something was going on. He knew the blue coats suspected
~~~

something was wrong. 'I wonder if they know we are in the draw?' he thought to himself. He turned his head and looked at the top of the hill to his left. He whispered to the brave next to him. "Watch the top of the hill. If you see bluecoats, tell me." The brave nodded his understanding. Naiche continued watching, wondering, and waiting.

~~~

Tye and Garrison were away from the others just far enough that they could not be heard. "What do you think of this, Lieutenant? Get several men up the hill where Jacobs was. He can lead them up there. Pick your best marksmen. You can take ten men and have them on the ground, guns pointing at the draw. I will take the horses of the men that are on the hill and run them by the draw. The sound of the horses will make them think we are coming into the trap and hopefully the Apaches will expose themselves to shoot. At the first shot have the men on the hill and the ones here open up on them. Have the rest of the men charge the draw and take care of as many Apaches as they can."

"What are the chances it will work?" Garrison asked.

Tye smiled that smile that always had a calming affect on nervous men. "If it doesn't, the Apaches have a sayin…" He was interrupted by Garrison.

"I know...I've heard it before, it's a good day to die," he said remembering the saying Tye said that the Apaches said sometimes
~~~

before going into battle. It still didn't make any sense to him that anyone could think any day was a good day to die. "Your plan makes sense Tye. I'll get Sergeants Arnold and Absher to get the men here where you can tell them your plan."

"You can tell them our plan," Tye said putting the emphasis on 'you'and 'our' plan. Garrison smiled. 'That's Tye,' he thought to himself. 'He's always making sure the men think the officers help with whatever plan he comes up with'

Tye stood beside Sandy studying the lay of the land before him. Fifty yards in front and to his right were the Apaches. To his left was a fairly steep hill but was barren of brush and rocks. He discounted that as a possible ambush spot. The land was flat in front and the horses should be able to run without breaking any legs. He looked to his right again and to the top of the hill where the sharpshooters would be. He scratched Sandy between the ears and tried to think of any reason this would not work beside him getting hit with the first shot.

~~~

McClellan had caught up to Buff and was listening to the scout explaining the situation to him.

"And they don't want us to help?" McClellan asked.

"No, Sir. Tha wus whut the private said Garrison told him ta tell yu."

McClellan asked. "How far behind are we?"
~~~

"Not fer, mabee a mile or mile and a half." McClellan nodded and turned to Sergeant Phipps.

"Get the men off their mounts but be ready to leave at a moments notice."

"Yes Sir," Phipps answered and started barking orders to the men who were more than ready to step down and rest their butts. Buff and McClellan stood beside their horses; staring into the distance listening for the gun fire they knew was coming.

~~~

Behind the hill on Tye's left, that he discounted because of the lack of cover, sat Asay and Ke-ah and almost a hundred warriors. Ke-ah had not told Naiche or Asay his plan for a double ambush. He told Asay only after they had left the braves in the arroyo. At the first shot, Asay would take one half of the band and go around the hill and attack the bluecoats from the front. He would take the remaining warriors and hit the bluecoats from the rear. With the soldiers fighting the men in the draw, they would not see him and Asay coming until it was too late. The three sided attack should confuse the bluecoats just long enough for the Apache to kill them all.

~~~

Tye took one last look around. The men should be on the hill by now. The riflemen by Tye were on one knee, barrels pointed to the ravine where the Apaches were hiding.

"Ready, Lieutenant?" he asked.

"We're ready, Tye." Tye nodded and kicked Sandy lightly with his heels. They were at a trot with ten horses less riders following Tye parallel to the draw. Tye's eyes were searching the draw for the first sign of an Apache. Five seconds later all hell broke loose.

Chapter Twenty Six

The Apaches rose up as one, to fire at the soldiers and immediately saw they had been tricked. Two fired at Tye but the scout was throwing his body from the saddle and the bullets whizzed harmlessly where he had been. Naiche, seeing the trap, shouted "TO THE PONIES," but it was too late. Rifle fire from the men on the ground and from behind them on the hill ripped into them. Half were dead before they took a step and more were wounded. Naiche rallied the survivors and begin firing back. Two of the soldiers on the ground were hit hard, dead before they hit the rocky soil. The soldiers that were still mounted charged the remaining Apaches firing their pistols. The dust raised by the horses and the smoke from the guns made seeing difficult.

Tye, seeing the Apaches coming from around the hill in front of them ran toward Garrison, screaming to get his attention but the lieutenant was too busy shouting orders and firing his pistol. As he ran Tye saw Apaches coming from the rear and knew they were trapped. Screaming at the top of his lungs, he finally was close enough to get Garrison's attention. He pointed toward the Apaches coming and when Garrison saw what he was pointing at his jaw dropped and his eyes widened as big as saucers.

The men on the hill were already firing at the warriors coming from the rear but hitting a man on a running horse is tricky even for a good marksman. Tye, reaching Garrison shouted to get the men in the draw quick but he knew it was too late for the men in the rear of the column. Sergeants Arnold and Absher were pushing and throwing the men into the ravine. Thirty men made it into the temporary safety of the ravine and immediately took positions and begin returning a deadly fire of their own knocking several warriors from their ponies. The Apaches in the ravine, those that were left, had escaped.

Tye, with his Henry repeater was taking a deadly toll on the Apaches as they raced by. After passing the soldiers, Ke-ah and his warriors joined Asay and the other warriors. Tye looked down the line at the soldiers faces as they stared at the Apaches. He could see fear etched on almost every one of them. Then he saw Arnold and Absher walking among them talking, encouraging and raising the men's hopes.

Tye shouted. "When they charge, fire your Sharps and then use your pistols. Try and stay bunched together. If they overrun us protect each others backs." He looked back toward the gathering horde and knew they were preparing to charge. It was then he noticed the huge warrior in front…"Ke-ah," he mumbled out loud. "Damn." He could kick himself for sending a man to tell Buff not to come. Things were fixing to get real nasty. He could see Ke-ah riding back and forth in front of the warriors, whipping them into frenzy.

~~~

A mile back Buff knew something was wrong. "Too manee shots Kaptain. Sumthang is wrong."

"Do you think we need to ride to them?" McClellan asked.

"Yes, I do. We don't need ta go chargin in but lets git a hell of a lot closer so mabee I can take a luk-see at whuts happening." About four minutes later after a run they pulled up.

"We shud be klose. Let me go ahead and see whut I can see." McClellan nodded and Buff walked his horse slowly ahead. Buff was afraid they were too late because of the lack of shots being fired now. Then he saw a soldier waving at him from the top of a hill, motioning him to come on. He turned, rode back to McClellan. "At tha furst shot lets ride in with guns blazing."

"D troop, form a skirmish line on me," McClellan ordered, urgency showing in his voice. "A troop, form fifty yards behind D troop." A minute later they were advancing, the butt of their cocked Sharps resting on their thigh, barrels pointing to the sky. Thirty
~~~

seconds later they heard the Apache screams and the soldiers kicked their mounts into a gallop.

"Here they come," Garrison screamed over the sound of close to a hundred ponies hooves pounding the rocky ground. The ground was trembling from the pounding, the screams of the Apaches was deafening and then gunshots added to the noise as they came into range. Bullets were striking the ground all around the rim of the ravine causing rock fragments to strike the men, stinging like hell. The sound a man could never forget, the sound of bullets striking flesh, could be heard everywhere. Tye had knocked four braves off their ponies with well placed shots from his repeater and he had seen several more fall. "Not near enough," he said to himself and braced himself for the Apaches who were now on them, throwing their bodies from their ponies onto the blue coats.

Tye swung his rifle like a club and split a braves head like a ripe watermelon. He pulled his Army Colt and fired point blank into the chest of another but went down with two Apaches on him. He swung his right fist and caught the one on top of him flush in the face, busting his nose and lips. He threw the unconscious warrior off him and turned his full attention on the other who was in the process of swinging a club at his head. He ducked. The club missed his head by an inch. As he ducked, he pulled the Bowie from his boot with his good hand and drove the ten inch shaft to the hilt in the surprised Apache's belly.

Garrison had his hands full too. He had one warrior dead at his feet, his saber stuck in his chest. He fired his Colt revolver with his left hand, striking another in the back. He turned to his left and shot another just as the Apache smashed a trooper in the side of the head with his war club splitting the man's skull. Then he was knocked down by two more Apaches.

Sergeant Absher and Arnold were standing back to back, fighting like mad men. Both were holding their Sharps by the barrel and using them as clubs. Three Apaches lay in front of Absher and two in front of Arnold. Everywhere one looked, men were grappling with each other fighting for their lives. It was pure hell in the ravine for both the soldiers and the Redman.

The sound of running horses reached the ears of both the Apaches and the soldiers in the ditch. The Apaches, seeing the approaching soldiers, were climbing out of the ravine and trying to mount their excited, skittish, ponies. Buff, McClellan and the rest of the soldiers were on them immediately. Bullets whizzed around like bees and everywhere one looked, an Apache was falling to the ground. A few blue coated bodies were falling from their horses also as the Apaches returned fire.

Tye came out of the ravine and was immediately attacked by a warrior with a Bowie in his hand. The warrior took a wild swipe at Tye's belly but Tye stepped back quickly and the razor sharp blade cut only empty air. Both men dropped into a crouch, their knife low to the ground, waiting on the other to make a move. The Apache cut loose with a scream and attacked. He came up with the blade of the Bowie intending to stab Tye in the belly but Tye caught the man's wrist and stopped the thrust and at the same time, stabbed at the Indian's stomach. He was surprised when a hand with a vice-like grip grabbed his wrist and held it. They stood chest to chest each trying to rip his knife hand loose from the other. Tye suddenly dropped to a low crouch, lowered his chin to his chest and like a battering ram, thrust himself up, the top of his head smashing into the surprised warriors face. Stunned, the man released Tye's hand and staggered back a couple steps. Tye immediately drove the Bowie into the man's chest, pulled it out and turning the blade sideways, slashed the man's throat. The Apache never uttered a sound as he fell limply to the ground. Tye quickly looked for another attacker but saw the fight had moved away from him a short distance and he rushed over to help.

He saw Buff take an Apache down with his steel bladed tomahawk he had gotten off a Blackfoot warrior years earlier. Buff turned toward Tye and screamed, "GET DOWN." Tye saw Buff throw the hatchet just as he dove to the ground. He heard the thud of the hatchet striking something and looked behind him. An Apache stood there like a statue looking at the hatchet buried in his chest and then slowly crumbled to the ground. Tye looked back at Buff and nodded his thanks.

Tye looked for Garrison but did not see him. McClellan was being pulled off his horse by two Apaches. Tye took three quick strides and jerked the one off the captains back, threw him viciously on the ground and immediately stabbed the man through the heart. McClellan almost decapitated the other with his saber. The captain looked at Tye and hollered thanks.

It was suddenly over, the only sound besides the moans of the wounded being the hoof beats of the Apaches that were left alive heading away from the scene. Men staggered to rocks and sat down, exhausted. An occasional shot signaled the end of a wounded Indian. Tye looked around and was astounded at the scene around him. Bodies lay everywhere, both Apache and soldiers.

Buff came over and stood beside him. "Wurst fight I ever did see," he said. Tye looked down at the little man and put his arm around him.

"I was never so glad to see anyone in my life," he said. "But why did you come after being told not too?"

"Thar wus just too much shuting fur thar not ta be a problem so we kame a running."

Tye smiled at him. "There are a whole lot of soldiers that are glad you did," he said slapping him on the back. "Let's see how many men we lost." They walked over to McClellan who was having his hand wrapped by a surgeon. As they walked up the surgeon said it was broken. McClellan grimaced in pain as he looked up at Tye and Buff. "Damn club caught me on the wrist." Tye nodded remembering his own hand and how it hurt awhile back after being hit with a stone club. His was not broken though and he could use it even though it hurt.

McClellan said. "That was hell on earth, Tye. I have Sergeant Absher getting me a casualty report." All eyes turned at the sound of the wagons with medical and other supplies arriving. "At least we have water and medical supplies now." He added.

Sergeant Absher came back with the casualty report. "Not good, Sir," he said. "We have nineteen dead and twenty seven wounded eight of them serious. One of the serious is Lieutenant Garrison. We counted forty-seven dead Apaches at first count. The men found eight more wounded and unable to escape. They were added to the list of the dead for a total of fifty-five dead. No telling how many are wounded."

"Thank you Sergeant. That will be all," McClellan said, returning the sergeants salute. Tye could tell by the anguished look on McClellan's face he was stressing over the number of men killed. He felt that was good and bad. Good in that the captain cared for his men. Tye had seen officers that were interested only in getting promotions and if men got killed in his winning them, so be it. It was bad in that it could affect his judgments on problems that might be coming up. McClellan ordered a private to get the surgeon started on the wounded and to get some men and put them in the shade of the cliff by the draw.

Tye smiled and knew the captain was alright. He and Buff walked off to find Garrison to see how bad he was wounded. He also wanted to look at the dead Apaches to see if Ke-ah was among them. Tye didn't know whether he hoped he was dead or alive. If he was still alive that would mean Tye would be chasing him and would probably end up killing him…or him killing me, he thought to himself.

Chapter Twenty Six

Ke-ah was not wounded in the fight…not physically anyway. He was the fox in his plan and the soldiers were the rabbit and he was sure of his kill. Then, the wolf showed up in the form of many bluecoats and ran the fox away. He had simply been tricked by his friend Watkins and it galled him that he had let it happen. He had seen the scout two or three times during the battle but never got close to him. He had shot two bluecoats and killed two more with his Bowie. The last one he killed was an officer and the knife apparently had stuck into bone because he could not remove it. He had noticed Asay and his Chiricahua warriors during the fight and they were fearless fighters as he had heard.

Ke-ah had twenty-three healthy warriors riding with him. They had seven more that were wounded but not so bad they could not ride. Asay was riding beside him but had said nothing. The Chiricahua was distraught over his friend, Naiche being one of the warriors killed. Ke-ah knew the feeling because a good many of his friends had been killed by the bluecoats. He had lost his best friend because of the war between the Apache and the white man…Scout Watkins.

He would lead the remaining warriors into Mexico. The bluecoats would not follow him there. He could rest, heal the wounded and make plans for another raid into Texas.

~~~

"Over here, Tye," Sergeant Phipps cried out. Tye and Buff hurried over to where Phipps was. Tye stopped in his tracks when he saw Garrison. He was laid out on a blanket, an Apache knife still in his chest. Tye could not move as he stared at this man, his friend, his companion on so many patrols that lay there dead on the blanket. Thoughts flashed through his numbed mind. He remembered the lieutenant's laughter and his love of the land and the job he had trying to make it safe for families to live here. He remembered how green Garrison was when he arrived at Fort Clark and how he had grown into a fine officer…and friend. He remembered the night that Garrison saved him from the Yancey gang. He kneeled down and placed his hand on Garrison's forehead. He shut his eyes and a tear rolled down his cheek. The men who were standing there all knew they were friends and walked away, leaving Tye alone with his friend. After a few moments, Tye gathered himself and stood up and looked at the knife in Garrison's chest. He knew that knife…he had seen it recently but where? He
~~~

thought about it for a moment and then it struck him…Ke-ah. It was Ke-ah's knife. He remembered seeing it in its beaded sheath on Ke-ah's waist. He had not seen a knife like that before with the twisted deer antler handle. He kneeled for a closer look and was sure it was Ke-ah's. "Sergeant, please get me a blanket and a canteen." In less than a minute, Tye had both. He took his kerchief off and poured water on it. He gently washed his friends face and the blood on his chin. He placed his hand under the lieutenant's head and raised it from off the ground and wiped the dirt from his hair. He lay his friend's head back down on the ground as gently as one would a baby and began smoothing out his clothes. He grabbed the knife and tried to remove it but it would not come out of Garrison's chest. He stood up and asked Buff to hold Garrison's shoulders and he jerked the knife out. He kneeled back down and stuck the knife in the sand and then pulled it out and wiped the blade clean. He pitched it handle first to Sergeant Christian, "Hold this for me for a moment." He finished straightening up Garrison's clothes and unfolded one leg that was bent under the lieutenant. He covered him with the blanket and raised his head looking at the men around him. "Would all of you leave me alone for a moment?"

He knelt back down and pulled the blanket from his friends face. He looked to heaven, "Lord, I haven't spoken to you in awhile and I'm ashamed for that but I'm asking you something now. I don't know if Lieutenant Garrison was a religious man or not.

Again I am sorry that he and I never discussed that. I know he was a good man, a good officer, and a good friend." He looked at the face of his friend and with tears streaming down his face and his lower lip trembling, he added, "take him to your bosom Lord and have mercy on his soul."

He gathered himself after a moment, stood up quickly and walked to where the others were. "I want to see all the dead Apaches, Sergeant Phipps."

"Okay, Tye…but why?"

"I'm looking for a particular Apache, the leader called Ke-ah." They walked to the stack of bodies and Phipps was rolling them off to where Tye could look at each one. After a few minutes Tye was satisfied Ke-ah was not one of the dead. An hour ago he did not know if he could kill his old friend or not…now he knew he could. He turned to Buff, "Let's go talk to McClellan." They passed Sergeant Christian and he handed the knife back to Tye.

"Whut yu want tha knife fur?" Buff asked.

"It belonged to my friend, Ke-ah. He killed Garrison and I'm going to kill him with it…his own knife."

It was mid-day and temporary camp had been set up. The wounded had been cared for and the more severely injured had been placed in one of the wagons that would head back to Clark. Tye found McClellan.

"I figure maybe twenty-five to thirty Apaches escaped, Sir, including Ke-ah, their leader. I know they have some wounded so I figure they are headed to Mexico to rest up and lick their wounds before coming back."

"Do you really think they will come back after the licking they took?"

"As sure as God made little green apples," Tye answered. "They will be back with vengeance in their hearts. I think we need to follow Thurston's plan about following him into Mexico and seeing if we can end it before he comes back to Texas."

"Tye," McClellan said holding up his throbbing hand, "I don't think I can…"

Tye cut him off. "I would not expect you to go with that hand. I would hope we can get fifteen or twenty volunteers…men with experience and men who won't quit when things get tough."

"I figure Sergeant Arnold should be able to wade through the volunteers for the men that you would approve of," McClellan said. "I will get the men together."

Tye sat down on a large flat rock and relaxed for the first time in what seemed an eternity. He rubbed his jaw feeling the two day growth of beard. He knew he stunk to high heaven with stale sweat, smoke, dust, and blood on his clothes. He stared in the direction the Apaches had fled. "Ke-ah you sonofabitch, I'm going to kill you and every one of your bloodthirsty friends riding with you if it's the last thing I do," he mumbled.

"Yu say sumthang, Tye?" Buff asked.

"Nah, just talking to myself." He could not believe he had just said that about his friend. Ke-ah was just an Apache trying his best to survive and doing what he had to do. He would do the same if he was in Ke-ah's place. The fact that he killed Garrison was just bad luck. He respected the Apache people and their way of life. He looked up at the sky and to himself said, "Lord, forgive me. I didn't mean those things I said just now about my friend. I…" his thought was interrupted by the men arriving and gathering in front of him.

Tye stood beside McClellan as the captain spoke. He explained the situation with the Apaches going into Mexico and they were going to pursue, not as soldiers but as civilians. They had brought clothes and extra horses with no army brands on them. Their weapons would not be military issue nor would the equipment. They would be a loose riding outfit with nothing showing they were military. Wanting only volunteers for the mission, McClellan said, "Each of you need to know that if you are caught by the Mexican soldiers and they prove you are military, you will be treated as a spy and you know what that means."

Tye stepped forward. "If you feel like you can handle the pressure, please move to where Buff is," Tye said pointing toward

Buff. Immediately almost every soldier stepped over to where Buff was. Tye smiled. He knew they would.

McClellan said. "Sergeant Arnold. Pick out fifteen men."

"Right away,Sir." Arnold looked at each man as he walked among them. He knew each one of them, their strengths as well as their weaknesses. "When I call your name you will step over to Tye. Private O'Riley, Private Garner, Private Smith, Private Jenkins, Private Garcia, Private Brody, Private Cahill, Private Ellison, Private Adams, Private Edwards, Private Greenwood, Private Wheeler, Private Dixon, Private Boggs and Corporal Johnson." McClellan took a pencil and paper out and handed them to Sergeant Christian.

"You have a good handwriting Sergeant. Please list each man's name that Arnold picked. Then add yours, Arnold's and Absher to the list and give it back to me." Christian lined the men up and as they passed him he wrote down their names. He gave the list to McClellan. "Thank you Sergeant," he said as he placed the paper in his pocket. He walked over to Tye. "You have men you can depend on Tye and with Sergeants Absher, Christian, and Arnold you have some of the best in the army."

Tye nodded. "I know I can depend on each of them, Sir." He turned to the men. "Go to the Wagon and find some clothes that fit you. Turn in all your army issue equipment. Pick up a canteen, saddle and blanket, saddlebags, guns and ammunition that have no military markings on them. Get three pounds of jerky and biscuits and put them in your saddlebags and report back here." He and Buff kept their mounts since neither was branded with the U.S. brand. Tye exchanged the blue cavalry pants for a pair of buckskins he had in his saddlebags. He would have liked to use some of the repeating rifles the dead Indians had but there was not enough ammunition to go around.

When everyone was dressed, supplied and mounted, they were ready to head to Mexico. "You should be at Clark late tomorrow if you don't drag your feet too much," Tye said to McClellan as he shook the captain's good hand. "Take care of your hand and the wounded men, Captain."

"You take care, Tye. Good Luck." McClellan took the men not going with Tye, the wagons, the wounded and the dead and headed back to Clark. Tye watched them for a few minutes then told the men to gather round him.

"I will say this one time only so listen up. You are no longer military but civilians so act like civilians. Do not ride in any formation and if we are stopped by the Mexican Army, make damn sure no army lingo comes out of your mouth. You will do what I or Buff say without question. Sergeants Arnold, Christian, and Absher will divide you up into three groups and they will be responsible for your actions. This will not be a stroll in the park men. You will have no friends over there only Apaches, bandits, and the Mexican Army. Any questions?"

Private Smith spoke up. "Let's just go get them red bastards, Tye." That was followed with a few whoops and hollers from the rest. Tye smiled.

"Let's move out then," Tye said. Tye smiled again at Smith's words. This was a fighting man. That's the reason as a ten year veteran and in his mid fifties, he was still a private. There was no telling how many times he had been promoted and then busted in rank or days he had spent in the guardhouse for fighting. He fought not only others of equal rank but officers too. Anyone who crossed him was fair game. He was a soldier though and a damn good one as long as he was sober. Tye thought his first name was Jim but wasn't sure but he was glad to have him along. He was the only man taller than Tye in the whole army that was stationed at Fort Clark. Tye chuckled at something Smith said awhile back. `

"Apaches don't want to kill me because of this." He took off his hat and showed his bald head. "Ain't no trophy for the buck that kills me so why bother." He laughed as well as Tye and the others that were around him that day.

About an hour before sunset, they came to the Rio Grande. Tye told the men they would camp here tonight and this would be the last chance to bathe. They could have a fire tonight for a hot supper but this would be the last until they returned. As the men sat around the fire and ate their jerky, Tye outlined his plan.

"We will attack the Apache at every opportunity. We will hit them," he said slamming his fist in the palm of his hand, "and hit them again and again not giving them time to rest or gather food. Be prepared to move faster and farther than you have ridden before. There will be danger everywhere so we will move as fast as possible and quite as possible. We will have guards at night. Sergeant Christian will set the duty roster. Do not pace back and forth like a military sentry. Find a place and sit. Just make sure you damn well stay awake. It's now full dark. Let's get some sleep. It may be awhile before you get another full night's rest."

Tye laid down on his blanket with Buff on one side and Absher on the other. It was quiet in camp. Missing was the usual chatter among the men before going to sleep. Everyone understood what Tye said about them going to be on the move just about twenty-four hours a day and figured they had better rest while they could.

Buff spoke in a low voice, almost a whisper. "Seed yu in tha fite today when thos two Apaches jumped yu. I tried ta shoot wun uf them but my Colt was out uf damn bullets." He laughed. "Luked like yu didn't need no help anyhow. Yu fighting thos two reminded me of yur pa. He wus like a madman when he got riled up. Hell, I don't think God kud put enuf Injuns on him tha he kudn't handle when he wus tha way: knife slashing and swinging that tomahawk and screaming like a crazy man. Tha wuns he didn't stab or bust thar heads he plum scared to death with his screaming." He chuckled again thinking of the many fights he had seen Ben in back in the Rockies. "Yep! Yu two are two peas in a pod."

"I glimpsed you today when you smashed that Indian with your tomahawk; looked like you could handle yourself pretty good…for an old codger." He laughed and turned on his side, his back to Buff. "Now go to sleep…old man."

Buff answered. "Yur tha wun tha had better git sum rest or yu won't be able ta sta up with this heer old codger tomorrow yu yung whippersnapper." He laughed and rolled the other way and was soon asleep.

Tye lay there listening to the night sounds, identifying each of them, his hearing becoming accustomed to each sound. This was a practice he did every night. It was one of the ten thousand things he pa had taught him. After going to sleep, any sound that was not normal would wake men like Tye immediately.

Dawn found the men crossing the Rio Grande and entering Mexico. They rode in a loose group with Private Wheeler bringing up the rear leading the pack horse with the water kegs and extra supplies. The land here was the same as they had left in Texas: rocky ground with little topsoil and lots of cactus, sage, cedar, chaparral and sparse grass. The terrain was gently rolling hills but in the distance was the blue shrouded mountains, maybe thirty or so miles away. That is where Tye figured the Apaches were headed. They would feel safe there and could regroup themselves. He didn't intend to let that happen.

Absher rode beside Tye and Buff. "I've been intending to ask you something, Tye."

Tye looked at him. "What is it?"

"Remember when we found where Lieutenant Braddock and his men were killed?

"I remember."

"The men were butchered up pretty bad. Why do Apaches do that?"

Tye had explained this many times but he knew Absher was new out here and probably hadn't heard. "Apaches are like other tribes in a lot of their beliefs, Sergeant. One of those beliefs is that when a man dies he goes into the hereafter just as he was when he left this life. An Apache does not want to meet an enemy in the hereafter that is as he was before. He had rather meet him with no eyes or no hands and not have to fight him again when he is whole."

"You mean the Apaches believe in God?"

"They worship several gods but they have one main one. He is Ussen, the creator or the life giver."

"I'll be damned. Who would have guessed that?"

Buff laughed. "Life's full uf surprises ain't it sonny." Tye and Absher laughed along with Buff.

Tye and Buff got back to the business of tracking the Apaches. It wasn't hard to do with thirty or so horses but they were mainly looking for ambush spots. Tye figured Ke-ah was aware they were being followed and also knew he had more men than Tye so an ambush was what he and Buff were watching for.

Fortunately, the land they were passing through was not very contusive to a surprise. There were no canyons, no arroyos to hide in, and no trees. The land was covered in short sage and cactus and not a chance of surprising anyone. From the tracks Tye could tell the Apaches were moving at a leisurely pace for some unknown reason and this bothered him. By mid-afternoon of that first day the men were only two or three hours behind the Apaches.

An hour before dusk, Buff spotted a warrior sitting on his pony. The warrior had stupidly sky lined himself for just a couple seconds and that was all it took to be seen. He disappeared quickly and was not seen again. The question Tye and Buff asked each other was the sighting accidental or on purpose. Tye knew an Apache warrior would not do that even accidentally but what purpose had it served.

Tye was looking for a good spot to make camp. He wanted one that would be both sheltered and easy to defend or one that was wide open with an open killing area all around. He found what he was looking for just before the sun set behind the hills in the west. The spot was absolutely flat and was covered in loose rocks and gravel.

It would be almost impossible, even for an Apache, to walk without making at least a little noise.

~~~

"Why you think bluecoats follow us?" Asay asked Ke-ah as they sat around the small fire. "Why they dressed as Texans instead of soldiers?"

"I do not know why they are dressed the way they are but I know why they come after us here in our homeland. We killed many bluecoats, maybe as many as Kah-tin-yay (30) yesterday. They want revenge so it does not surprise me they are coming. We will be in the mountains when the sun is at its highest tomorrow. We will then make plans to protect our father's land against them."

"The soldiers are close behind us. Should we not keep riding?" Asay asked.

"I have fought the bluecoats many times as you have. Do they not stop before dark and not start again until just before the sun appears?" Ke-ah asked.

Asay nodded. "What you say is true but something tells me these soldiers are doing things different."

Ke-ah laughed. "You worry too much my friend. They are soldiers and as such, predictable." He handed Asay some pemmican. "Eat," he said.
~~~

Chapter Twenty Seven

Tye woke up a little before midnight and lightly touched Buff's shoulder to wake him up. He placed his fingers over his lips, telling Buff to be quite. They both stood and walked to the edge of the camp.

"Whut's up?" Buff whispered.

"Thought you and I would take a little stroll." Tye whispered.

" Thar's whut I thought yu'd say."

Tye walked to the sentry and told him they would be back in an hour or so don't get trigger happy. They walked away from camp in the direction they had been going earlier.

"Are we going to find their camp?" Buff asked.

Tye nodded and spoke softly. "If we can find their camp we can hit them while they are asleep. We might get lucky and end this thing real quick and get out of this country." Buff nodded.

They moved through the brush and cactus as silently as one of the predators that lived in this country would. Thirty minutes later they both smelled it at the same time, smoke. Both dropped into a crouch and continued on, watchful for any sentries. Moving on silent feet they approached the camp, stopping when they were a hundred yards off. They could see the glow of the coals from the fire. Tye didn't like the terrain from what he could see by the light of the stars and the half moon. He tapped Buff on the shoulder and motioned with his head to go back. They carefully backed away before standing up and begin trotting back to their camp. Tye was concerned about the pony herd. He had hoped it would be on this side of the camp. It would have helped if they could have run their ponies off. It would hinder the Apaches some but not enough to make a difference, An Apache can cover forty miles a day on foot, more if necessary. A horse to an Apache is two things; a way to cover ground quickly and a source of food. They loved mule meat better than horse but ate both readily. A hundred yards out from their camp Tye hollered to get the guards attention.

"COME," the sentry said loud enough for them to hear. The walked into camp and woke up Sergeants Absher, Phipps, and Arnold. Together they all walked away from the sleeping men before Tye spoke.

"Buff and I took a little stroll and found the Apache camp. We need to wake the men up and go there. Complete silence is imperative. We can get within maybe seventy-five yards of the camp fifty if we are lucky. We will wait until they start stirring around before we attack. Maybe, with a little luck, they will sleep until almost light when the shooting will be easier. Any questions?" There were none. "Wake the men up then and let's move out. Leave three men here to watch the horses."

A half hour later the men were spread out in a skirmish line approaching the sleeping Apaches. They moved slowly, each step carefully placed so as not to dislodge any rocks. They were fifty yards out when Tye signaled them to hold up and take a knee. Since he and Buff had moccasins on and could move almost in complete silence they moved among the men whispering they were to hold their fire until Tye gave the signal. They were to fire their Sharps, then lay them down and rush the camp using their six shot Colts.

The stars were still out and the eastern sky had not begun to show any signs of turning gray with the rising sun. The men were still on one knee, not moving. The only way one could tell they were alive was by the rapid raising and falling of their chest, a sign of a nervous man going into a situation where men were going to die. They waited.

The first hint of gray in the eastern sky was showing over the hills when An Apache suddenly appeared in front of the men surprising both parties. Tye shot him and the men fired their rifles at the sleeping Indians in the camp. With a tremendous yell coming from each man's throat, they charged the camp. The Apaches were caught off guard but in a few seconds were organized and fought back as they retreated toward their pony herd. Bullets from the

Indian rifles and from the charging soldier's revolvers split the early morning air.

Tye glimpsed Ke-ah once during the fight but only for a second. The fight only lasted a little over thirty seconds as the Apaches reached their ponies and raced off. The men killed a couple of the Apaches that were wounded.

"Anyone hit?" Tye shouted. "Garner is hit in the shoulder, Tye." Tye nodded. "Anyone else?" Silence followed and Tye sat down by the blanket relieved.

"Luks like we kilt abut nine, Tye."

"Gather up their food, ammunition and whatever else they left," Tye ordered. "Stack it here," he said pointing to a blanket by his feet. Five minutes later he had an assortment of weapons from clubs, spears, a couple knives and nine rifles from the dead Apaches. There was some ammunition and several bags of pemmican, the favorite food of the Apache when on the move. The Apache were well stocked on repeating rifles but sorely short on bullets for them.

Private Jenkins pitched two bags of the food on the blanket. "What the hell is that stuff?"

"Pemmican," Tye said. "It's made from lean meat that is beat into a powder and then mixed with hot animal fat and then dried. It's actually pretty good…if you are hungry enough," Tye answered laughing. He walked over to where Arnold was bandaging up Garner's shoulder. "You okay?" he asked.

"Just a scratch, Tye. No problem," Garner answered. Tye nodded and spoke to Sergeant Christian. "Send a couple men back to camp and bring the horses." He noticed the men had already picked up their Sharps they had laid down. "While we are waiting on the horses, clean and load you guns," he told the men. "This is the way it will be. We will give them no rest, no chance to gather food. As soon as our horses are here, we will be after them again."

~~~

Ke-ah was livid. Twice now, Watkins had caught him off guard. He sat astride his pony and pounded his thigh in frustration. "It will not happen again," he mumbled to himself. He looked at Asay. "We will not be surprised by this scout again." Asay nodded.

"I see why your people think this man is part Apache. Once again as I said before, we must plan on doing what Apaches do or as he would think we would…then do the opposite to trap him." Ke-ah nodded his agreement. Ke-ah's mind was racing as fast as his pony's legs were. He knew before another sunrise there would again be another fight. He would be ready this time.

~~

The sun was well above the hills by the time Tye and the men moved out of the Apache camp. They were feeling good after the fight and thought things went well. Tye knew different. He knew that Ke-ah would be wary now that he had been caught twice by surprise and the third time was going to be a hell of a lot tougher.
~~~

He was trying to place himself in the Apache's position to see what he would do. His pa had preached this to him when he had a problem tracking someone or trying to figure their next step, just put yourself in their place to see what you would do. A man would be surprised how many times it worked.

Buff was riding beside him and the old trapper hadn't said a word in an hour which wasn't like him. "Buff, I've been thinking and when we make camp tonight I…"

Buff butted in. "We had better get ready fur an attack by yur friend…right?"

"Yes. That's what I figure." Tye laughed. "You been thinking too?" he asked.

"Wal, I've been up tha thar river an around tha bend manee times too. Onlee stands ta reason that he wud want ta pay his old friend back fur tha attack this morning."

"Since you're doing all this thinking, I suppose you have a plan?"

'Wal…no, I wus waiting on yu, to see whut yu come up with." There was silence for a moment. "I'm waiting?"

"I'm thinking. Give me some time."

The men were getting close to the mountains and the land was becoming more and more conducive to riding into a trap. Tye had nudged Sandy into a trot to where he was out front about a hundred yards and Buff was staying halfway between him and the rest of the men. Buff rode with his Sharps cocked, lying across his lap, trigger finger on the trigger and watching Tye's back.

Tye was pushing the men pretty hard. They had not stopped since leaving the Apache camp hours ago. No one was complaining though, as each man knew from what Tye said, this was the way it was going to be. They didn't have to volunteer but they had, so they were here to see this thing through,

Tye stopped, dismounted and kneeled to look at the tracks a little closer. He saw a pile of manure just ahead and walked to it. Using a stick, he poked the manure and pulled the stick out, studying the manure stuck to it. Buff rode up and Tye showed him the stick.

"Damn close to'um ain't we?" He straightened up in the saddle looking into the foothills at the base of the mountain range.

Tye nodded his agreement to Buff's assessment of how far behind they were. He figured an hour or less which was damn dangerous when tracking Apaches. Tye took a quick glance at the sun and figured they had about an hour of good light left. He had decided on a plan and wanted to talk it out with Buff, Arnold, Christian, and Absher to get their input.

"Thar's a good place over thar, Tye," Buff said nodding toward a high bluff. They both rode the quarter mile to take a look. The cliff had an overhang which prevented anyone from shooting down on them. One side had a ravine about twenty foot wide and maybe twenty or so foot deep with almost vertical sides. If you approached from the other two directions there was absolute no cover other than low shrubs and a few cactus for well over a hundred yards. It was as good a place as they could hope for.

Away from the rest of the men the three sergeants and Buff sat down with Tye. "The best guess Buff and I can come up with is, we are less than an hour behind the Apaches. That's close enough to expect trouble any second and I think trouble is headed our way shortly after dark."

Absher raised his hand and asked, "I thought Apaches don't fight at night?"

"Normally they don't except if they feel safe in doing so or if they are desperate. We hit them pretty hard this morning and I promise you, there is a hell of a lot of anger in them right now and they are going to vent that anger tonight…at least that's what Buff and I think." He looked up at the clouds moving in promising a chance of rain. "With the clouds moving in and if they remain through the night, it's going to be dark, real dark and I think the Apache will take advantage of it"

"What's your plan, Tye?" Arnold asked.

"There are good size pieces of dead wood in the ravine. We need to get a couple men down there and then with ropes lift them out and make a low wall here at the base of the cliff to lay behind for protection. After dark, I will take five men with me and we will wait along the edge of the ravine about thirty yards out from here. The remaining men will stay in camp behind the logs. If the Apache come they will be moving in slow and quite, their attention in front where the camp is. Hopefully, they won't know we have them flanked until it's too late."

"When do you think they will hit us?" Christian asked.

"Normally just about sunrise with the sun behind them. I think this bunch will hit us tonight, maybe about midnight or a little after."

"Why not at sunrise like they normally would?" Absher wondered.

"Because, they think I think like them, and Ke-ah is smart and I'm betting he will change what Apaches usually do just to fool me. Hopefully we can stay a step ahead."

"What if they don't come?" Arnold asked.

"Then all we have lost is some sleep," Tye answered. "What do you men think?" The men looked at each other and shrugged their shoulders. "Let's get the logs out of the ravine before it gets too dark," Christian said standing up and barking orders.

Within twenty minutes and just as the sun set, the dead wood had been stacked to make a wall about twenty feet long and three foot high. The men sat around eating jerky, drinking warm water from their canteens, and checking their weapons. There was none of the usual camp chatter among the men. The plan had been explained to them by the sergeants and all knew it was going to be a night of little sleep…or a very long sleep if things didn't go right.

Shortly after full dark, Tye took five men and quietly made their way thirty yards out and then to the right to the edge of the ravine. They lay down among the low sage to wait. Waiting for an Apache attack is the most stressful thing a man will ever go through. They waited in silence, each man lost in his own thoughts… waiting for hell to come their way.

Chapter Twenty Eight

The faces of the men with Tye were strained…frightened as their eyes tried to pierce the darkness of the night. The only sound a man could hear was the breathing of the man next to him. Tye figured the attack, if it came, would be within the next two hours which would be about midnight. If not by then, he felt it would not come.

The men, at the base of the cliff, were no less tense than the others. Every sound of the night resulted in heads jerking in the direction of the noise, muscles tensing, eyes struggling to penetrate the blackness. Under their breaths, every man cursed the clouds that prevented the faint light of the stars and the quarter moon from helping them.

Seventy-five yards away, Ke-ah, Asay, and eighteen warriors quietly approached the soldier's camp. Each warrior held cocked repeaters in front of their body, ready to fire at the first movement or sound. After the first shot, they were to drop their rifles and charge the bluecoats and kill them with their war clubs and knives. Ke-ah was searching for the sentries who would have to be the first to die. They moved silently on the soft soled moccasins which, unlike the leather sole boots of the soldiers, allowed them to feel each rock or twig and avoid making noise. They were thirty yards from the base of the cliff and the tension on both the white man and redman was strained to the breaking point.

Suddenly Tye felt, more than saw or heard a form a few feet from him. He raised the Sharps to waist level and squeezed the trigger. The flare from the barrel of the Sharps illuminated the terrain for a second and the men saw the Apaches. The Apache, Tye shot, crumbled to the ground and then everything was chaos. The noise of thirty or more rifles from the Apaches and the soldiers resounded across the land. From the flame of the guns that were flashing everywhere, Tye saw several Apaches go down. He also heard the thump of bullets hitting flesh close to him. After the initial sound and flare of the rifles, it was Apache war cries that pierced the still night.

In the darkness, it was hard to tell friend from foe. Asay smashed a soldiers head with his club and then was clubbed from behind by Private Smith. He almost went down but managed to twist his body and tried to hurl himself into the white soldier. Smith swung the gun again and caught Asay in the left temple busting his head open… he fell silently to the ground.

Tye jumped an Indian from behind and threw him to the ground on his back and was on him instantly stabbing the warrior in the chest. Buff buried his Black Foot hatchet in the head of an Indian and then was knocked to the ground from behind. Despite his age, his agility helped him roll quickly to the right as a knife was buried in the dirt where his chest had been an instant earlier. He pulled his Bowie from the sheath and faced the warrior who was much larger than his one hundred and thirty pounds. He stepped back and sucked in his belly as the warrior took a wild swipe at it. Buff deftly blocked with his blade another attempt to gut him and instantly turned his blade sideways and cut the man's belly open. The Apache stepped back and looked down at his insides oozing from the wound. Buff ended it by burying the blade of his Bowie to the hilt in the man's heart.

Sergeant Absher had a knife stuck in his left shoulder but stood his ground swinging his Sharps with one hand and screaming as loud as the Apaches. Other struggles, between soldier and warriors, were everywhere and then there were none as the Apache broke off the attack. The clouds had opened up and the stars came out. The men could see a little better and they all were appalled at the sight. The smell of blood and powder struck every man's nostrils.

Each man had struggled with an Apache and some won and some lost. It was all over in less than two minutes. Tye had heard Apaches running away, their knee high moccasin boots scraping against the sage as they ran. "Check the Apaches that are down and make sure they're all dead," Tye shouted. A pistol shot followed and then all was quiet. "Assemble around me," Tye ordered.

Seven men stood around him. "Spread out and find the others and if they are wounded, take them over there behind the logs. If they are dead, put them over there," he said pointing to a large flat rock.

Five minutes later, five men were laid out on the rock and seven were behind the wall with various wounds, none life threatening but most could not continue the chase. Privates Garcia, Adams, Edwards, Boggs, and Wheeler were wrapped in blankets. Sergeants Arnold and Christian were tending to the wounded the best they could. Absher had a knife wound in his shoulder, Privates O'Riley, Garner, and Jenkins had busted arms from fending off the deadly war clubs. Privates Brody and Cahill were still unconscious from head wounds and Private Ellison had a knife buried in his upper thigh.

"Buff, see if can you find out how many dead Apaches we have here. Private Adams, you and Greenwood help him. Put the dead ones over there," he said nodding toward a spot that was clear of sage and cactus. He watched as the dead warriors were dragged to the spot and stacked in a pile. He was looking for Ke-ah. The men circled the area again and found no more. There were thirteen Apaches in the pile.

"We're trimming them down some," Private Smith commented.

"Yeah, we have, but they have trimmed us a mite too," Tye replied back. "I think they have four or five left and we have eight healthy men. I'd say the field is about even."

"Are we going after them now?" Corporal Johnson asked.

Tye looked over at the wounded men. "Not now. We'll wait till morning when we can pick up the tracks. Besides, we need to take care of our dead." He turned to Christian; "How about the wounded?"

"Four definitely cannot continue. I won't know about Brody and Cahill until they come around. They both caught glancing blows from a club and are still unconscious. Garner has a bruised left forearm and probably can continue, but O'Riley and Jenkins both have broken arms and are in a lot of pain. Absher and Ellison need to return to the Fort and have their knife wounds treated before infection sets in."

Tye thought for a moment before speaking. "Each of you did a great job. That was as tough as it gets. We will send the wounded and dead back in the morning. Sergeant Absher can take himself and the others back to the fort. As for what is left of the night, let's get some sleep. Arnold, set the guard schedule."

Tye lay awake watching the clouds as they moved across the sky temporarily blocking what little light there was from the stars. The wind whipped up a little bit and the warmth left the land. The men became chilled to the bone. “No reason not to light a fire,” Tye said. Two were lit and the warmth from each felt good to the men and they lay back down on their blankets and were soon asleep.

As tired as Tye was, sleep did not come. Thoughts of Rebecca came as they always did, especially at night time. He closed his eyes and Garrison’s face was there, laughing like no one else could. He quickly opened his eyes. Garrison’s face was no longer there but the thought of him was. Tye remembered the first time the lieutenant met Buff. Buff was telling one of his stories about his days as a mountain man and Garrison kept interrupting him, asking question. Buff told everyone that this story was going to take a while because of this here greener. Greener was the term mountain men gave other trappers that knew nothing about nothing.

Tye smiled as he remembered the many good times he and Garrison had and tears suddenly welled up as he thought about how much the man had grown, not in size but as an officer. Tye figured he had the mettle and smarts to go far in the military. All that was gone now and nothing could change it. He knew Thurston would be highly upset at losing not only a good officer but a man he could trust. If a commanding officer could ever consider an officer under his command a friend, Garrison was that friend. Tye listened to the night sounds as always and just before he fell asleep a coyote’s lonely wailing could be heard. ‘That’s appropriate,’ he thought to himself and drifted off into a restless sleep.

~~~

Ke-ah could see the fires of the soldiers. He had not gone far after the disastrous fight. For the first time as a leader of the Lipan, he felt humiliation and feeling he was a disgrace to his people. Never before had he been defeated in battle and now, this white man had outsmarted him three times in two days. He had only three men with him and two of them were Chiricahua and they were going back to their homeland. He would never go back to his people like this…in shame.

He remembered long ago when he was only ten winters old and his friendship with this man Watkins. 'How did it come to this?' he wondered. 'Why could I not have been killed along with my brothers or why could not Watkins have been killed. Now, it would be a fight between me and him. To kill the great scout is the only way I can regain some respect from my people and once again hold my head high. He walked to his blanket and sat down. He spoke to his fellow Lipan warrior. "When the sun rises I will meet Watkins in battle. When it is over, if things go bad, return to our people and tell my father and mother I died like an Apache should die." He lay down and quickly fell asleep, but his sleep was a troubled sleep.

~~~

Dawn found Tye leading what was left of the soldiers west, following Ke-ah's tracks. Ten minutes later he pulled up sharply. Ke-ah and another warrior were sitting on their ponies in the middle of the trail. The men behind Tye spread out in a skirmish line pulling their rifles from the saddle scabbard.

Tye sat beside Buff on their mounts, waiting to see what was happening. Both men's eyes scanned the terrain for hidden trouble but saw none. Finally, Ke-ah's pony moved forward a few steps. Tye heard rifles being cocked behind and beside him.

"Hold it a minute 'till we see what is happening," he told the men. He kneed Sandy lightly and they moved forward toward Ke-ah. Both men held up their mounts when they were five yards apart. The two men sat staring at each other, neither speaking for almost half a minute. The other men, including Buff, stayed back away from the two men. Buff knew what was coming. He spoke in a hushed tone.

"Yu boys' ar fixing ta see a great fite. That Injun is going ta challenge Tye." Christian surprised at the statement asked.

"Why do you say that?"

"That Apache has lost face and the only way he can regain it is to kill Tye and that's the sad part of it."

"What do mean by that?" Arnold questioned.

"Those two use to be best of friends. When they were youngsters, Tye saved his life. A couple of days ago, he saved Tye's. Now one is going to have to kill the other."

"My God," said one of the men.

Tye shifted in the saddle and spoke. “It does not have to be this way Ke-ah. Just ride away.”

“You know I cannot do that. I have lost face with my people.”

Tye nodded. “I know that, but pride has killed a lot of men.”

“When last we spoke, I told you the next time we meet will be as Apache and white man and one would die.” He slid off his pony and stood facing Tye. He rolled his shoulders and flexed his massive muscles. Tye stepped off Sandy and faced his old friend. Ke-ah slid his knife out of the beaded sheath holding it in his right hand. Tye slid the knife out of his boot, making sure Ke-ah saw it.

“I took your knife from my friend’s chest,” Tye said. “I intended to give it back to you one way or another.” Ke-ah stood still, eyes transfixed on the knife.

“The leader, he was your friend?” Tye nodded. Both knew the talk was over and they dropped into a crouch, the knives held low to the ground in their right hands. They circled each other shuffling their feet watching each other’s eyes, waiting for the other to make a move.

The rest of the men sat on their mounts, mesmerized by what was going on before their eyes. Buff had dismounted and held the reins of his and Tye’s horses. He prayed that Tye would kill the red bastard and not get himself killed. He sure didn’t want to have to tell Rebecca that her husband was dead but more than that, he did not want to lose his friend.

Tye feinted with his blade and Ke-ah moved to block it then immediately slashed at Tye's mid-section. Tye stepped back quickly and the tip of the blade skimmed across his leather buckskin shirt. Tye slashed down and his blade cut deep in Ke-ah's forearm of his right arm and the blade fell from the big Apache's hand. Tye stepped back breathing hard. "It is over Ke-ah. Go home to your woman and children."

Ke-ah, holding his left hand over the cut said, "I have no woman. I have no children. Bluecoats killed them all. Now, you have killed me."

"You are still standing."

"Apache warrior has nothing if he loses face with his people. You know this."

"I know living is better than dying regardless," Tye answered.

"That is difference between white man and Apache. Apache not afraid to die," Ke-ah said and suddenly dropped to the ground and grabbed his knife with his left hand, rolled and came to his feet facing Tye again.

"This does not have to end this way, Ke-ah."

"It can end no other way," Ke-ah said rushing in and catching Tye off guard. Their bodies came together hard and somehow Tye managed to grab the warrior's knife hand just above the wrist with his left hand and desperately held on as Ke-ah tried to jerk it free.

Tye's knife hand was also grabbed by Ke-ah's bloody right hand and held tightly.

This was the biggest and strongest Apache Tye had ever fought, and he knew that somehow he had to end it quickly because he was not sure he could overpower this man as he had done to so many men in the past. They stood like frozen statues for a couple seconds then the Apache fell backwards suddenly, pulling Tye with him. As he fell backwards, the two separated slightly and Ke-ah came up with his right leg in Tye's midsection and when he hit the ground straightened his leg throwing Tye in a high somersault through the air. Tye's reflexes that had grown to a razor's edge now saved him. Even before he hit the ground he was rolling to his left so he hit the ground on his left shoulder instead of his back and rolled and was instantly on his feet surprising Ke-ah who was preparing to jump him while he was on the ground.

The men watching sat motionless, saying nothing, totally enthralled by the fight. Buff was watching too but was not frozen like the others. He moved, he feinted, just as if he was fighting. As a survivor of many knife fights, he knew exactly what each man was thinking and doing before they did.

Once again the two old friends faced each other, knives in hand each wanting to kill but yet…not wanting to kill. It was a strange, bizarre situation that neither wanted but neither had a choice either. It was kill or be killed.

Ke-ah rushed in again but this time Tye was ready. He caught the apache flush on the nose with a smashing left fist. Ke-ah was caught by surprise and staggered back, blood rushing from his broken nose and his eyes watering, hindering his vision. He shook his head trying to clear his head. He had never even seen what hit him, and he was now leery and unsure of himself. He had killed dozens of enemies with his blade but was not so sure he could this man, as he had been earlier. This white man was all that his people had made him out to be. If he had been born Apache, he would have been a great chief and maybe between him and me fighting the invaders the white man would not be here in their land

He had lost a lot of blood from the deep cut on his arm and Ke-ah could feel some of his great strength flowing from his body. This fight had to end quickly if he was to live. He kicked Tye's left knee hard and Tye felt the blow and the instant pain as he was falling on his back. Ke-ah was on him immediately and stabbed at the white man's chest. He was shocked when his wrist was grabbed and the downward thrust of his arm stopped…and held. He had Tye's knife hand but because of the blood on his hand was not a solid hold and he could feel his grip slipping as Tye tried to pull free. Tye twisted his body and rolled on top of Ke-ah.

Tye was pushing down hard with the hand holding his knife; or rather Ke-ah's knife. Ke-ah, had a grip on Tye's hand and was holding the tip of the blade about an inch from his chest. Tye was doing the same with the warrior's knife hand. For a moment it was a stalemate, then Ke-ah felt it, his strength quickly fading. He knew he had lost to his friend. He looked Tye in the eyes. "Remember me my friend…my brother." He suddenly released his grip on Tye's wrist and before Tye realized this; his blade plunged deep into Ke-ah's chest.

Tye was stunned. He rolled off Ke-ah and sat on his butt looking at his friend. Ke-ah turned his head slightly and looked at Tye, a slight smile appeared on his lips and he nodded…and died. Tye could not help himself; tears filled his eyes and rolled down his cheeks. He placed his hand on his friend's forehead, shut his eyes, remembering the good times they had as youngsters and the wasted years they were apart. He removed Ke-ah's knife that was in the warrior's chest. He stuck it into the ground and pulled it out and wiped it clean. He placed the knife in his friend's sheath. He took Ke-ah's arms and folded them across his chest.

Buff held the men back. "Stay here. Let him be fer a minute."

Tye got hold of his emotions and stood up and the men came to him. They were slapping him on the back, congratulating him but he paid them no mind. He walked away. Buff came over to him and they both sat down.

"Yu okay?"

"I guess," Tye answered. "Well as a man can be that lost a good friend yesterday and killed a friend today." He shook his head.

"Things get kind of complicated sometimes, making it hard to figure out why things work out the way they do."

Buff put his hand on his friend's shoulder. "Can't say I kno how yu feel abut killing a friend but I kno a lot abut losing them. You just have ta muve on, keep going." He paused for a minute then continued. "Speaking of muving on we need ta git bac across that river. We made a lot uf noise over here. Sumbody could be looking fer us."

Tye raised his eyes and looked at his friend and smiled for the first time in awhile. "You're right but I have to do something first."

He walked back to where Ke-ah lay. The men were standing around him staring at the biggest damn Apache they ever saw. Tye picked up a stout limb and began to scratch out a shallow hole in the rocky dirt. The men realizing he was not just going to leave his friend for the buzzards begin one by one to find sticks of their own and help dig the hole.

Private Greenwood put his hand on Tye's shoulder and said. "Just you go over there and sit down, Tye. We'll take care of this for you." Tye looked at Greenwood then the rest of the men who were looking at him.

"Thanks men," he said. "You'll need to gather some rocks too." All of them heard a horse approaching and looking up saw the Apache that had been with Ke-ah. They scrambled for their weapons.

"HOLD IT MEN…RELAX," Tye hollered.

The men stopped and looked at Tye and then the Apache. The Apache had his right hand held up, palm forward showing he was coming in unarmed. "Stay here," Tye said and walked toward the Apache. The warrior slid off his pony and walked to Tye and spoke in broken English.

"It good you honor your friend…and my friend by this," he said motioning to the hole the men were scraping out. Apaches do not speak a person's name that had died, so he spoke to Tye referring to Ke-ah as simply his friend or him. He nodded toward Ke-ah and said. "Him great warrior, much respected among our people, the Lipan; I would like to honor my friend by taking him back to his people for proper Apache burial." Tye nodded.

"That is good," Tye said. "I know he was a great warrior and he was my friend."

"Lipan will hear of this, Watkins. They already respect you and after this, the way you handled your friend's death, your name will be remembered in all our camps. I go now." He walked over to where the body lay and he started to pick Ke-ah up but was stopped by a firm hand on his shoulder. Two soldiers picked up Ke-ah and carried him to his pony and lay him gently across the pony's back. They stepped back and the Apache nodded and then jumped on his horse, gave the peace sign and rode off leading the other horse. Tye and the men watched as he disappeared over the crest of a hill. Tye stood there for a moment. Greenwood spoke up.

"Been fighting them devils all my life and just now…" he paused for a second. "Hell, they are people just like us." Tye smiled and the thought hit him that maybe his friend's death may not have been in vain if it caused better feelings among the two races.

Tye walked over to Sandy and stepped into the saddle. He took out the makings and rolled himself a smoke. It only took a couple of minutes for the men to mount up and moved over to where Tye was. "Let's go home," Tye said.

Chapter Twenty Nine

A day and a half later, Tye and the weary men with him rode into Fort Clark. It was April 9, 1869, and would be a day Tye would remember for the rest of his life. After giving an oral report on what happened to a much relieved Major Thurston, Tye headed home. Buff had gone on home to tell Rebecca he was here. He was almost there when he saw Rebecca coming toward him…walking not running as she usually did. He noticed this and knew it was unusual but didn't think anymore about it. They hugged each other and after a kiss Rebecca stepped back and did her usual thing when Tye came home after a scout... stepped back and held her nose. They both laughed.

"Where's Buff?' Tye asked looking around when they entered their home.

"He had a bath while you were at the major's and then said he had some errands to do and would see us later."

"What errands?" Tye asked.

"Staying out of the way errands," She said pushing Tye toward the tub filled with hot water. "Get out of them smelly clothes and get your tail in the tub and please, scrub hard." She pitched him the soap and laughed.

He stepped out of his clothes and sat slowly down in the hot water. He lay back and shut his eyes and relaxed. A couple minutes later he opened his eyes when he heard her voice. "You going to stay in there all day or you going to come here?"

He looked through the door and saw Rebecca sitting in bed, naked and patting the bed beside her. "Hurry up," she said.

Later, Tye, Rebecca, and Buff were sitting at the table trying to finish what little was left in their plates. "Sure you got enough, honey," Tye kidded. "Never saw you eat that much before."

"You have to when you are eating for two people," she replied. Tye, a spoon of beans half way to his mouth froze. He placed the spoon back in the plate.

"What did you say?"

"Just that for now; I have to eat enough for two people."

Tye thought for a second. "You mean you…I mean me…" he was stuttering trying to get the correct words out. "I mean are we going to have a baby?" She nodded. "My God…Buff! Did you hear that? I'm going to be a father. I'm going to be a father," he repeated. He hugged Rebecca and then hugged Buff. Tears ran down all three of their cheeks. He looked at Rebecca. "Is it going to be a boy…a girl? What's it going to be, honey," then realized just how a stupid of a question that was. He looked her in the eyes and said it didn't matter whether it was a boy or not…it was theirs and that's what's important.

Tye jumped up. "I've got to tell the O'Malley's."

"Just sit down, Tye. They already know. In fact we are going to their house tonight to eat." Tye sat back down.

"I love you, Rebecca and right now is the happiest day of my life…except," he added quickly, "the day you married me." They all three laughed and hugged each other.

A few minutes later, sitting at the table, Tye asked. "Did you hear about Lieutenant Garrison?"

Rebecca nodded and said. "I'm so sorry Tye. He was such a good man and a real gentleman. I liked him so much. They are burying him and the others in the morning," she said. Tye nodded. She added. "I heard you lost another friend too…one I didn't know about."

Tye lowered his head. "I had forgotten about Ke-ah. I had not seen him for fifteen or sixteen years and figured he was dead. He was a man, honey. You should have seen him. He was…" he stopped. He did not really want to talk about him right now. Rebecca, realizing this, changed the subject.

"Major Thurston and Captain McClellan will be at the O'Malley's tonight also," she said.

Tye nodded. "That's great. By the way, how's the kids?" he asked referring to the Turley kids that the O'Malley's had adopted. The children were the grandkids of very good friends of Tye's that were killed by some Apaches led by Tanza and few months ago. Tye had tracked down the Apache and after killing him, brought the kids home.

"They're fine. I'm helping them with their schooling and both of them are bright youngsters. They seem very happy."

"That's good," Tye said. "I'm so happy for them." He hugged Rebecca again and held her face in the palms of his rough, calloused hands. "I love you honey and I'm so happy about the baby." He kissed her.

"I've got to get ready to go to the O'Malley's," she said. Tye and Buff stepped outside and sat on the porch, neither saying anything. Tye was looking forward to tonight but dreaded the funeral of his friend and the other men in the morning. But tonight he was going to relax with friends and enjoy the thought of his becoming a father.

www.ingramcontent.com/pod-product-compliance
Lightning Source LLC
LaVergne TN
LVHW091022080826
845145LV00002B/331

* 9 7 8 0 9 8 0 0 8 5 4 7 1 *